PRAISE FOR

North of the Sunlit River

"At once mystical and firmly grounded in nature, *North of the Sunlit River* takes the reader on a journey into the Alaskan tundra. Jessica Bryant Klagmann's characters are beautiful, flawed, and curious, their relationships rich and complicated, their secrets compelling. This book is beautifully written and unlike anything else I've read; I could not put it down."

— Suzy Krause, author of *I Think We've Been Here Before*

This Impossible Brightness

"An original and inherently fascinating novel by an especially gifted author, *This Impossible Brightness* by Jessica Bryant Klagmann will have a particular attraction for readers with an interest in family life / women's domestic life novels whose deft crafting raises them to an impressive level of literary excellence."

—*Midwest Book Review*

"At once haunting and visionary, Jessica Bryant Klagmann's *This Impossible Brightness* asks us to consider ghosts in their many forms—literal ghosts, the ghosts of grief that follow all of us, and the ghost of a present-but-disappearing earth amid climate devastation. In the face of sweeping loss, this novel resists despair by weaving an expansive web of interconnectedness and also of hope. Klagmann's debut is both wildly imaginative and gorgeously moving."

—Anne Valente, author of *Our Hearts Will Burn Us Down*

"In the eyes of *This Impossible Brightness*, humans bear a particular mark of distinction, one that's spiritual or psychological rather than physical. We are the species that tries to change direction in midair; we attempt, impossibly, to take our fall and transform it into an ascent. Jessica Bryant Klagmann's writing seems motivated by this same desire. Everywhere in her novel's pages, you sense some force yearning to turn the future into the past—to forestall the autumn of the world, spin it around, and allow it to burst into spring. Through her focus on this effort, she produces a feeling that's sustained and powerful, a clear-eyed grief leavened by a mad hope."

—Kevin Brockmeier, author of *The Ghost Variations*

"Part ghost story, part adventure yarn, part death meditation, Jessica Bryant Klagmann's *This Impossible Brightness* is a tour de force of storytelling. Spinning us through multiple time frames and character perspectives, Klagmann captures the beauty and largeness of nature and our tenuous place in the world. A wonderful debut novel from a remarkable new voice."

—David Nikki Crouse, author of *Copy Cats* and *The Man Back There*

NORTH
OF
THE
SUNLIT
RIVER

ALSO BY JESSICA BRYANT KLAGMANN

This Impossible Brightness

NORTH OF THE SUNLIT RIVER

A Novel

JESSICA BRYANT KLAGMANN

LAKE UNION
PUBLISHING

This is a work of fiction. Names, characters, organizations, places, events, and incidents are either products of the author's imagination or are used fictitiously. Otherwise, any resemblance to actual persons, living or dead, is purely coincidental.

Text copyright © 2025 by Jessica Klagmann
All rights reserved.

No part of this book may be reproduced, or stored in a retrieval system, or transmitted in any form or by any means, electronic, mechanical, photocopying, recording, or otherwise, without express written permission of the publisher.

Published by Lake Union Publishing, Seattle

www.apub.com

Amazon, the Amazon logo, and Lake Union Publishing are trademarks of Amazon.com, Inc., or its affiliates.

EU product safety contact:
Amazon Media EU S. à r.l.
38, avenue John F. Kennedy, L-1855 Luxembourg
amazonpublishing-gpsr@amazon.com

ISBN-13: 9781662534713 (hardcover)
ISBN-13: 9781662520174 (paperback)
ISBN-13: 9781662520181 (digital)

Cover design by Faceout Studio, Spencer Fuller
Cover image: © AnnstasAg, © Bodega, © Valerii_M, © vellot / Shutterstock;
© Ron Mellott, © Cameron Zegers, © J. Anthony,
© Christian Tisdale / Stocksy United
Interior image: Courtesy Donna Bryant

Printed in the United States of America

First edition

For my father, who never did get to Alaska

Imagine there is purpose in this, in all of this—that there is meaning beyond ritual. Imagine that the world ends in light, that what love floods your veins is a gleaming of stars.
—Anne Valente, "How to Let Go"

PROLOGUE

The beginning is always the same.

First, she says goodbye. Then Eila Jacobsen holds both his hands in hers, and she looks at their knuckles pressed together as she says: "I think, when we're together, we're invincible. Like nothing could hurt us, nothing could stop us. I'm going to live my life that way, from now on, because of you. With no fear."

Jackson Hyder stands on the bridge over the Chena River, staring into the water, trying to shake the image of Eila and this dream he's been having for days on end. It's more than a dream. He's experienced visions like this before and knows that it's not something he can simply ignore. There's a truth to it, an inevitability.

Usually, the visions involve animals, but they are varied in their timing and consequences. Once, he'd dreamed of finding a dead loon, only to then stumble on one dying in the grass. Another time, he'd seen a raven heckling a man at an outdoor restaurant days before it actually happened. Last winter, he'd known somehow that as he walked the path from his cabin to the outhouse, a moose would wander right in his way and force him to wait.

So he is certain this dream of Eila—and the terrible thing that happens just after she says that because of him, because of *them*, she is going to throw caution to the wind and live a life without fear—will eventually come to pass. It's only a matter of when.

Unless.

The river carries slabs of ice toward him, and he watches them vanish beneath the bridge as they continue downstream. It's a clear spring day, the Alaska Range visible in the distance, peaks like sharply carved alabaster. Despite the buildings that line the river's shore—the lodges and restaurants and two-storied offices and the riverboat with its paddle wheel frozen like a cog in a broken clock—the area is strangely absent of people, and there is so much stillness that Jackson considers for the first time that someone might be watching.

The weight of decision presses on him. He needs to feel lightness in his body, so he hoists himself over the railing, grasping it from behind and hanging on as he leans forward. He is not afraid at first, which is partially because he's done this very thing so many times before and partially because he's never been afraid.

Until now.

Now he is terrified, and this fact is what scares him most of all. That he's experiencing fear as he realizes how much he loves her. And if he doesn't do something, she'll be gone. He hangs there, suspended over the river. He closes his eyes and he sees it again. Unstoppable, unshakable.

In the dream, after Eila says the words and releases his hands, the scenery changes and he's at the edge of another river, somewhere north of here, and she's standing on the other side. She doesn't see him—his presence is elusive, as if he's observing it all from the outside.

From behind her, hundreds of caribou approach. They move as one, invisibly connected. Their heads bob forward and back, building momentum as they approach the river. At the water's edge, they divert around her. She is a statue among them as they charge chest deep against the current. This crossing is a typical part of their migration, an obstacle they've encountered for centuries. But that doesn't make it safe—rituals may still be wrought with peril.

Eila doesn't move—she is frozen there, she who is never cold. She who is a sister to the caribou. She who is fearless, who believes now that she is invincible.

North of the Sunlit River

Then something draws her attention upstream. Jackson's gaze follows Eila's, and he spots the wolf. Everything about its body—its dart-like tail, the intensity of its eyes, the sharpness of its nose—indicates that it's picked a target and will not let it go.

The caribou changes direction, but the wolf intercepts it as it reaches the bank and leaps onto its back, locking its jaws beneath the shoulder. They run together for a few steps, the wolf losing and regaining its grip, the caribou falling and nearly giving up, but then standing again and thrashing the wolf around as it bolts. Then the wolf falls and takes hold of the caribou's back leg, and the two wrestle to the ground one last time.

The other caribou scatter out of instinct, briefly frightened, but they quickly regain their composure and fall back into their focused forward motion, pushing into the current. Jackson can't take his eyes off the wolf and caribou, struggling together, snow falling on their tangled bodies.

But when he looks for Eila again, he sees the tragedy of his mistake—that the wolf was not the center of the moment. It was simply a distraction. In the time he turned his eyes from her, the caribou also seemed to forget she was there. In the chaos of the wolf's attack, they've overtaken her, trampled her. She is swept away by a flood of fierce, dark water.

Jackson opens his eyes now to the roaring river below. It is abyssal and colder than he can imagine. He stares into it deeply, as if within he will find the answer. Or perhaps he will wake up. But the truth is, he knows beyond all doubt that this is no ordinary dream, that what he has seen will unfold whether his eyes are open or closed, and it will be he who causes it, and there is nothing—*almost* nothing—he can do to stop it.

PART 1

1

Eila Jacobsen

The first touches of daylight are brushing the windowsill when Eila Jacobsen wakes on the couch. She scratches her shoulder where the corduroy seams of the cushions have left striped indentations. Because she is actively trying not to dwell on details of the past, like why she slept on the couch last night in the first place, she turns her attention to the first task of the day, of every day—food and coffee. From the couch, it's a mere four steps to the fridge, where she finds no eggs, no yogurt. Cold rice is unappealing. She opens a cabinet. Even the cereal is gone. There's a full five-gallon jug of water by the sink—she made sure to stop at the spring to refill it on the way home last night—but the jar of coffee grounds on the counter is also empty, and this is unacceptable.

Four steps back to the couch. There's a flashlight on the coffee table, and as she picks it up, flicks it on and off again, the events of the previous night come back to her. After she returned home from bedding down the reindeer in the barn, she sat with her laptop, attempting to write the speech she's expected to give at the Large Mammal Research Conference in a week. Despite it being the middle of an Alaskan winter, she left the window open so she could hear the soft sounds of the forest. And, as often happens, she was distracted by the snapping of a branch outside. Her attention was pulled away from the computer, and before she knew it, she was on all fours in the snow, looking for tracks. Then she saw the light bouncing down the dirt road, so she brushed the snow from her pants and shook hands with her neighbor, Lev. From the crystals of ice that fringed his wool hat, she guessed he'd already been out walking for at least an hour.

"Dogs got out again," he said. "Not all of them, just the two naughty ones. Daisy and—"

"Timber," Eila finished. She shook her head and put her hands on her hips, scanning the dark woods. It wouldn't be the first time she'd helped him look for them.

"They've already gotten into one fight from the sound of it." Lev sighed, shifting his weight from one leg to the other. He was thrown from a horse when he was younger and has walked with a bit of a limp ever since. Maybe that's what inspired Eila to help him search for his rogue sled dogs, but probably not. More likely, it was an excuse to walk through dark, snowy woods instead of writing a speech she had no idea how to begin.

The presentation has been weighing on her, and not because she isn't qualified or equipped to stand on a stage and provide scientific facts or argue data trends. It's the part she has to play—the purely professional scientist—that troubles her. Because she knows one way or another, she always reveals the fascination she has with the caribou that goes beyond science.

It's something she internalized as a child. The first time she went mushing, she was with her father in a village in northeast Alaska, where her father was learning to make snowshoes with a local Athabascan man. They were invited to go caribou hunting on dogsleds, and there—startled but amazed by the sight of a caribou cow lying dead in the snow—Eila was drawn into the honoring of the animals' spirits. Into the belief in the cycle of rebirth that means when a caribou dies, its soul is passed on to another.

Eila is certain that every caribou that has ever lived still walks the earth now.

In school, when she wrote papers or competed in a science fair, she was left with the feeling that people didn't take her seriously. The school counselors told her that philosophy or mythology would be better subjects than biology, if that's what she really wanted to research. She tried to refocus, stick more closely to the facts. But eventually, as a graduate student, she traveled again to remote parts of Alaska, wrapping tracking collars around the caribou's necks. Once, she locked eyes with one that had already been netted and blindfolded by senior teammates, and as she fastened the collar, the blindfold came loose. Eila held the caribou's warm muzzle in her palm, and when their eyes connected, she felt a flood of oxygen, and there it was—a sense of time stopping but also rushing past them. She blinked and looked around, and the rest of her teammates had disappeared. She was alone with this caribou, surrounded by dwarf trees and songbirds, and it might have been centuries before. The moment passed, of course, and they were in the present again, the crew chatting away, and she pulled the blindfold back up to keep the caribou calm.

Whenever she and the caribou share a moment, she gets the same feeling. More and more, she can't suppress the desire to share it. Her heart and her head are in constant battle when she talks with other scientists. It will inevitably come out at the conference, this spiritual connection, unless she can force herself to stick to the script. But even the script is proving difficult.

When she heard Lev outside, she'd jumped at the chance for distraction. Eila and Lev separated, and she pushed through the snowy pines on one side of the road, calling the dogs' names and casting the beam of her flashlight on anything that seemed to move. Her breath rose in clouds and she shouted until her throat was hoarse, but she was never so comfortable as this—a wild being. When the northern lights appeared in green ripples above the treetops, she tipped her head back and lost herself for a moment—the swells of the aurora carrying Jackson Hyder back to her on its waves. As they always did. Then she refocused on what was in front of her, on the ground and the snow that fell silently, dampening all sounds, wrapping her in the quiet comfort of the woods.

A few hours later, she saw four eyes reflecting the light back at her. The two pups had stuck together. They were jumping and wrestling like it wasn't the middle of the night. Eila was lucky to have some dog treats in her pocket—a longtime habit because she never knew when she'd run into a pup while walking. And as she knelt to let the dogs fight for the dried salmon in her palm, a feeling that something wasn't right came over her. The feeling followed her back to the road, back to Lev's house, where she found him grumbling and just about to give up for the night. The mysterious weight of it pressed on her as she walked home, closed the laptop without looking at the blank page, and dropped to the couch.

The feeling twists in her stomach again now as she tugs her fingers through tangles of long black hair and puts on a baseball hat. Her father will at least have coffee, and perhaps he can reassure her that the world has not turned upside down once again. Still in her work pants from the day before—caked with dried mud and straw—Eila pulls on her muddy boots and zips her canvas coat and begins walking Halley Road.

It's a bright winter morning—all the brighter for the layers of ice. The road is snow-packed and glistening, icicles hanging like gems from the spruce and birch that line the unpaved street. Her boots make a crunch-creaking sound with each step. She has walked, run, biked, and cartwheeled down this road all her life—90 percent of the time with Jackson by her side. Now, alone, she marches, head down with determination until halfway there, when she passes the place where the two birches curve in opposite directions against reason, one branch of each entangled with the other. The place that marks the entrance to the woods, where, just a few steps from the road, a deer path leads to the tree house Jackson built.

They were thirteen when he disappeared for a month to work on it in secret. She'd see him at school, then he'd be gone immediately after, and she couldn't track him down. He was always finding new interests to explore and getting lost in them—juggling behind his back or solving a Rubik's Cube in under a minute or crafting arrows from pinewood and deer antlers—so she hadn't thought much of his absence. But two days after she failed a biology exam (she'd based her essay on the theory that the heart plays a bigger role than the brain in guiding Arctic terns in their migration), he dragged her by the hand, blindfolded, down the path. She'd been crying, and the bandanna he'd tied around her eyes stuck to her face. But since he was walking in front of her, grasping both her hands with his behind him, she didn't dare steal a hand back to adjust it.

When he stopped and removed the blindfold, she jumped at his fingers brushing her temples. Then he jumped, too, and she saw a flicker of something like fear in his eyes. She shook her gaze away and leaned to see past him. Wedged into a sprawling oak was a tree house—a scaled-down but otherwise perfect replica of every one of her father's cabins. With the bandanna hanging around her neck, she climbed the ladder to a square room with a desk and a round table. A stack of pillows was arranged in the shape of a couch. He'd carved a wooden cabinet to look like a fridge, a bucket with a watering can suspended over it for a sink faucet. But this, most of all: on the desk, he'd set up a microscope—an old one, he explained, that he'd found at a thrift store. There was a box of plastic bags, a kit with tweezers and clippers, safety goggles, a field notebook, and a weathered paperback called *Incredibly Wild Stories of Migration*.

"See these windows?" he said, pointing to six openings in the walls, each with a differently angled blind. "Like your dad's. The light comes in no matter what time or what season. And the design on the ceiling . . . I wasn't able to make it exactly the way he does, but it's my first one."

It was impressive, what he'd managed to learn simply by watching her father. But in that moment, she didn't give him enough credit for his carpentry. She'd always wished she could go back and praise him more, spend at least a few more seconds focused on him. But all she saw was that microscope. That field notebook. That space that belonged to her—to them—because he had listened and taken her seriously.

She can hear him now, saying "Facts are boring. They're dead. They have nowhere else to go. Theories are more interesting. They're *alive*."

Every time she's here, she thinks of that moment, Jackson pulling down the bandanna and the glimmer of fear in his eyes just before she saw the tree house. It wasn't until many years later that she realized what that look was. He was afraid that his creation—his attempt to emulate her father's effortless artistry—might not be good enough.

The air smells fresh and vacant, although it's an unsettling smell. Eila tries to place it, searching the clear sky and the woods around her, then realizes that it's the absence of a smell. There should be woodsmoke thickening the air, and there isn't. It happens then, finally, when she reaches her father's cabin and finds that the door is wide open, a mound of windblown snow gathered in the doorway. Eila is running, her feet disconnected from her brain. She's running as the sense of foreboding from the night before dissolves—ice melting in her chest—dread and perfect certainty replacing it.

There's a pile of frozen clothes on the mat by the front door, and too much silence. Inside, Eila stops at the door to her father's bedroom, wanting to fling it open but worried about being dramatic and invading his privacy. Instead, she backs away and her hands and feet move involuntarily, reaching for a towel and crouching by the door, mopping the water with a quiet numbness. Waiting to find out what this is. She wrings the towel, folds the clothes and refolds them, then returns to the puddles on the floor.

She is thrusting at the hardwood planks with the waterlogged towel in nauseatingly repetitive circles when she looks up, and he's there. Stefan Jacobsen, a bear risen from hibernation, standing before her with confusion and terror in his eyes.

2

Stefan Jacobsen

Stefan Jacobsen wakes in his bed, though he can't remember getting into it. His skull feels hollow, as if something large and important has vacated it. He steps out from the back room and finds his daughter, Eila, on her hands and knees, mopping water from the floor with an old towel.

"What happened?" she says, pointing to the clothes he was wearing the night before, which he apparently shed when coming through the door. They're in a pile next to his boots, heavy and dripping with water.

"I don't know," he says, and he isn't lying. He has no idea what happened. "It's freezing in here."

Eila looks like she's already been to the research station, her overalls caked with dried mud and hay that's mixing with the water on the floor and creating more of a mess. Still, she keeps scrubbing with the soaked towel in pointless circles. He wants to be useful, to light a fire in the woodstove, but he can't remember where he put his lighter. And for some reason, he can't think of the word for the thing you strike to spark a flame.

"The door was wide open. Also, Lev's dogs got out last night. Got in a fight with some other dogs down the road. Did you see the gate open when you got home?"

"I don't know," Stefan says again, raising a hand to his beard, scratching, thinking. "Actually, it's possible . . . I might have opened it."

Eila looks up, and Stefan realizes he's been watching her for the last few moments as if she were a child again. Small, timid, sweet. When she rises, she again grows into the tall, strong image of her mother that she's been for many years now—beneath a baseball hat, her long black hair is full of twigs and tangled, loose strands curling around her ears. The look on her face is her mother's as well. "This isn't like you," she says in a matching tone. He cringes a little as she wrings the towel out in the sink.

"I mean, it's not the kind of thing *anyone* does. Something isn't adding up." Her eyes are pleading and tired. "You have to try to remember."

Stefan sits on the couch, feeling more and more like a child who has done something punishable. His cabin is small, like all the cabins he's built—two rooms and a loft. The couch faces the sink and stove, with just enough room for a round kitchen table in between.

"What if you retrace what you did last night? It might come back to you."

He hums a little, rocking back and forth. There was a loss of vision, pain in his temples, confusion. It all boils down to that. One big confusing knot. Stefan's legs are jumpy, so he stands again quickly and says, "Maybe if I go out there."

He pulls a wool hat onto his bald head and a heavy coat over his shoulders. Outside, the sky is a well of blue. It's later than he thought and warmer. Probably almost noon already, and maybe five degrees. He walks to the end of the driveway toward the ceaseless yipping sounds.

The gate is latched again, and Stefan hesitates briefly before opening it, a flicker of something familiar bursting and then fading. Inside the kennel, he says, "Shh, shh." He sits on his heels and rests his hand on the chest of a tan-and-white husky pup. Her body heaves with hurried, anticipating breaths.

The other dogs jump to the tops of their houses and then down again. They do this over and over, as if they can't decide on their preferred vantage point. Some just keep up their frantic circles. Stefan feels dizzy again as he stands and reaches out for the fence. The sound of the metal reverberating and the sight of the dogs pulling on their chains. Suddenly, it's there.

The hammer, the ladder.

The path through the woods, the moon.

3

Stefan knew he left the hammer at the building site, but he couldn't recall where. He dropped to his knees, swiping through snow with gloved hands, the cold sending a chill like a circuit through his bones. The hammer wasn't that important. There were others. But things couldn't be left like that, no matter how inconsequential—forgotten and locked between a frozen ground and its rind of snow.

The light was fading. Not slow and steady. The apricot sky darkened in leaps.

He'd spent the last two months tending to the needs of his cabin tenants. An oil tank that needed to be filled, another that needed closing up while the occupants headed to warmer climates. He'd been repairing light fixtures and electrical outlets. The cold, dark months of the Alaskan winter had left all Fairbanks wrapped in quiet. Those who stuck around did so because they liked this way of being. A world tucked in and sleeping. In winter, Stefan always thought of light, despite the impulse to slow down, shut down.

Hibernate.

Stefan stood and kicked the snow with his boots around the perimeter of the cabin's foundation. He ventured within the tree line at the edge of the property, finding nothing. When he saw the ladder leaning against the side of the cabin frame, he knew with complete certainty that the hammer was up there, on one of the exposed ceiling beams. Climbing down that ladder was one of the last things he remembered before the cold came on with its calm persistence, sure to stay.

He'd secured the ladder and climbed. As he knew it would be, the hammer was resting on a beam a few feet from his reach. He straddled the beam and slid toward it, eyes focused on the tip of a spruce at the edge of the yard. He didn't look down, though he wasn't really worried.

This is what Stefan Jacobsen does for a living: he defies gravity.

From up high, he could see the valley darkening and slipping into frigid stillness. Some might call it bleak or too stark, but Stefan's eyes have always sought out the glow hovering over surfaces. He was suspended nearly twenty feet above the ground when he noticed the first flicker, like a bulb blinking out. He rubbed his left eye. After another moment, his vision on that side dimmed out completely and the world began to tilt. The slivered moon fell, sliding down the slope of the sky like a shaving of ice from a spoon. His balance faltered and his hands gripped the beam for support. He closed both eyes, hoping to restore some stability, but the world continued to spin even when he'd shut it out.

His temples stung.

Stefan lay flat on his stomach and shimmied backward to the ladder. His right foot reached, feeling for the top rung. When he found it, he wedged his boot against the metal and used it to drag himself the rest of the way. His left foot fumbled for the next rung and Stefan paused for a moment, face down, his torso pressed against the frozen beam, his eyelashes grazing the snow on its surface. Below, the cabin floor flooded up toward him, but he told himself it wasn't real. He could still feel the ladder, the beam, the air moving between his body and the ground. He rested, trying to breathe slowly, then began to lower himself down one rung at a time. It was simple from here, a pattern he could predict. Hand beneath hand, foot beneath foot.

Eventually he found both his boots on the ground again, yet still he felt as if he was sinking. Turning, Stefan looked for the road, but it was already so much darker than when he'd gone up the ladder. His truck was there, but the shape of it seemed wrong. The unlit headlights looked like the eyes of some creature he'd never seen.

Another option: Take the path through the woods back to his cabin. He knew it would be quicker, but he wasn't convinced he could find it in his state.

He tried.

Stefan covered his left eye with his palm, as if he were reading a chart on a wall. Tears seeped from the other eye, stinging as they froze on his cheek. It had dropped to twenty degrees below zero, yet his neck was sweating beneath a tightly wound scarf. He tugged to loosen it and stumbled toward the woods, left hand over his eye, right hand still clutching the hammer.

He tripped more than once, landing on his knees in the snow. Fireworks went off behind his eyes. Tiny explosions. The path was barely visible. On the ground around him, he saw animal tracks and thought that at least he wasn't completely lost. Stefan pulled himself to his feet and kept walking, following the tracks the moose and deer had made. They were creatures of habit. He paused to touch anything that would tell him which way was up, down, forward. An old, abandoned washing machine. A tire. A rusted oilcan.

Ahead, the moon glinted off some shred of metal, and Stefan aimed for it. A place to rest, to gather his wits. Confusion and fear were not feelings he was used to. He was a man of clear decisions, solid purpose, straightforward resolve. The glittering reflection of the moon turned out to be wire fencing, taller than he was. The sled dogs inside were sleeping, but when they heard his boots in the snow and caught his scent, their ears perked and they began yipping and running in manic circles.

A tan-and-white husky approached the fence and bared her teeth, pressing her nose to the wire. Stefan wrapped his fingers around the cold metal, pulling himself along the dog yard perimeter until he saw the road, wide and bright in the moonlight. His coat sleeve snagged on the wire, and he yanked it free, leaving behind the sound of shaking metal and dogs barking in the snow-blue shadows.

The road—moonlit and full of deep divots—was finally something familiar. Stefan had traveled it thousands of times, by car, on bicycle, and on foot. He began to run. When his boot caught on a moose antler beneath a crab apple tree at the edge of a driveway, he knew he'd made it.

Eila was somehow always finding these antlers—an odd talent that she constantly worried meant she was an attracter of death—and when her front yard got too cluttered with them, she started bringing them over to his.

Ice crystals had formed on Stefan's beard, tingling as they spread across his face and neck. His eyelashes stuck together with the same frost, and he blinked it away. The headaches dissipated in an instant, leaving his head empty and clear. He couldn't remember what the pain felt like. The hammer dropped from his fingers onto the porch, and he jumped at the sound. His sight flickered back too—not fully, but like little bubbles of light filtering into view and transforming into recognizable objects. The fallen hammer, the rubber tips of his boots, chunks of ice clinging like Velcro to his gloves. He opened the door and collapsed inside, exhausted, leaving behind the sound of sled dogs howling—a sound that seemed to come from too many directions at once.

4

There is reassurance in remembering—but also distress. As he leans against the dog kennel, Stefan feels the aching cold of the night forest in his lungs. His hands begin to shake as he tries to hang on to the tangible memory he just had in his grasp.

He isn't sure what he's doing here.

Eila is making breakfast when he returns to the cabin, jabbing at eggs in a pan, bacon frying on the next burner. She glances over her shoulder and points to a steaming mug of coffee on the table. He pulls out a chair, scans the kitchen counter, asks for crackers when he means sugar.

A week later and Stefan is sitting in the hospital waiting room. He's never been in this kind of sterile, too-bright facility for this long before, never longer than for a quick checkup or stitches. He is both appreciative of this fact and searching for some familiarity in the situation. The headaches have come and gone, but after that first night, the vision in his left eye never returned. He began to forget more as well—an appointment with a prospective tenant, which road led back home from town, the name of what he was looking for when Eila found him half under the front porch without a jacket. He forgot, sometimes, that he was cold. He felt particularly bad when, needing to deposit his tenants' rent, he called and interrupted her funding presentation to ask the name of his bank.

Finally, he surrendered to tests. A neurological exam to check his hearing and vision. Another for balance and coordination—basic skills that had always been part of the work and art of living. An MRI, CT scans.

Now he waits. He sits in a floral-patterned chair with his eyes closed, knuckles massaging his eyelids. The intense light manages to seep through anyway. He's waiting for information. News. Somehow, he knows it won't be good; it's just the degree that he's anticipating.

The man in the chair across from him is nodding off, reeling forward and then jerking his head upright. He's alone. But Stefan is not, and for this he is grateful. Eila is behind a door somewhere, speaking to the doctors, getting the hard truth so she can shape it into a more digestible kind of truth for him. She's been gone less than ten minutes, but it feels like so much longer. He folds his hands over his stomach and leans back. Someone is pushed by in a wheelchair, a pebble caught in the wheel clicking with each rotation.

It's the most recent memories that are lost. The distant past remains, another thing to be grateful for. And so he takes comfort in history, giving in easily to anything that his senses fall toward. Any stories his mind allows him to conjure. He might start writing them down.

A door flies open and two doctors come through, leaning in toward each other, speaking in hushed voices, consulting some paper on a clipboard.

Laughter floats from down the hall as the doors close.

Stefan remembers to breathe.

Eila returns, finally. Her dark hair is spun into a knot at the base of her skull, bangs pushed to the side. She's twisting her wool hat in her hands. She kneels down and forces the words "It's okay," when he can see what she means is the opposite.

"Let's do this at home," he says, waving away the serious talk.

She's smiling as she nods, but he knows her better. Her eyes are like the snow—clear and incandescent. They reflect everything.

Eila has never left Alaska as an adult. Despite being captivated by the idea of migration, she has remained here, gathering this landscape and everything that comes with it—all its bitter cold and endless darkness and incredible radiance—deep within her. Stefan has wondered if she is pulled by other places, as her beloved caribou are drawn to move, but regardless, she has stayed here, with him.

"You were made for this place," he says, then reconsiders his words and says, "Made *of* this place." He realizes this probably seems disconnected from the present moment. She probably thinks he's lost his words again.

Eila smiles once more, and this time it is genuine.

On the drive home, the train crosses the tracks in front of them, and Stefan rests his forehead on the passenger window. He watches a man drive a team of sled dogs through the snow parallel to the road. Snow flies out behind the sled in his wake. The dogs curve right in unison, and the whole chain of them slides off into the trees, the man disappearing last. Stefan blinks, the window cold on his forehead. When the musher and dogs are gone, the snow settles and all that is left are the tracks that have been carved into the powder.

5

Eila Jacobsen

When they get back to her father's cabin, they each half sit on one arm of the couch, feet on the floor. Eila opens the window behind them and they share a cigarette, leaning back toward the screen, where a draft sucks both smoke and heat from the room. This is something they have done, once in a while, when the world around them seems too absurd for regular conversation. Too upside down to comprehend. No doubt, sometime soon they'll have to be more responsible and give this up. Both of them.

Eila hands her father the cigarette and stands, anxious, but goes nowhere. A week ago, when she found his wet clothes on the floor and the woodstove cold, a panic immediately rushed through her. Her body flew straight to fear, but there weren't words for what she was so afraid of. Now there are, and it's nothing she could have anticipated.

Their roles switched in an instant. A daughter now tasked with taking care of her father.

She sits down again and says, "When you realized it was you who opened the kennel and let those dogs out, I thought you must have been drunk. Either that or you had some really good reason. I couldn't imagine any other possibility."

"Yet here we are." He wraps a hand around his bearded chin, shakes his head, and shrugs. "Okay. Let's have it."

Eila turns her head, watches through the window as a squirrel outside scrambles up the crab apple tree. When it reaches the height of one of the bird feeders, it leaps toward it, clinging with its claws, the feeder swinging. It gets its bearings and lifts the feeder lid, peering at the speckled seeds inside.

"You're going to need surgery. But they don't, they can't, it won't be possible to . . ."

She stops, still staring hard out the window.

The feeders are Eila's. She put them there to draw the wild around him. She has never needed to draw them to herself—they just come. She's never asked for them to follow her, never done anything to lure them close. Yet they find her all the same. Wild creatures linger by her windows, always watching. Today, she stares at the scene blankly; the squirrel swings back and forth against a clouded sky, nibbling away at the food it's stolen.

"Well," Stefan says, "I always liked to think anything is possible. We can say that for sure now. Here we are, in paradise, and when you live in paradise, it's probably good to leave some tough things to be discovered. Otherwise, you'll get bored or happy." He drops the cigarette into an ashtray on the windowsill, his eyes focused on something far off, though there's a wall of snow-laden trees within spitting distance, blocking the view. A world awash in silver. "I mean, *look* at it. The colors."

"That's funny," Eila says, knowing he isn't joking. Not even a little. He's always seen beauty in the most ordinary details. A kaleidoscope even in the palest of landscapes. "Obviously, it's a hard place to live sometimes. But it really is a kind of paradise, isn't it? The second those doctors told me you were going to . . . I thought, 'But how? This is fucking paradise. It's *my* paradise. This can't happen here.'"

Stefan throws up his hands. "This happens everywhere. Even in paradise."

"The other thing I thought," she says, pausing for just a moment, afraid to let something out that can't be taken back in, "was, 'Not you too.'"

There are no words to ease the ache of losses past or future. He leans over and gently touches his palm to the window screen. "It's getting too damn cold. Let's shut this place up. If we're going to be stupid, we can at least be warm and stupid."

They drive two miles to Ivory Jack's, the bar where Stefan often played guitar when he first came to Alaska. When they get there, Eila is hit with the newness of her father's illness, that only the two of them know about it. He shouldn't be smoking *or* drinking, but they look at the beers on the table and then at each other, deciding without words to allow themselves one last night of normalcy.

They've given him six months to live, a cancer that's winding its fingers through his brain, taking over, causing memory loss and confusion and pain. They sit at a table in the corner. On the other side of the room, beneath a dartboard and a series of tacked-up rugby jerseys, a young man is setting up an amp and plugging in his guitar.

"When you were little," Stefan tells her, "I used to play here all the time. And I was good, too, not to brag. I knew I was good because no one ever paid attention. I just blended into the background."

"You're still good," she says. "But I knew you were good then too. I remember drinking Shirley Temples and eating olives at the bar. I thought, 'Yep, that's my dad.' It didn't bother you that people weren't watching?"

"Nah. That was the only way I could just sort of lose myself. And I could tell everyone was enjoying themselves too much. But there was one time, one time I got them all sobbing and staring into their beers. I can't remember the set I was playing, but I remember the room that night."

"Why? What made it different?"

She sees him reaching back, gathering a memory. "There was this woman, wearing a shimmery—no, *sequiny*—black dress. Like a disco ball.

Had all the guys' heads turning, but she was obviously out of place. She sat at the bar, and I kept playing and singing, and she cried so much the guys actually got tired and stopped looking. I felt bad. When I finally finished, she yelled something—a song she wanted me to play, it turned out."

Stefan squeezes the bridge of his nose, rubs his forehead. He hesitates. "I asked her to say it again, so she did. I still couldn't make it out, so I just said, 'That's it, folks' and packed up my stuff and got a drink. She came and sat next to me and kicked her shoes off. I asked if everything was okay, a simple question. A nice gesture. She reached over and touched my arm. It was the first time—" He stops. "This is stupid. We're getting way off track."

"We were never on a track to begin with," Eila says, smiling. "What happened next?"

"Well, nothing happened. She touched my arm, and I froze, and she said, 'You couldn't just play fucking "Angel from Montgomery."' And she got up and left without her shoes. You were there, by the way. You were four, tossing a lime back and forth with one of the waitresses, and I saw you running and giggling. When I looked at that woman walking out the door, all I could think was how I didn't care if anyone else was happy, as long as you were. No, not that. That's not it. I just couldn't be responsible for anyone else's joy, except yours."

Eila sips her beer, wondering if she's happy enough, by her standards and by his. She asked for the story, perhaps to reassure him that he still has stories in him. That even if he doesn't live much longer, he did live, once. He met people and had conversations and made choices and traveled the paths created by those choices.

Her father retreats inward again, fishing up something, anything, from the sea of everything. "Remember that day when Jackson found the dead bird? Came busting down the door on that poor woman at the college." He looks apologetic, perhaps sorry he brought up an old hurt while she's still processing this new one.

But the truth is, the hurt is never far out of reach. "Yes," she says, "of course."

6

When Eila was sixteen, she and Stefan had gone to the university for a talk about sandhill cranes. They were sitting in the back row, and the speaker was clearly nervous. Only half the seats were filled when the woman walked to the podium and spread her papers out. She started by saying in a shaky voice that she was sure they'd all seen the cranes that migrated to Alaska for the summer, and could all recognize the birds' loud rattling call too. The call was produced by their long, coiling windpipes. Like a trumpet, she said.

Stefan leaned over and whispered to Eila that dear god, he hated jazz, except for that one time he'd seen—and heard—a pair of cranes dancing in the marsh behind his cabin. "They were obviously in love," he whispered. "Mate for life, but I'm sure she'll get to that. Sorry. Aren't you glad you invited me?"

Eila faked a quiet chuckle and shook her head as she bent forward to pull up her socks.

The talk went on for thirty minutes before it happened. The woman was elaborating on the cranes' depiction in art by various cultures across the globe. The same cranes that summered in Alaska and inspired Athabascan art wintered in New Mexico and became part of the Pueblo people's imagination. The lights were turned off, and she was clicking through a slide show of ancient artwork. Just as she said, "These birds have been around for millions of years," the door swung open, banging against the wall.

Jackson stormed in and flipped on the lights, and the woman stopped in the middle of her sentence. Every head in the room turned to Jackson, standing bare chested, his T-shirt balled under his arm like a football. He ignored the surprised faces—Eila wasn't sure he even knew she and Stefan were there—and rushed directly to the podium. He placed the bloody shirt on a table, unwrapping it to expose the bleeding body of a red loon. He took the bird in his hands.

The speaker, so timid before, grew suddenly confident. "What the hell are you doing?" she demanded, flashing looks around the room. To Jackson, the audience, the ceiling lights, the bird. He held the loon out to her like an offering, its neck limp.

"You have to fix it," he said as he dropped the bird into her hands. "Please, I need you to fix this." His pleading seemed so personal, as if they weren't exchanging a bird at all, but some larger, unsolvable injustice.

"You can't just—" she said, reluctantly accepting the loon. "It doesn't work that way."

"It has to," he said. "Just please do *something*."

This obviously made her angry: not only that a stranger had interrupted her presentation, but also that he'd had the audacity to suggest that she wasn't doing all she could. But despite any anger she might have felt, something changed in her demeanor—a switch flipped. Perhaps she finally saw that need in his eyes. She laid the loon on the table, its gray neck feathers sticky and matted. She put her hand on its chest, listening through her fingers, then bit her lip as if she might cry.

"It's dead already," she said, shaking her head.

Eila learned later that Jackson had found the loon on the trail past the pond. The two of them had been out there picking blueberries the weekend before, and she'd been struck by his spontaneous dive into the murky water. If she was honest, she was struck, really, by his back muscles, which had grown chiseled over the past year.

But in the university room, he looked older and beaten down, leaning against the wall and wiping his bloody hands on his shorts. His eyes remained focused on his muddy shoes, though Eila kept trying to get his attention, to tell him in their unspoken language that it was going to be okay.

7

Eila drags a finger through the puddle of condensation that has dripped from her glass onto the table. Sadness wells up in her, not because of the loon, not because of that moment death stepped into the room and held them all. It comes not from the loss of Jackson—a loss she lives with daily. This new sadness comes from the realization that the shared memory is far enough in the past that Stefan can still easily recall it.

The music starts—an energetic acoustic guitar.

Stefan clears his throat and says, "But hey, you know what I remember most about that day?"

"What's that?"

"Before the bird talk, we went for pizza. We were sitting and Jackson came into the place, all sweaty. Ordered six slices and ate them all standing right there, then just took off running again. Man, that kid could eat." Stefan leans in his chair, laughing. His legs are so long he almost topples it backward.

She remembers it, too, the way Jackson hugged her as he strode up to the counter. The way his shirt, drenched from running, also smelled like his mother's cabin—woodsmoke and incense. The way light shone in his eyes even though his mother had just left him, even though he had to fend for himself now.

For a moment, Eila forgets her father's news. She laughs, too, not sure how to say that what she remembers best about that evening is the sunlight on their bike ride from the pizza place to the bird talk. Stefan was ahead, pedaling hard up the hill. Eila pushed to keep up, the sun beating down on her shoulders. It was five o'clock in the evening, and the sun wasn't even close to setting.

Everything seemed infinite. The days were long, so many hours of light yet to go.

8

Vern Graves

Vern Graves is driving to town beneath the ice fog that hovers all winter. The veil separates the street and buildings from the atmosphere above. It's claustrophobic, but to be perfectly honest, this isn't why Vern despises being in town. There are a handful of instances when he relents to the three-story buildings and two-lane traffic: the grocery store, the bank, and of course, this—the local sled dog race. It begins in downtown Fairbanks each year, beneath the bridge that crosses the frozen Chena River. It's a shorter-than-usual, more laid-back race that ends in Coldfoot, and it's even better attended by Fairbanksians than the big races because there's less media and noise about it all.

Vern is here to flip pancakes and dish out eggs and bacon at the mushers' lodge before the race. How he ended up with this particular decades-long commitment is murky, but he believes he signed up by accident during a spell of awkward anxiety mixed with disappointment at Sadie Watkins's farmers market booth. After Sadie—a little too pleased, it seemed—had informed him later of his volunteer status, she remained vigilant about reminding him to show up with a smile every winter. Sadie's father—long dead now—had founded the race; otherwise, Vern suspects she wouldn't be here either.

The parking lot is full of the mushers' trucks, beds stacked with the dogs' traveling compartments. Black noses and white ears protrude from each little hole, the dogs anxious to get out so they can eat and stretch and do their business.

Vern groans as he parks in the icy lot where a sign says **Reserved for Volunteers**. He squats to yank the cord from beneath the front bumper and plugs it into an empty outlet. He uses the hood to hoist himself back up and walks to the lodge with his hands in his coat pockets, turning his eyes to the ground when he catches sight of the bridge over the Chena River—the last place Jackson Hyder was seen five years ago. Before his presumed fall. Vern always finds it interesting that suicide was never suspected. He supposes they all knew Jackson too well, and they assumed whatever he was doing on that bridge was rooted in gathering life experience, the opposite of some intentionally quick end.

Collective hypothesis aside, it's not the last place that Vern saw Jackson. But the reporters hadn't asked Vern, so Vern kept his mouth shut and let the bridge become the end of the legend that was Jackson Hyder.

Or perhaps it was the end of one legend and the beginning of another.

For the last five years, whenever Vern comes downtown for this event and sees the bridge, he almost backs out of the whole breakfast ordeal. He's not sure he can bring himself to step onto the bridge anymore—too many secrets there, things he's unable to speak of—but inevitably, he tucks his chin, digs his hands deeper in his pockets, and heads into the lodge.

Inside, it's warm, bright. There are long wooden tables with blue-and-yellow paper tablecloths. People weave between them, wearing parkas and insulated coveralls and half-pushed-back wool hats, dodging one another with plates of pancakes and scrambled eggs held high. Excited dogs dart between their legs. Bored dogs lie under the tables, and expectant dogs sit and beg.

Along the back wall there are more tables with aluminum trays full of barely warm breakfast foods. It doesn't look terribly appetizing, but it's free and no one seems to mind as the volunteer servers choose this pancake or that slice of bacon for them.

Sadie stands behind a back table, one hand clamped around a pair of metal tongs, waiting for her next hungry, pink-cheeked customer. She's wearing a maroon sweater with a deer on it, a white-collared shirt peeking out. Her head is adorned with fake reindeer antlers, woven with holly and tiny blinking lights. Vern tries not to stare and inevitably fails. She's been donning this same holiday outfit for as long as they've been doing this job, relatively unchanged. But Vern has watched Sadie change inside it—her face creased now but also softer, her hair a swirl of silver and dark gray.

When she sees Vern, her forehead wrinkles. She averts her eyes and occupies herself with rearranging bacon on a tray, nudging the slices around idly.

Vern takes a few exaggerated strides toward her. "Morning, Sadie," he says louder than necessary. She ignores him, slapping a few pancakes onto a man's plate. Vern grunts and wanders into the kitchen to grab an apron, tying it around his waist before returning to the table.

"You're late, Vern." A wafting sort of response, over her shoulder.

"I—"

"Quit giving them so much food, Vern. We won't have anything left for the latecomers."

"I thought I was the—"

"Shut up, Vern."

Sadie is pricklier than usual—*usual* being the frigid state of their friendship after not seeing each other for many weeks. Such is the season. Sadie likes to keep to herself for the dark winter months, this event the one exception. This time of year, the months slip by, both of them all but hibernating in their cabins, locked in by snow and the certainty that energy can be stored up and better used when the warmth returns.

"Have a good one," Vern says to a family of three as they leave the buffet with their plates piled high. "Enjoy the race."

"Aren't you friendly, Vern." Sadie glares at him over her shoulder. She's well aware that the one thing she can do to get under his skin is say his name just so at the end of a sentence. Don't give out too many pancakes, *Vern*. No one cares what you think, *Vern*.

But she doesn't usually say it like this. Not quite so fiercely.

"This is one of the coldest yet, isn't it?" he says to an older couple, the next in line, and Sadie shakes her head. He glances sidelong at her.

Shut up, *Vern*.

He shrugs.

For the rest of breakfast, Sadie keeps her distance, turning away each time he comes close. When she bends to pick up a fallen spatula from beneath the table, she comes up and accidentally looks right at him, and he sees tears in her eyes.

The room is almost empty, the race about to begin.

Vern tries to ask if she's okay, but as he begins to say "Listen, Sadie"—she turns to him abruptly and her cheeks are red and glistening.

"Well, what is it?" he says instead, and it comes out all confrontational, all wrong.

Some recognition suddenly crosses her face, and she shakes her head slowly and says, "Oh my god, Vern. You don't know?"

Vern's arms begin shaking under the weight of ceramic plates when he hears about Stefan's illness and the short projection of the time he has left. Dizzy, he turns away without a word and busies himself, gathering more dishes—too many dishes—onto the stack. His mind is ping-ponging. He makes his way around the tables, struggling to name his feelings.

9

The pang that strikes Vern hard in the chest is an old but familiar one. He hasn't felt it in so many years, he'd almost forgotten it was ever there at all. Of course Stefan told Sadie first. Of course he confided in her, let her see him at his most vulnerable. Vern allows himself to briefly imagine how the scene unfolded—Sadie's arms wrapped around Stefan's shoulders, tears in their eyes, both of them attempting to be strong. Stefan has never cried in front of Vern. He's shown fear maybe once or twice. They've shared many moments, but none so fragile and heavy as this one.

Vern isn't jealous. He's buried jealousy when it comes to Stefan and Sadie. He doesn't allow himself that feeling anymore—it cost him too much. The truth is, he doesn't know what he is now. Hurt, perhaps, at the confirmation that he will always come in second. Possibly even last, depending on how long the line is.

By the time the tables are empty, all the plates piled in the kitchen for washing, Vern has burned through his hurt and is simply terrified. His mind spins through hundreds of scenarios. They all end the same way—the way the doctors have predicted. Perhaps because his imagination is limited, he can think of no other scenarios, nothing miraculous.

Until he's putting away the maple syrup and sees the jar of honey, a glistening amber droplet running down its side.

The answer is there—hiding within years of abandoned research, an abandoned cabin hundreds of miles north—and it's so clear that he could be the one to solve this. And he convinces himself that he's over not being told first, at least enough to include Sadie now. To let her take some of the credit. It's only fair. It's her greenhouse. Technically, they're her bees that would be the real heroes of this story.

Vern and Sadie avoid each other until the kitchen is clean and the trash has been taken out, and then Vern stops Sadie by the back door. The distant voice of a race announcer out on the frozen river, and the sounds of a hundred yipping sled dogs, can barely be heard through the thick walls of the lodge.

"Do you think it's still there?" Vern asks. "Do you think it's all still the same?"

"What?" she says, pretending not to hear.

"We could fix this, Sadie," Vern says in a loud whisper, much more forcefully, and pleadingly, than he'd intended. "We could *save* him."

Sadie must have known they'd have to revisit what they'd done one day. What did she think, that their silence was going to last forever? She plays ignorant for another moment, avoiding his eyes and twisting her expression into a look of innocent curiosity. But she knows exactly what Vern is talking about, and he's persistent, if nothing else. "You *know* we can fix this," he repeats, a little louder, more urgently. He reaches for Sadie's hand, his fingers shaking.

"All right, shush," Sadie says, pulling her hand back and searching the room for listening ears. But the room is quiet, as vacant as the hundreds of miles of tundra that separate Fairbanks from the abandoned cabin.

Vern rolls his eyes, whispers instead. "Well," he says. "I think we have an obligation."

"Obligation," Sadie repeats sourly, turning her hand into a little chattering puppet. "We went through all this back then, how many times? Hundreds? Thousands? We settled. We said *no matter what*."

But even as her mouth forms the words, Vern hears a hesitation, thinks he sees her gears turning, chinking together inside her brain.

It's Stefan, after all. What if...

"What we know could help Stefan. Sure, in the past, I preached about saving millions. But what about right now, with this one person? Our *friend*. What if we just did that?"

"I wish," Sadie says, but her voice trails off and she thinks for an agonizingly long time, her fists clenched. Vern wonders how she has such conviction to go against what she really wants. "Even this one person. That's what *no matter what* means."

"Please, Sadie." He wonders why he's trying to convince her at all, rather than simply doing whatever he'd like behind her back. It would be easier. It would be more successful. Of course he knows the answer. He's made a promise, and it's not just the promise to hide their discovery. It's a promise to himself—to never break another promise.

Sadie says, "You know that if what we found got into the wrong hands, life as we know it would be over. That's a certainty. We promised we wouldn't let that happen."

"Just once, Sadie. Please. We'll put it in the right hands."

"There's no such thing as just once, *Vern*. And there's no such thing as the right hands. How would we even get up there right now? No one's going to want to fly us. We can't drive the whole way, and we're too damn old to be backpacking across the tundra, especially in winter. There's no way."

"Ten teams of sled dogs are going to Coldfoot. Right now."

Sadie just looks at him, and he knows it was a ridiculous suggestion, but he won't let it go. "We can figure something out," he says. "We *should* figure something out. There *has* to be a way."

"There isn't even enough time," she says. "By the time we... We'd be too late anyway."

"Too late?" He knows what she means—it's not like they have a magic pill Stefan could just swallow. So many more tests would need to be done to determine the safety and the soundness of their research.

And real scientists would have to synthesize the compound into some kind of serum or capsule or who even knows. Vern can feel himself wincing at what he knows is callousness as he says, "So, you've already given up on him then."

"Of course not," Sadie says. She puts her hands on her hips and narrows her eyes. "Faith may be invisible, but it's not nothing. Giving up on people is what *you* do, Vern."

Vern grips the warped wooden doorframe to keep his onset of dizziness at bay. The fake antlers on Sadie's head wobble, suddenly seeming so absurd. He wishes they would disappear and take their false Christmas spirit with them.

"We can't" is all Sadie says before pounding the side of her fist into the door and storming into the cold. He watches as the door swings shut, the icy draft sweeping in and mingling with the warm air inside the lodge. Vern shivers. Once the cold has dissipated, he looks around to see that he is truly alone once again.

10

It's thirty degrees below zero. Vern grips the bridge railing tightly anyway, a pure, hostile cold penetrating his stiff fingers. He holds on as if afraid he might be inspired to let go, and he's aware of the possibility that his fifty-two-year-old muscles may fail him anyway. Then he gets scared, feeling the stickiness of metal fusing to his bare hands, afraid he won't be able to let go—even if he wants to.

He peers down at the thick, charcoal gray ice.

Sadie is nowhere to be found. She may be concealed among the throngs of people, but more likely, she's booked it home. More likely she's already rounding the bend by the lake, turning onto Goldstream Road, the little dot of her cabin barely visible on its sleek, white curve of hill.

Vern considers what she said, that giving up on people is what he does. He wonders if it is in his nature, something he's bound to do again and again. Yes, he's done regrettable things in his past. Yes, giving up is one of them. Does it define him? On a different day, he might be able to talk himself out of the idea. But the fact is, the impulse to run away tends to come when heartbreak is involved. The greater the hurt, the farther Vern wishes he could bolt.

Vern closes his eyes and sees bees. He hears the steady vibration of wings inside his skull. He pictures a greenhouse swarming with them, surrounded by every color of vibrant flower. How many bees would there be by now? Thousands, maybe hundreds of thousands.

He remembers the day he and Sadie boarded up their greenhouse and left their years of work behind. They left their hives of bees and the strange platonic life they had created: amateur horticulturist and beekeeper with one goal in mind—the most beautiful, most resilient flower the Arctic had ever seen.

They were serious about their quest for beauty, for vitality. It was a devastating waste to turn their backs on it. In the end, the beautiful union they'd been striving for had only created a greater rift. He's sure they never recovered. For one, she'd stopped inviting him over for hot buttered rum on Tuesday evenings, offering no explanation. And though he missed the buzz those drinks gave him—and the slippery, salty sweetness—he never asked why, and they just went on as if this were the normal way of things when it very much was not.

The day they walked away, a roll of heavy tape hung around Sadie's wrist like a bracelet, and Vern stretched the thick plastic over every possible opening. When they were done patching up potential holes, they stepped outside. Sadie pushed the abundance of flowers back in through a crack in the door and held them, pulling her arms out at the last second as Vern slammed the door and threw the dead bolt. Then they draped another heavy plastic sheet over the whole greenhouse, got the hammer and nails, and secured it all with planks. They could still hear the thrumming of the bees.

When they finished and stood back to look at the monstrosity they'd created, Sadie turned to him horrified, as if she only then realized that insects breathe air just like everyone else. Vern's eyes traveled the whole of the greenhouse, and he sighed heavily. They both knew it didn't matter. The lack of oxygen might have meant death for other creatures, other insects. But not these. These bees would live forever. They wouldn't need air or water or sunlight to do so.

A decision had been made and could not be taken back. Sadie would never allow it. Vern had agreed, albeit reluctantly, to lock up what they'd found, to make absolutely sure it would never be released, to walk away for good.

And that's what they did.

The crowd moves along the sidewalk and down to the river. Lines of dog teams are careening into place, every single dog driven by a force that apparently requires ample yipping and bouncing to satisfy. They jump in their neon booties and piss and shit right on the ice. They're driven by a singular notion: *Go, go, go.*

Vern catches little snippets of spectator conversation. *Look, there's the guy who won last year; probably will again. That newcomer is supposed to be the next you-know-who. And musher so-and-so was disqualified for treating his dogs poorly. Shit, I hope the car starts when this is over—I forgot to plug it in. You dropped your mitten. It's cold. Zip your coat up and quit complaining.*

The Alaska Range is in the distance, covered by a white snowy veil. Everything else is the same washed-out gray, with touches of pink and blue. Vern lingers a few moments, his mind shifting from Stefan to Eila and all that she must be going through, and then inevitably to Jackson Hyder, standing in this very spot five years ago. Vern wonders what Jackson was thinking about, if he'd had doubts, and who it was that saw him dangling from the railing here and became the authority on his last moments on Earth. Then he says goodbye to Jackson for what seems like the hundredth time, though it has never—not the first time, and certainly not this time—felt true.

By the time the race begins, Vern is already opening his car door. He leaves town, the concrete buildings behind him, smoke erupting in stacks that rise and merge with the ice fog—the low, drifting cloud that never dissipates. He drives the snow-packed roads home, his hands tensing around the wheel when he approaches the intersection of Halley and Snowdrift Roads. An intersection so small as to have no streetlights or stop signs. But an intersection full of meaning nonetheless. A right turn would take him home, while a left would take him to Stefan Jacobsen's cabin. His car inching forward, Vern has never experienced such conflict, such indecision as the one that pulls on him now.

He wonders again why, after more than two decades of friendship, after everything they've been through, Stefan chose not to tell him first about his illness. Perhaps he told Sadie by accident, a slip. Or perhaps Stefan had been trying to protect him. Or perhaps there was no explanation at all. The scared often do strange, nonsensical things, he decides, accepting the truth of this. Despite the hurt burrowing into him, he is something of an expert on the subject.

Alaska had been his plan to start over. It was where he would forget all the disappointment and hurt of his previous life. He had no choice—it was the only way to escape the crippling helplessness he felt. But, surprise, it has simply brought him the long way around, right back to feeling just as much hurt, but in a slightly different form.

Usually, when he reaches this part of the road, Vern turns left without a second thought, stopping at Stefan's for a quick hello or to linger on the porch with a drink, chewing on ideas that mean nothing and everything at once. The lightest of things—the unique differences of color that streak like watercolors through the nasturtium petals, or the way the black spruce cast striped shadows across the dirt road. They might marvel at a strip of sunlight running vertically down the cabin wall, slanting as the better part of an hour passed. Stefan would likely report, with endless joy and pride, something Eila had done.

But today, Vern can think of nothing light to say. Today, the trees' shadows are imprisoning and the variations of flower petals so far off—it's been months since any flowers have bloomed. Today, the thought of Eila makes his chest cinch tight, because he knows how much pain she must be feeling.

Today, he can think only of the unkindness of the universe. Of darkness. Of running again. Vern prepares to turn the wheel right. Yes. He'll make a hasty trip to his cabin, rush to pack his bags. He'll leave behind anything unessential. He'll leave without a trace. No notes, no clues. Disappear to another place, farther away, even more remote, where there is truly no possibility of forming friendships.

This is what he decides. With conviction.

Then he hears Sadie again—*Giving up is what you do, Vern*—and he knows there is no going anywhere. There is no giving up, no evading, no escaping the fate of the man who has excelled in all the ways Vern has failed as a father, and as a friend. No running from the substantial role he could play in lightening the darkness. The answer is so clear, and he tried to involve Sadie, to get her blessing. It wasn't a mistake to ask her. But her stubbornness can't be helped.

Vern leans forward over the wheel. In the sky above Halley Road, a sun dog is carving a brilliant fragmented arc—perfectly spaced parentheses of reflected rainbow light around the sun. That shining orb at the center is a blurry, half-hidden beacon of something that resembles hope.

Light, he thinks. *The light is its own reason.*

Turning left means he could change, maybe, this time. Left means he could prevail where he's never prevailed before. Left is light. Left is hope.

In the sunlit snow, Vern turns left.

11

Shindigs. That's what Sadie liked to call them. Simple cookouts, that's all they were. Just Vern and Stefan and Eila eating black bean burgers and roasted potatoes at Sadie's house—the big place on the hill that they all envied for its indoor plumbing, central heat, and garage. A long field sprawled out before it, backed by thick woods. Along the field's perimeter, Sadie kept fifteen beehives. She thought the place was too extravagant, but she'd inherited it from her parents.

They'd started getting together like this not long after Vern had introduced Stefan to Sadie at the farmers market, where they'd stopped by Sadie's booth to buy some honey. Vern wonders now if Stefan even remembers this part of the story—Vern's responsibility for them meeting. Stefan was new to Fairbanks, though only slightly newer than Vern. He'd shaken Sadie's hand, smiling wide when she invited them both to her first shindig. This thing she was going to try out. Being social.

Of course, then there was *the* shindig. Shindig number six or seven. The one that changed things.

Sadie's menu on *that* evening was grilled garden vegetables and homemade bread and an enormous potato salad with green beans and dill. Eila played in the grass, distracted by grasshoppers when she was supposed to be searching for dandelions. Sadie had offered to pay a dollar per basket so she could make dandelion wine.

Sadie was making herself seem much busier than she actually was. She kept retreating to the kitchen to get just one more thing. It was on one of those hasty trips back and forth that Vern caught sight of it. She was on her way out of the kitchen and Stefan was on his way in. They passed awkwardly in the doorway, sidestepping with a giggle, and Stefan's hand brushed hers as they finally parted ways. For the rest of the evening, Vern said little, too preoccupied with what he thought he'd seen. He was too afraid to ask, lest it be exactly what he was thinking. When they said good night, and Stefan and Vern walked down the long driveway, Eila on Stefan's shoulders, Vern noticed that Stefan turned back toward the house rather than his car.

Vern drove a bit down the street before he pulled over, his heart pounding. *Ridiculous* was the word that came to mind when he looked down at his shaking hands. There was nothing wrong with two people deciding that they like each other. He had romantic feelings for neither of them. So why were his fingers trembling?

Opening his wallet, Vern pulled out a little folded note. It was simple notebook paper, torn on one edge. It had Sadie's name at the top, and the address and the usual dates for the Tanana Valley Farmers Market. The words *Fairbanks, AK* were underlined twice.

This. This was why his fingers were trembling.

He stuffed the note back into his wallet and exited the car, sneaking across Sadie's open field in the dark. The moonlight painted the grass silver. He made it as far as the trees, then sat on a rock and counted the lights in Sadie's house. One in the top-right window. Two on the bottom floor. He strained to see movement inside. Sadie appeared in a downstairs window, and Vern felt for a moment like she was looking directly at him, though there was no way she could see him, the woods as dark as they were and the window so brightly lit. She was a brief fixture; then Vern heard a high-pitched sound from inside the house—the whistling of a kettle—and Sadie left to attend to it.

A moment later, the lamp in the top window went out, and then strings of lights illuminated the back deck. Sadie stepped outside with the teakettle in hand, a towel wrapped around her torso. She emptied the steaming contents of the kettle into an outdoor bathtub beneath the lights and dropped her towel to the ground. Vern held his breath, closed his eyes, opened them again to see Stefan stepping out to the deck, wearing only a pair of shorts. The two slid into the tub.

Vern didn't know what he'd expected, but this wasn't it. And of course, he should have left, should have looked away at the very least. But he couldn't. Even though he knew he was doing something terribly wrong, he couldn't help coming back every night for the next week, wondering what else they might be keeping from him. He brought binoculars and tea in a thermos. Somehow, he convinced himself that if they were going to keep this from him, then it was their fault, not his, that he had to spy. He had no other choice if he wanted to know what was going on.

It was on the eighth night that he burned that little note he kept folded in his wallet. Vern watched Sadie and Stefan emerge from the back door in the moonlight, fill the bathtub, drop their towels. But this time, they didn't get in the water right away. This time, Sadie brought her hands to her face, covering her eyes, and through his binoculars, Vern saw her shoulders shaking. She was crying. Stefan, his back to Vern, his arms gathering Sadie close to him, was crying too.

Vern was hypnotized, then flustered. This was too much. He'd gone too far, invaded too much of their privacy. He unfolded the yellowed piece of notebook paper—this memento he'd been keeping, this thing that had brought him to Alaska. He'd kept it long enough, and it was silly, really. He was here now, whether or not Sadie remembered writing her name and saying "If you're ever up my way." It was embarrassing, the stock he'd put in it. The time for reminding her had passed, he decided, and now, he didn't deserve whatever it was he'd been hoping for anyway.

He lit the paper's edge with a lighter, dropping it when the flame singed his fingertips. He watched the fire go out, then turned and ran back across the field, tripping, his glasses flying into the tall grass. On his hands and knees he searched, but his fingers found only dried leaves and dirt. He combed the grass until it became clear that whether he should continue feeling around in the dark or drive home with less-than-perfect vision wasn't really a choice.

That night, he calculated how long it was acceptable for Stefan and Sadie to keep their relationship private. He added some padding for this new development—whatever they'd been so upset about—because that would likely make it harder to reveal. But he never expected it to take as long as it did—forever. They never told him. As far as he could tell, they eventually stopped seeing each other, though they remained good friends. And they never told Vern why they'd been crying, not even later. Not even after what happened next.

12

He finds Stefan in the Arctic entryway using a broom to swipe cobwebs from the top corners of the room. Vern peeks his head in and clears his throat. When Stefan turns, they both jump. Stefan had probably planned on telling him about his illness at some point, Vern realizes, but on his own terms. He's clearly thrown by Vern's impromptu visit. Vern glances at the thin web dangling from the broom and shakes off the feeling. It's too late now.

"What's this?" Vern asks. "Spring cleaning in the dead of winter?" He forces himself to laugh at his idiotic joke. The room has been stripped of clutter, a trash bag in the center of the floor spilling over with old insulation and dead wasps.

"I'm just doing what I can, now, you know. Before. Listen, Vern, I have to tell you—"

"Forget it," Vern interjects, waving a hand. "I already know. It's okay. I mean, of course it's *not* okay. It's just okay that you didn't tell me."

Stefan tilts his head, then says, "Well, I was going to tell you. But I was advised to stay close to home this week. My brain is doing things to me now. And I forgot where I put all the phone numbers."

"Sadie . . ."

"Oh, right. Eila ran into her at the store the other day. I guess Sadie got worried when she saw Eila in line at the pharmacy. Eila let the cat out."

Vern hides his relief by running his hand over the doorframe, wincing when a jagged sliver lodges in his palm. He pulls his hand back, and Stefan swoops to grab the trash bag and says, "Let's go inside and have some tea."

They settle at the kitchen table, two steaming mugs between them, the sweet-spicy smell of cinnamon and cardamom. Through the window, Vern watches an icicle break free from the gutter and fall into the snow.

"So," Vern says, unsure where to begin. "What's the plan? Are they going to have you on radiation, chemo?"

"Surgery first," Stefan says. "In a couple of days. It's standard protocol, I guess. Even though . . . you know. The chances are, well, the chances are basically zero."

"I'm going to get right to it," Vern says, straightening in his chair. "It doesn't have to be this way. I have something that can help. Sadie and I . . ."

Stefan leans over his teacup. "Listen," he says. "I know about the greenhouse full of bees and whatever life-regenerating mutation they have inside those little bodies, and I'm not interested. There's no way I'm going anywhere near it." He waves his hand as if to erase the idea from the space between them.

"You *know*? Oh . . ." Vern, the wrench returning to his gut, turns and scans the cabin, as if Sadie might be hiding behind the sofa. "Where is she? She got here before me? Well, for the record, it was my idea. Sadie didn't want to tell you. I was the one who tried to convince *her*."

"No, no," Stefan says. "She told me years ago. Back when it all happened."

Vern didn't think it was possible, but somehow this stabs even harder than being last to learn Stefan's news. Once again, he imagines the moment—Sadie telling Stefan about their big discovery, the two of them acknowledging the gravity, but also laughing at the absurdity of hiding it. Who in their right mind hides *immortality*? Or maybe they laughed at the fact that Sadie had been so adamant that Vern keep their secret, only to reveal it to Stefan behind his back. *I guess I just can't keep anything from you,* she'd have said coyly.

"All this time, and you knew," Vern says, slumping back in his chair. "The secrets you two kept."

"Didn't you have a secret or two of your own?" Stefan asks. "This big discovery, among other things, that you never told me about. You left me out."

"Yes, but that's different. Sadie made me promise not to tell a soul. I didn't want to leave you out. You let me go on thinking I was keeping a secret from you, when you were keeping a secret from me. You both could have just told me. About this . . . about everything."

"I'm with you there, Vern. Here's what I'm finding. That now, when the end is in sight, I feel like confessing. I don't even know what I have to confess anymore, but I want to remember it all, want to get it all out there. Before it's gone for good. And I want to listen too."

"Yeah," Vern says, straightening up a little. "Of course."

"Do you have anything you want to say?"

Vern thinks hard but can't come up with a single thing he's willing to dig up for Stefan, or Sadie, or anyone he knows here in Fairbanks. His worst deeds are all so far in the past, and he's worked hard to keep them there. He's not about to dig them up. "Are you looking for a eulogy or something? Because that's not what I'm here for. I'm not going to talk to you about death, or take a walk down memory lane. I'm here to talk you *out* of this whole dying thing."

"No."

"Please."

"Remember that day we met?" Stefan asks. "Out in the mountains. Remember what we talked about?"

"Yeah, sure. Adaptation. Resilience. That's exactly what I'm—"

"No," Stefan says. "We talked about the beauty of *nature*."

13

Vern doesn't realize how tightly he's squeezing the wheel until his dry knuckles begin to ache. He's also holding his breath. It's almost too ridiculous to believe. All the agonizing over betraying Sadie and offering this brilliant solution to Stefan, only to be turned down. And not just turned down, but humiliated again. Reminded that he's still, somehow, a third wheel to their secret, if short-lived, romance.

At the end of Halley Road, he shakes himself out of his trance and hits the gas harder than he intends. He pulls onto Goldstream at the same moment a man on a bicycle slips past the nose of his car. Vern's foot jerks to the brake, sending his heart into frantic palpitations. No excuse that a bicyclist isn't common in the middle of winter—this is plain carelessness. Distraction. No wonder he's losing everything.

Vern flinches, his eyes pinched shut. He shouts at the windshield—an ugly sort of scream that frightens even him as he realizes the two enormous, irreversible mistakes he has made in life. One is so obvious: That he left behind a family that needed him to be loving and caring and responsible—a need he stupidly took for a burden. Instead, he ran straight for some vast frontier, some blank canvas. But two: That the canvas turned out to be not quite as empty as he'd expected. He'd only found more people who, though they might not *need* him in the same way as his wife and daughter, had also come to deserve his love. His *friendship*. And has he lived up to the obligations this time? Adequately reciprocated the affection on this second go-round? Thinking of all that's happened, and of Stefan now—facing his inevitable end—Vern is pretty positive he hasn't.

He watches the bicyclist—bound in cold-weather gear from the toes up, only his eyes peeking through—shrink into a tiny red bead rolling across the icy road. Vern looks again in both directions and crosses the intersection at a crawl.

14

Eila Jacobsen

Playing music at Ivory Jack's was a big part of Stefan's beginnings in Alaska—vital to the reinvention of himself here. So when he wakes in a panic at the thought of forgetting, of losing this aspect of himself, he tells Eila he wants to play there one last time. The decision is short lived, though, because soon after, he panics again, worried that he'll forget the music or the lyrics or both.

Eila convinces him to play in the living room. She invites Vern, who—through a half-opened front door—promptly turns his eyes to his shoes and says he's not available, even though she hasn't yet mentioned a date or time. Sadie's eyes immediately well up, and she resumes shoveling snow madly, rambling about how she wouldn't last one song. Far too heartbreaking, she says over her shoulder, especially if he played *that* one. Eila doesn't ask which one she means because she knows already, and she also knows that he will play it, because it's the earliest song he wrote, and that makes it the safest given his memory.

Before she has time to think of a reasonable explanation for the absence of his best friends, her father waves her off and says he's happier if it's just her. "I was only ever really playing for you anyway," he says.

In a red-and-black-checkered bathrobe and wool slippers, he sits on a stool with his guitar balanced on his knee, and the instrument looks suddenly small. Eila knows it's a trick, that he's grown heavier because of his medications, but it seems like more than that. Like somehow, his overall presence has expanded. A sigh to dispel jitters and then his voice fills the room—low and raspy—and she snaps the one Polaroid he agreed to, because he knows he doesn't look like himself anymore.

He plays three songs without forgetting a single word or chord, and the last is *that* one—the one he called "The Sunlit River"—and she listens carefully to the lyrics. She knows she's hearing them for the last time. The song is full of imagination and exploration and burnt-parchment maps. It's full of cold, rushing rivers and endless valleys of fireweed and the haunting blush of summer nights on the tundra.

The music conjures an image that rests at the edge of Eila's memory. Perhaps, she thinks, it's because she's heard this song so many times. Perhaps it's because the song is based on her childhood. Either way, it has come to life over the years by way of repetition.

She lets the tears fall because there's no stopping them anyway—and why not let him know he's that loved, that his absence will create a chasm in her life? They don't talk directly about what's coming anymore—there's nothing they haven't said already—so Eila wipes her cheek with the heel of her palm and attempts to be tough. Her father tears up for a moment, too, until he also straightens his back and clears his throat with a forced, theatrical "Ahem." They both laugh at the melting display of sentimentality. A thing they'd promised not to do, a place they wouldn't go.

"We should go for a walk," he says. "Before the mosquitoes come out."

She looks at his thin calves beneath the bathrobe. Though he looks larger, it's a trick, because the truth is, he's lost so much muscle. They haven't gone walking in weeks. "Aren't you tired?" she asks.

He shrugs, nestling the guitar into its stand. "Absurdly," he says, and he might mean *absolutely*, but *absurdly* does the trick too.

"We should have pizza."

He thinks for a moment, and she knows he's searching for a word. He nods and says, "Yes. Let's do the garden instead."

She's used every inch of space in the gated garden, growing herbs, flowers, and vegetables in an intricate system of garden beds, tiered barrels, and vertical hangers. He helped her put up the fence to keep the moose and hares out. It's still too early to grow anything outside, but there are herbs in the greenhouse. Eila watches him snip basil, his hands shaky. He studies the leaves, and she studies her hands, which have always seemed capable to her. Capable because of the way he raised her. Though right now they seem useless, unable to fix the one thing that really needs fixing.

"I always liked that lyric," she says, "about wild minds and needing to tell stories."

"That's always the easiest line to remember," he says, dropping the basil into a basket. "It's the first one I wrote. If we're going to survive in this world, we need wild imaginations. And we need to wander to cultivate those imaginations, and we need wild places to wander in. And we need to imagine a future in which those wild places are still here. It's all a cycle. But I'm rambling."

"No," she says, taking the basket, shaking off the words *survive* and *future*. "You're not."

"You're really good at this," he says, lifting a mint plant that is leaning heavily from its pot. He surveys the small greenhouse teeming with greenery so early in the season—a difficult feat perhaps, but not for someone who studies Arctic vegetation for a living. He seems lost in thought, then says, "I bet you could have solved it. Sadie and Vern."

This takes Eila by surprise. "What about them needed solving?"

"Oh." He ponders this. "The, um . . . the lupine. The ash flower. The project, the problem, the anomaly, the abomination. I bet you could have fixed it."

She's curious—it sounds ominous and even a little bit exciting—but she doesn't ask for more explanation, because it's frustrating for him to be questioned when he's having trouble saying what he means. Times like this, when the words get jumbled and don't make sense together, she usually changes the subject. "Parsley? Inside, we have zucchini, bell peppers, broccoli, onions. Bacon, of course."

"All of it. Everything. Pile it on, as much as possible, before the thing collapses."

"You're becoming poetic," she says.

"Happiness is pizza."

"See what I mean."

After dinner, once he's gone to bed, Eila takes the empty water jugs to the spring just outside town. This is part of living here—chores that would seem ludicrous in warmer climates. But it is never something she minds doing. Sometimes, it's a joy. Sometimes, she's emotionally exhausted and just needs the quiet.

She pulls into the parking lot where the spring flows through two metal spouts inside a shed. She lifts the four blue jugs from the back of her car, places them on the ice beneath the streams. The water pours in and Eila taps her boot against a hanging icicle, zipping her heavy canvas work coat higher, rubbing her hands together. It's more out of impatience than anything—she doesn't really understand what cold is.

Hands in her pockets, she leans back and looks up to the black sky, a few stray flakes of snow drifting down. A chickadee zips past her head and wedges itself into the smallest crack in the shed roof. Sawdust falls onto Eila's shoulder. The bird squeezes its body in to roost and ride out the night. Eila marvels at its natural adaptation. It will lower its internal temperature to fifteen degrees, burning all night long the enormous amount of fat that it's stored throughout the day.

Last year, one of the station's undergrad interns wrote a paper about the dangers faced by wintering birds. *Finding a roost for the night is the most important task. Without shelter, they wouldn't survive the night in this kind of cold. Without that place to huddle up—even if they have to flatten themselves into a hole the size of a cherry—all of the day's hard work would be for nothing. They can never lose sight of this mission. They must find shelter.*

Eila remembers the shocking repetition of this fact—the critical task of finding a place of refuge each night. When she's particularly tired, her mind has an irritating tendency to wander to darker places, and it travels quickly from the chickadees to the image of her father stumbling home in the dark, confused and alone, lost in the very place where he'd previously found familiarity and comfort. She picks up the icicle, squeezes it in her fist, feels it begin to stick to her skin, and then lets it fall to the pavement.

Rather than going home, she drives to the station, though it's after hours, and she finds the animals are exactly as they should be. The muskoxen and reindeer are bedded down, chewing their cud, snow collecting like thick blankets on their well-insulated backs. Everyone else has gone home, except for Drew, who's leaning on the reindeer pen, watching one of the calves, Charley, the calf that didn't attempt to walk within minutes, like other reindeer. Charley, who stumbled and couldn't extend her legs because of contracted tendons. It took her over a week just to get off the ground, and she still hasn't taken more than a few steps. The veterinary students put a splint on her front legs, and they've been watching her, hoping she'll learn to walk on her own before she turns one.

Charley's mother lingers nearby. In the wild, she might have left her calf behind; Charley would have been the weakest in the herd and easy prey. But here, her mother seems pulled by opposing forces: the wild instinct to preserve the herd and the domestic one that tells her to care for her calf at all costs. She can afford to here.

Drew turns toward Eila, snowflakes caught on his eyelashes. He looks like some wild creature that's just emerged from the forest. "I'm supposed to be fixing this gate," he says. His hands are hidden from the cold in enormous puffy gloves, and he's holding an axe.

A few days before, one of the muskoxen rammed into the post, splintering it. Drew stayed late to chop it down and put in a new one, but the thick post is hacked at and half-mutilated. It looks as if he's given up.

"Who taught you to use an axe?" she asks.

"My uncle?" Drew deliberates. "No one?"

She grabs the axe with her ungloved hands.

Drew winces. "Don't—" he begins. She knows it disturbs him that she never wears gloves, even when touching metal in the dead of winter. It's absurd, it's dangerous, but she's never felt the need.

She cuts the post down with one determined blow.

Drew rolls his eyes. "Show-off. I'm not incapable, Jacobsen."

On a daily basis, Eila and Drew pretend that there was never anything between them—brief and halfhearted as it was for both of them, back when Eila thought she might be able to love someone who wasn't Jackson. They've managed to become good friends and even better coworkers.

"Everything good?" she asks, standing on tiptoes, peering over the fence.

"Why wouldn't it be?" he asks. "Yeah, everything's fine."

She's still thinking of chickadees, and of her father's resilience the night before everything changed, but voicing it now would only give the gut-twisting feeling more life. She's about to say something trivial instead, something about the kids who came by the station on a field trip earlier that morning—dressed like butterflies and bumblebees. But the snow stops and Drew looks up, pointing with his cartoonishly large hands.

Eila tips her head back to see that the clouds have cleared and the northern lights are snaking across the sky, each green ripple smudged upward and fading into the void.

"Who taught *you* to use an axe?" Drew asks, looking up.

Eila is lost in thought—the swells of the aurora always carry Jackson back to her on their waves. Drew nudges her with his elbow. "My father," she says quickly. "Apparently, I was a natural. At least that's how he tells it."

"Check it out," he says. "She's doing it." Eila's eyes flick back down to Charley. He's right. The calf is ambling around the perimeter on tentative but strong legs. Charley pauses at the fence, her long neck stretching, her eyes gazing into the dark, maybe beyond the corral and the many acres of frozen land. Beyond the train tracks and the hills that rise at the edge of town and continue on for what seems like eternity.

15

Her father starts writing it all down. Sometimes just a detail here or there, other times whole paragraphs. Occasionally the memories are pages long. He does this as soon as the urge hits, which is why he's begun carrying a notebook around the house while he and Eila pass in opposing circles. She, clockwise, from the kitchen to the living room to the bedroom. He, counterclockwise, from the bedroom to the living room to the kitchen.

It's an unspoken system. Eila makes breakfast and coffee while he dresses. They meet on the couch in front of the large window, the sun rising pink behind them, and she sips her coffee slowly and glances over her shoulder at the moose and fox that visit the yard. He pauses between bites of oatmeal or sips of tea and jots something down in his book. When they finish, he insists on taking the dishes to the sink and washing them, one by one, careful not to waste water since he isn't the one driving to the spring or carrying the heavy jugs. Yet, there is always some water that dribbles into the bucket beneath the sink. Eila moves into the bedroom, where she refills his medicine boxes and makes sure the floor is clear of clothing and shoes so he doesn't trip on anything.

She watches him one morning, his hands shaking and eyes closing every so often, as if the stories are written there, just behind his eyelids. And it's one of the harder things she does in those final days before he dies, promising to read it all, every page, after he's gone.

And then he *is* gone, as they'd come to accept that he would be. Though how is one ever ready for it?

Eila brings him home in an alderwood urn. It is simple and rectangular, with minimalistic carvings—a mountain, a sun, two bears. The house, she finds, is not quiet, the way she expected. Quite the opposite, actually, every sound suddenly revealed. The ticking of a branch against the window, the creak of the couch. When the kettle whistles on the stove, it's almost unbearably loud. And that sink water— each drop in the slop bucket jolts her.

Eventually, she uses the tip of her boot to gently nudge his bedroom door open, half expecting something to jump out and surprise her, though she knows the room will contain only cold, dusty objects that now belong to her.

His bookshelf holds a disorganized collection of naturalists. Most books have multiple bookmarks wedged in, torn pieces of paper that point to either his rushed reading or his hunger to keep track of it all.

He left the notebook for her on the bedside table. On the faded cover, he'd written a quote: *"Chaos was the law of nature; Order was the dream of man."* *H. Adams.* The bedroom doubled as his office. His drafting table is piled with blueprints, his filing cabinet full of his tenants' account information. She will have to attend to these eventually, find someone who can take over his business.

Maps hang on the walls—not of prospective cabin sites or places he planned to visit one day. These are maps of rivers he'd once traveled along, of mountain ranges he'd driven through, all probably before she was born. Each yellowing sheet marks a point of transition. They are pictures of change, of his deliberate migrations. Eila has never looked closely before, and she's surprised to see how far he'd gone—the extent of his travels and the impressive reach of his life.

16

He'd told Eila many times he didn't want a traditional funeral, and to please scatter his ashes one day in the mountains, so she puts off any kind of ceremony for as long as possible. But in May, Sadie comes knocking, insisting that they do *something*.

"It's not for him," she says. "It's for us." She glances over her shoulder, noting Vern's absence. "Well, me." There's a need deep in Sadie's eyes, and Eila reminds herself that, though he was her father, he was something else to Sadie, to everyone who knew him. So, on the next decent Friday, Eila, Sadie, and Vern stand around Stefan's firepit in exactly the kind of awkward manner that Eila had expected. Breakup is just beginning—mud and mosquitoes feel like the only certainties in life—and the light is returning gently. They avoid eye contact despite their tiny circle, swatting at insects and shielding their faces from a surprisingly intense evening sun.

Vern opens his mouth multiple times but changes his mind. Eila assumes he's feeling just as she is—the pressure to share some detail they can reminisce over—something thoroughly and uniquely Stefan, and meaningful to all of them too. Every memory seems too personal, though. Sure, they'd been to the same midnight baseball games, state fairs, sled dog races. But when Eila tries to remember these moments, she can't recall a single specific thing that either Vern or Sadie was doing. It had to be the same for them.

Eila wonders if she should have brought her father's urn out to the fire, then decides he would prefer being exactly where he is—in the cabin, surrounded by the smell of cedar and pine. She tries to redirect her thoughts from the borrowed hospital bed that's still in there, waiting to be taken away. Not much more cheerful, she touches her flannel shirt pocket, almost pulling out the last picture she took of him. She's even tempted to toss it into the fire because she regrets taking it—he hadn't wanted his face to be remembered that way—but Sadie looks like she might burst into tears if the wind blows the wrong direction, and Vern's arms are crossed over his chest and he buries his chin into his jacket collar. He whistles quietly, a tune that Eila doesn't recognize but is a good enough distraction. When he stops briefly, Eila and Sadie both look up, startled, as if they might now be expected to speak.

It's beginning to feel like they'll never find a way off this train speeding straight into a cave of irreversible sorrow, when Sadie says, "How was he so good at everything?"

"Ha!" Vern laughs. "Remember, that son of a . . . he won the Nenana Ice Classic three years in a row? I still say that was pure luck, because you can't predict river ice cracking to the minute based on science."

"I actually think luck counts as something you can be good at," Sadie says.

"Well, he did win the marathon too," Vern adds. "A couple of times, if memory serves."

"And wait," Sadie continues. "How many times did he win the Chatanika Outhouse Races?"

"That was *all* of us," says Vern. "A team effort."

"Oh please, you think we'd ever have won if it wasn't for him?"

They pause for a moment, and Eila's afraid they're looking at her, so she keeps her eyes on the fire, waiting for them to continue. But the pause stretches on, as if they're unsure about this new train they've boarded. She remembers only one of these races, when they'd decorated the outhouse to look like a penguin, fabric wings and yellow wooden beak and everything. The teams were supposed to be five—two people pushing on either side of the outhouse, and one riding inside—but instead, they'd buckled Eila and Jackson to the toilet seat, then Sadie and Vern pushed one side, and Stefan did the work of two people on the other.

"There was the flamingo year. We won that time, right?" asks Vern.

"Yes, and the peacock year," Sadie adds.

There it is. The gap between their memories. Eila feels slightly lost, then tries, for her father's sake, to take part. "The penguin," she says. "That's the only one I remember."

"The majestic penguin!" Vern says. "The year we retired the old bird."

"The last race," Sadie laments. "I don't even know how we won, because that year one of the skis broke off, remember? Stefan went sliding on his ass across the snow to get it, and we got off kilter because it was just the two of us on one side, and he left his damn post."

Eila cracks a smile, surprised by how visceral the memory is—the shaking of their bathroom-racing structure around her, Jackson's presence, the view of the snowy tracks suddenly turning to the crowd on the sidelines and the trees behind, the feeling of spinning out of control, everyone shouting to push harder. She can see her breath and Jackson's breath, and her knees next to Jackson's knees, both of them in jeans stiff from the cold.

"We recovered, though," Vern says, holding up an emphatic finger. "He made it back in time. Saved our precious cargo"—he gestures to Eila—"*and* won the race."

"Wait," Eila says. "What happened to the outhouse after?"

"Oh, Prometheus!" the three of them say at the same time, laughing, because Stefan Jacobsen couldn't just burn something without also becoming a fire god.

He'd dismantled the outhouse and stacked the wood high. Eila, Sadie, Vern, and Jackson stood around the firepit on a muddy spring night not unlike the current one, wondering where her father was, until a ball of fire behind them caught their eyes. From the cabin deck, her father shouted, "I give you humans fire!" and the flaming ball flew toward them and struck the firepit, and the burn pile exploded into a mighty blaze. Turned out, her father had run fishing line from the deck to the firepit, then hid behind the charcoal grill. After his great proclamation, he'd slid a flaming roll of toilet paper down the line toward the gasoline-soaked mountain of wood.

"I give you humans fire," Sadie says, shaking her head.

Vern kicks one of the firepit stones and grunts, perhaps at their small fire. "We should have done better," he says.

Sadie clears her throat. "Are you going north this year for research?" she asks Eila.

Vern's eyes flash up to Sadie, then to Eila, then to the flames again like he knows something, but he says nothing.

"No," Eila says, her heart leaping from her chest into the fire. Yet another subject that hurts to talk about. "It's my turn to stay back at the station."

Vern looks relieved and Eila's annoyed. Does he think her research trips are vacations, and what, it's too soon for her to enjoy life again? She jams more wood into the already-full firepit, sparks flying and ash floating up. When she stands, smoke stings her nostrils. She mumbles that she needs to grab something from the cabin and turns to go.

Inside, she looks around for a bag of chips or something she can "grab" but decides to open her laptop and the caribou tracking app instead. The herd is moving toward the coastal plain for calving, and Eila closes her eyes to see chartreuse fields dotted with wildflowers. She smells wet earth and new buds and fresh grass.

It seems unbearably cruel that her father had to close his eyes for the last time when the world was finally coming back to life. Now is not the time for hibernation. Now is the time for waking up.

17

Vern Graves

When Sadie's house burned, she lost the house, but also her twelve acres of cultivated flowers and all her hives. Stefan offered to rebuild the place, but she refused to put another house on the same ground. Too many memories that she'd rather leave behind; that was all she said. But her family had some remote land up north, east of Coldfoot. It was an old homestead, a small log cabin and some garden beds, left untouched for generations. That's where she would move.

It was the middle of summer when Sadie showed them where it was on the map. Since the fire, she'd been staying in one of Stefan's near-finished cabins on Halley Road. Vern had his elbows resting on the back porch railing, binoculars held to his eyes. He was tracking a bird. He remembers exactly what bird it was—a northern goshawk—because he was just about to call for Stefan to come out and have a look when Sadie marched up the back steps in a magenta swimsuit, a towel wrapped around her head, rolled-up map in hand.

Vern guessed she'd just come from the sauna behind Stefan's cabin. Her eyes grew wide when she saw Vern, and he almost left. But Stefan asked him to stay, so the three of them stood around the kitchen table with the map spread out, chunks of quartz and granite holding down the corners. With a pen, Sadie marked a little dot along a thin blue line of river, in the middle of all that endless green and brown. That's where her family homestead was.

"Do you think it's possible?" Sadie asked. Strands of wet hair escaped the towel, twisting down to her collarbone. "It must be pretty run down."

"It should be," Stefan said. "If you don't need running water, and you'll only be there for the summer months. We can go up there now, and it should be ready before winter. Getting supplies out there will be tricky, but we can manage it."

Vern glanced around the room, involuntarily looking for signs of Sadie's life there. He couldn't stop himself from asking, "Where are you going to live the rest of the year?"

Sadie and Stefan exchanged a glance. "I think, here?" Sadie said, her words more of a question than a statement, as if she had only just thought of it and needed confirmation. She laughed self-consciously. "Not *here*. I mean, in the cabin down the street. Where I'm staying now. I'll buy it."

"It's almost done," Stefan said, shrugging, "and no tenants lined up."

Vern tried to keep his mouth shut, but his brain circled back to this remote land in the North, this homestead she'd never mentioned before. "And what are you planning to do up there all summer?"

Sadie whirled around to face Vern, her eyebrows narrowed. "What exactly are you doing here again?" she asked.

Vern flinched, feeling caught, guilty. She must know, he thought. He waited a moment, then said, "Honestly, I don't know! I was going to leave." He almost did get up and leave but instead said, "But I do know that when I'm asked to participate in something, I participate."

Sadie's face twisted with incredulity. "Well, I don't recall asking you to participate!"

There was a moment of awkward silence in which they all focused on the map instead of each other. Then Sadie broke the quiet with uncontrolled laughter, and Stefan joined her a moment later, leaning back in his chair, letting loose his deep, roaring chortle.

Stefan elbowed Vern and shot him a look, so Vern forced a smile, gaze still fixed on the table.

Sadie dabbed at her eyes with her towel and turned to Vern again, suddenly serious. "Hey, weren't you, like, a scientist or something?" she asked.

"Horticulturist," Vern said. "I was a high school horticulture teacher."

"Hmm," Sadie said, squinting. She and Stefan shared another look that Vern couldn't quite decipher. Then Stefan shrugged, and Sadie shrugged and said, "Well, I'm going to get dressed. I guess you could show him, Stef, if you want. Who knows, maybe he can help."

Vern knew he'd lost the right to feel left out, if he'd ever had the right in the first place. He knew, especially after spying on them, and then after—gulp—the fire, that he didn't deserve to know everything that was going on. So he bit his tongue and feigned curiosity as Sadie pulled one of Stefan's hoodies over her swimsuit, slid the rocks from the map's corners, rolled the paper tightly, and left through the back door.

Once she was gone, Stefan took Vern to his small backyard greenhouse. The two stood, shoulders touching, as Stefan opened a wooden box. Inside was the cut blossom of an Arctic lupine. It was so deeply and radiantly violet that Vern thought his eyes were clouding up, and he blinked in an attempt to make the glow disappear. He'd never seen anything so remarkably full of color and light.

"It's incredible," Vern said.

"Sadie found this in the ash, where the beehives were. It was the only thing that didn't burn. It was just growing there, perfect. It hasn't changed since she brought it over, and it's been cut for weeks."

Vern fished out the loupe he kept in the pocket of his flannel shirt. He peered closely at the flower. "May I?"

Stefan moved the box closer, and Vern pushed and pulled gently on the petals with shaking fingers.

"I don't know what to think," Vern said.

"It's impossible, right?"

"I mean, Arctic flowers are more resilient than those that grow in warmer places, and they have certain adaptations that help them survive, but this . . . No, I don't know what to think. Are there more?"

"This was the only one. She isn't sure if it had something to do with the fire, or the bees, or if it's just the flower. But she wants to build a greenhouse up north, next to the existing cabin, where she can experiment with it."

Vern was sweating now, partially from the greenhouse's heat and tight quarters and partially because he was trying to keep his heart from beating so madly. He didn't dare ask if he could be part of whatever this was, but he wanted to, desperately. "What kinds of experiments?" he asked. "And is she in touch with a botanist or something? Someone who can help her?"

"Sadie has this idea," Stefan said, "that maybe you could help? She doesn't really want to tell anyone about it, just yet. She doesn't want anyone, especially any outside scientists, to come up here and—how do I say it—change the dynamic. She's feeling kind of low on trust, given the fire."

"Oh," Vern said, trying not to look as guilty as he felt. As he *was*. "Does she, you know? Did you tell her?"

Stefan looked at the ground. "No. I don't know what she's thinking."

Vern curled his hands into fists to keep them from touching the flower. He tried to hide how much he wanted to accept by relatching the box with great care. "I'll see if I can clear my schedule."

They spent the rest of the summer on Sadie's family's land. Stefan hauled roofing to the site by ATV, and Vern went out to the surrounding forest to cut and mill the lumber he needed. The greenhouse was a feat, requiring metal framing and rolls of sheet plastic. Eila helped Sadie prepare soil while Stefan and Vern worked on the house—repairing the broken-down door and shattered windows.

Vern felt, for much of that time, inferior in more ways than one. Not only was he terrible at building things, but he watched an enviable father-daughter relationship bloom right before his eyes. Being a single parent wasn't something Stefan had ever expected, he'd told Vern over a backyard beer once, but it was the hand he'd been dealt. His partner, Maisie, had never intended to become a parent at all, and she left one night—a simple note tacked to the front door begging him not to follow. Despite being thrust into the role, Stefan managed to do things like climb a ladder to the roof and balance himself on the peak, all while keeping his eyes on Eila playing by the river. When Vern noticed Eila wandering off toward a stand of stunted spruce, he almost asked Stefan if he should run and grab her. But before he had a chance, he saw Stefan was already watching her, hammer poised above a nail as his eyes followed her toward the tree line.

"Wait for it," Stefan said, and sure enough, Eila reached out to touch a low spruce bough, then turned and ran, full of laughter, back to the house. "She's just testing boundaries."

And on top of it all, being a father didn't stop Stefan from being himself. Once the cabin was done and the greenhouse built, the garden beds filled and set to rest for the coming winter, they built a fire in the woodstove and sat around the living room. It was meant to be a celebration, but they were all so tired that they just sat in silence. Vern read a book, Sadie knitted, and Eila built towers with the extra kindling. Stefan, on the floor with a sketchbook in his lap, made quick, light strokes with a thin black marker.

The following spring, Sadie moved in. She got new bees and shipped them to the nearby village of Cloud Creek, then drove them by ATV to the homestead. She made a plan for how she and Vern would experiment and track their research on the flower.

Vern made a show of explaining how he was still currently seeking employment but could do this other, equally important work anywhere in the meantime. For now. The truth was he had nothing better to do than study Sadie's incredible discovery.

Despite his initial shame at accepting the invitation from Sadie, whom he'd not only harmed terribly but whose privacy he'd also grossly invaded, Vern allowed himself to enjoy each long drive up the Dalton

Highway to Coldfoot. The car shook and rattled over the cratered dirt road as the great expanse of tundra spun by outside the window. They had to yell sometimes to hear one another, but they'd pass the time chatting about crossbreeding flowers or the latest health supplement for bees that had popped up in the news.

He was breathless on every frightening flight from Coldfoot to that remote patch of land at the edge of the Yukon River tributary. Flights where he once—just once—was so scared he reached over and grabbed Sadie's hand without thinking, and the fact that she'd grabbed his back was so much more terrifying than the shuddering Cessna itself.

He never let himself think past it. He never allowed himself to wonder if he shouldn't have burned that little note. He reminded himself that he had a job to do, and to do it, he'd have to keep his friends at a distance. That's how they wanted it, too, it seemed.

Side by side, Sadie and Vern opened the greenhouse every spring to the garden beds they'd turned over and prepared the previous fall, the earthy smell of soil filling their nostrils. Then they'd work together all summer, pulling out the pages of notes they'd written the year before and retracing the lines, attempting to do even better. Attempting to re-create, through precise, deliberate interactions between Sadie's bees and Vern's new flowers, flowers like the one Sadie had found after the fire.

The original lupine survived only two years, but they still knew it had been beyond special. No annual plant should live that long, especially through the Arctic winter. They tried other plants, thinking that maybe, if they worked with the known adaptations of all Arctic plants, they might find whatever it was that had made the lupine survive so long.

Vern had read once as a horticulture student that sometimes it's the wildest, craziest ideas in plant breeding that lead to the most exciting results. For example, a green tomato plant may actually be carrying the gene for the deepest red. The more diversity he and Sadie introduced, the more variations, the better. They needed to start with the widest range of flower traits and then keep the ones closest to their goal. They tried everything.

They crossed Arctic willows with dwarf willows, aiming to capture the qualities of both—the natural pesticide and fuzzy leaves produced by the Arctic willow, as well as the broad shape of the dwarf willow's leaves. They tried to retain the Arctic poppies' light petals for camouflage and the shallow spread of their root systems in addition to the wooly stems of Arctic lupines, which could better trap heat. The cup-shaped flowers of tundra roses gather ample sunlight, bloom earlier in the spring, and take root in the sandy soils of south-facing slopes, so they attempted to merge these traits with the cushiony shape of moss campion, which hugs the ground to preserve warmth.

They tested each plant against the elements, even taking some back to Fairbanks for the winter to see how long they could survive at forty below zero. Once, they tried watering the flowers with liquid smoke, an effort to re-create the conditions for the first flower's adaptation. It had grown from the ash, after all.

For some of their experiments, it took generations of evolving one plant type for them to realize it wasn't going to work. They'd create a new list of ideas and move on.

Then one spring—what would turn out to be the last spring—they opened the greenhouse door to find it buzzing with bees and bursting with poppies. It was all impossible, of course. It all should have been long dead, as it had been every year before. Sadie and Vern looked at each other with matching expressions of shock: *Are you seeing what I'm seeing? Is this real? Does this even have anything to do with us?* It was real, but it also seemed like coincidence. At least, it couldn't have been the result of something they'd done intentionally.

When they dissected and analyzed the poppies, the only unusual thing they found was extremely high levels of calcium. But where and how they'd acquired it, neither Vern nor Sadie could tell. Their minds spiraled to the possible uses for such a mutation. But before they went any further, they had to be sure. So they spent the next week trying to kill both the bees and flowers. First, they used the obvious tactic, snipping a blossom clean off the stem with a pair of garden shears. They cut the flower on day one, and by day two, it had grown back to its full vibrancy. They tried this again on day three. But by day four, they were almost positive that the new blossom looked even healthier than the old one.

They attempted to drown some of the poppies by dropping them in a bucket and filling it with water. They threw some bees in there, too, dear god. The poppies sank, the bees struggled to swim, and Vern and Sadie covered the bucket with a lid so as not to witness their own heartless deeds. When they lifted the lid a few days later, the poppies were floating on the surface, fanning their petals out, brilliant as ever. The bees rested on the petals as if on little lifeboats.

On day five, they threw the bees and flowers into a can, then topped it with crumpled paper and lit it on fire. All the paper burned up, smoke spiraling into the sunlit night sky, flowers and bees remaining unscathed at the bottom of the bucket.

As a last attempt, Vern and Sadie laid the flowers in the freezer, zipped a handful of bees into a plastic sandwich bag, and laid them in there too. When they opened the freezer door the next morning, the bees were still bouncing around, trying to escape the plastic, and somehow the flowers had developed additional buds.

They wondered if this—this clear demonstration of what could only be infinite adaptability, immortality even—was what had happened with the first lupine, or if it was something new entirely. Perhaps, after all these years, they hadn't actually known what they were looking for, or how it would reveal itself to them.

Perhaps it didn't matter.

Every experiment revealed the same thing: The bees could not be killed. The flowers pollinated by the bees didn't die either. They weren't sure which had come first—the immortal bees or the immortal flowers—but Vern and Sadie had very different views on what to do about them.

The joy of their years spent in pursuit of a beautiful, resilient flower disappeared. All that was left was argument.

"We *have* to share this," Vern said.

Sadie didn't even have to think. She shook her head and said, "Absolutely not."

"Think of the problems this could solve."

"Share it with who?" Sadie asked defensively. "What could this possibly solve? You realize what something like this would do to the balance of nature? You think things are messed up now, just try introducing something that *lives forever*. Tamper with it, and everything will get worse. Much, much worse."

"There are new diseases every year, Sadie. We could potentially fix that. It's not a small thing."

"You're right. It's an enormous thing. The biggest thing. And what happens when we cure all diseases, Vern? The human population grows bigger and wreaks even more havoc on the planet, and there are even fewer resources, even less space? What then?"

"You're jumping way ahead, Sadie. We can't imagine that far into the future."

"We have to imagine it, Vern. That's what imagination is for—to show us what might be *if*. As far into the future as we can possibly comprehend."

"We'd only allow it to be used in the most serious cases. Or for the most terrible, uncurable diseases. There has to be a way to distill this so it's just for healing, to keep it from being used for the immortality aspect."

"Good luck with that. You can't trust people to use a discovery like this responsibly. The moment you offer it up, it'll be out of your hands. Out of control. You won't have a say in what it's *allowed* to be used for. No. We can't."

"But . . . ," Vern began, even as he realized he had no further arguments.

"I don't want anyone else here," she said. "Just us. No outsiders, no questions."

"You never thought we'd actually find it, did you? You were just passing time."

Sadie waved him off as she turned to leave the greenhouse. "As if you weren't just passing time yourself. This is my place, you know. You're here to help me, and I appreciate your help and your opinions, I do. But that doesn't change the fact that what's here belongs to me."

Stung, Vern closed his notebook and walked out of the greenhouse.

He went days without speaking to Sadie. Perhaps he thought she would come to her senses after she had more time to contemplate their discovery, all its potential uses. More than once, he considered going rogue—stealing the science and leaving in the night, using it for something good. Of course, he knew she had a point, even if it was tempting, after a life bursting with failures, to finally make a savior of himself.

18

Vern makes a drink and stands at the back window, where the plastic sheet that he heat-sealed to the pane is peeling at the edges. It's clear that he waited too long to put the barrier up. The glass was already too cold for the adhesive to work properly, but it's doing a decent job regardless, keeping much of the frigid air out, helping with his diesel bill. But a decent job is far from a stellar job. It's not perfection. And when perfection is possible, attainable . . .

He glances at the wall beside the window. He's hung every calendar that he and Sadie have x-ed their way through over the years. Free calendars from the phone company and a few nice store-bought ones that Sadie purchased when she was feeling inspired.

Vern shudders, remembering their attempts to murder the bees and flowers. Goose bumps rise on his arms beneath his heavy sweater, which he blames on his strong drink. Looking back, it seems like such a horrible experiment, but it had to be done. They had to be sure.

The heater in Vern's tiny cabin turns on, the loud fan puffing streams of hot air into the room, and the breeze it creates lifts one of the calendars, flapping it against the others until it detaches from its nail and flutters to the floor. The calendar lies open on the rug. Vern refuses to look. Finally, he glances down, not surprised to find it's the oldest, most worn out. The year: 2002. The month: June. The beginning of everything.

Vern kicks the calendar across the room, sending it sliding under the sink. It hits the slop bucket—which needs emptying, but his back hurts—and stops. He turns back to the window.

A snowshoe hare sits in the middle of the half-circle backyard, where pointed black spruce trees form a curved perimeter. Vern watches as a fox—the one he sees almost every afternoon—tiptoes out from the tree line. The hare shuffles forward a little, balancing on its broad front paws.

The days are beginning to lengthen again, coming out on the other side of darkness, folding forward and expanding. Somehow time feels more precious, even now, as with each dip of the sun below the horizon, Vern knows that the return will come leaps and bounds sooner than the day before. The hare's ears, pointed to the sky, twitch. The fur of its back legs has fully changed from its soft winter white to a flecked summer brown. Its back is camouflaged against a landscape still waiting to bloom. The fox, too, is changing color.

For both creatures, life is constant transformation, anticipation. Not so different from everyone else, Vern thinks. But what if—what if, what if, *what if*—it didn't have to be so hard?

PART 2

19

Lark Audette

In New Mexico, thousands of miles south of Fairbanks, Lark Audette is nothing like the bird she is named for. She does not have a pretty song—her voice is low and throaty to the point of sounding hoarse, so much so that kids in grade school used to ask if she was a boy when she took her turn discussing the weather chart. Her face is more colorful than the lark's as well—she blushes so easily, more like a red finch than anything, whenever someone draws attention to her. The birds have short bills, while her long nose can be traced back to her French Canadian heritage. They have short necks and rounded heads, while she is tall and lithe. The lark doesn't mind places that have been overrun by civilization, but Lark the girl is terribly disturbed by them.

The one thing she has control over, she does to imitate the horned lark—her blond hair, always twisted into two buns at the top of her head.

Despite being nothing like the lark, she was enamored with birds from the moment she saw her first hummingbird at age three. At least that's how her aunt tells the story. In her memory, she was five and it wasn't a hummingbird, but a goshawk.

She's harnessed that obsession through her final year of college, studying biology. Her specific track will eventually take her on to graduate school for ornithology, but for now, she hangs in a kind of limbo.

Lark is pulling weeds from the desert refuge's irrigation canals. It's a tedious job that causes her shoulder muscles to ache, but it's vital for the survival of the birds and animals at Bosque del Apache, where she both works and lives. It's all interconnected. The water running through the canals must be regulated—they use dams and floodgates to raise and lower the water level, to flood or drain areas intentionally so the natural marsh habitats can flourish.

She uses a rake to yank up knots of sedges and smartweed that have become entangled along the canal banks over the winter. A coyote slinks across the sand, stops to look at her as it crosses the little wooden bridge, and then disappears. A line of young quail skips down the path almost immediately after, and Lark holds her breath, hoping the coyote doesn't change its mind and turn around.

Lark is up to her thighs in the muddy water when she hears a voice say "Is that saltcedar down there? Or tamarisk?"

Out of breath, Lark stops pulling weeds and looks up, the sun in her eyes. The man is pointing behind himself, downstream, where the invasive plant is thriving—its wispy branches speckled with purple tufts of flowers. Lark says, "They're the same thing. And yes."

He flips through a small book, his elbows resting on the bridge railing. From where Lark is standing, rays of sunlight radiate from his tall, bent body.

"You have mud on your nose," the man says, not looking up from his book, and Lark does nothing to remedy the situation. She continues dragging masses of dead grass from the water, watching from the corner of her eye the way he carefully writes in a notebook.

"Do you want to get a coffee?" the man asks out of nowhere.

Lark doesn't need to wait for the inevitable burning in her cheeks to know they are the color of the saltcedar flowers. "Like right now?" She can think of few situations in which she's felt less attractive.

The man shrugs. He opens a map of the grounds and scans it. This part of the trail is close to the beginning of a three-mile walking tour through the Bosque. Lark guesses that he hasn't seen anything yet, besides some ducks on the pond and the cormorant that nests near the trailhead. He couldn't possibly mean right now.

"I have to finish here," she says, when he doesn't answer. She piles an armful of thick branches on the bank. "Maybe at lunchtime. If you're still in the area." She reaches for a branch that's floating away and stacks it on top of the others.

20

They meet in town later, after Lark has showered and changed from thigh-high rubber waders into hiking sandals. She couldn't decide between a loose, hippie-style top and a more athletic tank, unsure if she was about to go on a date. Getting coffee with a stranger could really be only one thing, a date—*what is she even doing*. She decides she's not interested in making a show of her carefree hippie side or the lean muscle in her arms. She chooses a black T-shirt with the white drawing of a roadrunner on it, the words *hey paisano* scrawled in cursive beneath.

Lark leaves her hair as is but tucks the stray wisps behind her ears.

It isn't until she's walking into the café that she realizes she has no idea what he actually looks like—the sun was directly behind him earlier, all his features darkened in shadow. But of course, he recognizes her blond buns and the pink of her cheeks, and he waves from a table in the back.

"Do you always accept invitations from strangers so quickly?" he asks. She notices his hands, tanned but clean—cleaner than hers—and clasped together on the mosaic-tiled table.

Her face is hot, but she smiles and says, "Only when I think I can get free lunch out of the deal, or at least a coffee. We're in a public place, after all. Do you always ask women out after speaking a mere two sentences to them?"

"Fair enough."

"It's true, though. I don't even know your name."

"Jude. Yours?"

"Lark. Like the songbird."

"You don't seem anything like a—"

"I'm aware of that." She's suddenly self-conscious of her low, raspy voice. She clears her throat and blinks up at the waitress, who comes with perfect timing. Lark orders a breakfast burrito with extra green chile, her usual for any meal of the day.

Jude sticks to coffee.

"So, what is it you do at the refuge?" he asks.

"I take care of the grounds. I regulate the water level—flooding it or draining it, depending on the season. I remove invasive species—like your saltcedar, which does nothing at all for the wildlife—and replace them with cottonwoods and willows. Basically, I try to keep things as natural as possible. For the birds and the rest of the wildlife."

"Wouldn't it be more natural *not* to do anything at all?"

"Well, no." She can't help looking at him like he's a naive child. Her expressions have never been within her control. "Because people have already fucked up the equation. They introduced plants they thought would help with erosion, and those plants took over, choking out useful native species. Even though they were never meant to be there to begin with. And the droughts we've had these last few years have destroyed the wetlands. The canal I was clearing earlier is vital to the migratory bird habitat. We now have to work constantly to maintain it, or the birds may not come."

"Won't they just go somewhere else?"

"They need places like this to stop and rest. How far could *you* travel before your legs were literally too tired to walk anymore? Probably not half as far as their tiny wings take them every day."

Thankfully, her burrito arrives. Her chest is heaving and she's starting to sweat again. Lark tries to think of something else to say. She lowers her voice, takes a deep breath, and calmly asks, "What do you do, by the way?"

"I'm just a photographer," Jude says, sipping his coffee. He seems amused by the passionate diatribe about her work.

Lark takes a bite of spicy eggs and potatoes and nods, unsure what he means by *just* a photographer, but her mouth is too full to ask. She motions to his camera, and he clicks through some of his photos, pausing to show her a wood stork.

"I swear, he came straight for me."

Sure enough, the wood stork got closer and closer to the camera, while the railing of the viewing deck stayed the same size. He shows her blue grosbeaks and scarlet tanagers and a great blue heron. The pictures impress her more than she expected, given that she sees these birds daily. But she is struck by something fresh in the photos, like getting to meet an old friend for the first time again. She doesn't know anything about this person who's paying for lunch. She doesn't know where he lives, if he's even curious about seeing her again. And yet, he talks to her like they've known each other for years.

"I've never seen anyone eat so fast," he says, setting the camera down and taking another sip of coffee. "What's that?" he asks, reaching across the table and almost touching the necklace that's half-tucked into the collar of her shirt. She pulls it out and lets it rest against her chest.

"It's a tiny fragment of a sixty-two-million-year-old bird dinosaur fossil. Found here in New Mexico. My aunt gave it to me. She was working with the paleontologists who found the rest of the pieces. She's been everywhere."

"And how about you?"

"How about me, what?"

"Where've you been?"

Lark thinks a moment. "Nowhere really," she says, gathering up the last of the green chile and melted cheese with a strip of tortilla and stuffing it in her mouth. "Nowhere but here."

21

She returns to her casita—a small adobe house behind her aunt's larger one—and finds her mail on the kitchen table. The letter on the top is hand-addressed from Fairbanks, Alaska. Inside is a letter inviting her to work for two months at a youth camp based at a migratory bird refuge called Creamer's Field. It's where the sandhill cranes make their summer home.

She considers whether she'll see Jude again, and if she even wants to. She considers the lie she told him about never having gone anywhere. The truth is, she's never been anywhere else in her adult life. But as a child, she traveled a lot with her aunt. After her mother died when she was five, she watched the northern goshawk migration at a sanctuary in Pennsylvania. She remembers the sloping yellow mountains, the leaf-fringed trails, the setting sun peeking around the corner of a granite boulder, its frayed light dispersed across the sky. The goshawks, which migrate alone and only roughly every ten years, do so with an abruptness that has been described as violent and alarming. Lark remembers the chaos of it, but also an unexpected clarity that birds would be her family, her home.

She remembers being eight, after the longest flight of her life, standing on a cliffside in Australia, watching short-tailed shearwaters dance over the sea. That was when her aunt told her about her father, a quitter of a man who chose to run when he should have stayed, and Lark thought the timing was interesting; she couldn't help but feel a brief understanding as she witnessed the untethered freedom of the diving seabirds.

"I'm sure he had his reasons," she said.

"Well," her aunt laughed, "that's very generous of you. But the reasons certainly weren't good enough."

As an adult, though, Lark has only ever lived in New Mexico—rarely even leaving the Bosque in the few years since graduating from college—and the idea of seeing somewhere different now, meeting new people, is tempting. But it also seems odd that this place, thousands of miles away, would reach out to her of all people. Who is she anyway? Lark Audette, Queen of Birds? What can she possibly offer them that someone in Alaska cannot?

Lark looks the refuge up on a map, drawing an imaginary line with her finger, the distance between here and there unfathomable somehow—and yet it also feels right, like it's something she's meant to do. A migration of her own.

When she finds her aunt later, after the last tour of the evening, she shows her the letter. Hidden in her first glimpse, there's a flicker of something. Recognition? Pain?

"Do you know this place?" Lark asks.

Her aunt has put her glasses on and turned back to a list of the birds they saw on the tour. She says distantly, "I've been there once. It's a beautiful place. And quiet. I gave a talk years ago at the university."

Something about her aunt's short sentences, followed by an in-breath that never becomes a word, makes Lark feel like she wants to say more. But nothing more comes.

"Do you think I should go?"

Behind her aunt, sunlight glitters orange on the pond, where the snow geese are returning for the evening. An egret and several cormorants are perched on a branch, and each time one of them moves, the others shuffle around as well, repositioning.

Again, her aunt hesitates. "I . . ." She looks beyond Lark at the cottonwoods. It seems like she's calculating something more than just losing a niece or an employee for a couple of months. "Yes. I think, if you want to go, you should."

22

Lark is good at sitting still, letting the world and wildlife spin around her. It's an art she has practiced all her life.

In fifth grade science class, they did an experiment that involved the life cycle of fruit flies. The class peeled a banana and placed it at the bottom of a large glass jar, and Mr. Montoya opened a plastic box that contained live fruit fly cultures. Then they closed up both the fruit and the fruit flies, draping a paper towel over the mouth of the jar and securing it with a rubber band. Then they watched.

After a few days, they wrote in their logbooks about the tiny white flecks, the eggs that had appeared on the banana. Then they made drawings of the wormlike larvae that had burrowed into the fruit, and the next stage, too, the pupae, that had attached to the side of the glass jar. By day ten, new fruit flies had emerged. A full metamorphosis in just shy of two weeks.

But when Craig Fortier was flipping pencils into the ceiling panels at his desk, he kicked the jar and it shattered on the floor. That's when the infestation began.

Mr. Montoya made the class a deal. For every fruit fly they captured and brought back to him, they would be rewarded with one jelly bean. A bean per fly. "Remember, they'll be laying more eggs in, like, two days, so get to work," he said.

While her classmates scrambled through every classroom, jumping from chairs with nets, Lark Audette sat in the hallway with a cup that contained an overripe plum and vinegar that she'd stolen from the school cafeteria. She sat in the same spot as long as she was allowed by her class schedule. The fruit flies came to her, and she went home with a bagful of jelly beans.

23

Before dawn, Lark is sitting cross-legged on one of the viewing decks. Red-winged blackbirds dart in and out of the long grass, and ducks congregate on the water. The sandhill cranes come in as if riding an invisible wave, thousands of birds against the backdrop of a peach desert sky. Their long legs stretch, reaching for the ground. The volume of their rattling calls rises as the thunder of their wings dies down and they gather in the field. They step across the field with a combination of clumsiness and grace, with their bloodred stained foreheads and black-tipped wings.

Lark stays put, even when the sun finally rises over those mountains, her binoculars hanging untouched around her neck. Jude said he was going to come say goodbye, even though they've only met twice and owe each other absolutely nothing. He'll be leaving anyway, returning home, a five-hour drive north.

She closes her eyes. There is one thing, she realizes, that she'll never be able to explain to anyone: that she doesn't even need to *see* the birds. That she feels their movements in her chest, thousands upon thousands of beating wings.

Jude's voice comes out of nowhere. "Did you know the cranes make tandem sounds? It's a unique call that, I guess, cements their bond as a couple."

"Of course I knew that," she says. "I study birds for a living."

"I find it so fascinating," he says, and Lark can't help but nod because it is. He points to the binoculars slung around her neck. "Can I borrow those?"

Lark flinches. The thought of letting anyone else look through them makes her almost physically ill, even someone she's at least mildly attracted to. But she pulls them off and says, "Just be careful, they belonged to . . . never mind. Just please don't drop them in the damn water."

He takes them cautiously, holds them up, fiddles with the focus. "I just can't believe how many of them there are. It's insane." He lowers the binoculars and turns, bumping his elbow on the railing. The binoculars spring from his hands. They land in the tall grass just at the edge of the water, and Jude lets out a shout. "Oh my god! I'm so sorry. I'm such an idiot. And you said that, too, 'Don't drop them' . . . fuck. I'll get them."

"Goddammit," Lark whispers. "It's fine. At least they're not in the water. I got it."

"We haven't spent enough time together for you to know this, but there it is. I'm the clumsiest person in the world."

This makes her smile, though she tries to hide it as she slips through the bars and drops to the long marsh grass. "You might have mentioned that before I let you borrow them."

"I'll make it up to you."

"Oh yeah? How?"

She climbs back on the deck with the binoculars, and Jude is holding out a book called *The Humming of a Northern Heart*. On the cover, there's a winding path that snakes through a wide golden tundra set ablaze with clusters of purple fireweed.

"It's just a gift. But also . . ." He reaches for her hand, turns her palm down, uses his teeth to pull the cap off a black permanent marker, and writes something on her skin. "One of my favorite quotes from it."

She examines the back of her hand, where the words *perhaps the future* are scrawled. It takes up all the space, like a trail leading off a page.

Lark leaves later that morning, the cranes and geese and her aunt and Jude behind her. She is a magnet to winged creatures, but she hates to fly herself. She tosses her canvas bag and camera into the passenger seat of her truck and begins driving to Fairbanks, truly alone for the first time in her adult life.

Her eyes catch the looping words on her hand every time she turns the wheel, and the possibilities of new futures—maybe even revised pasts—suddenly seem endless.

24

Eila Jacobsen

Eila is half wearing her sweater. Her arms are in the sleeves but only up to her elbows, the rest of the sweater in a pile on the desk. She can never decide what to put on in the spring.

On a computer screen in front of her, little orange dots representing the Porcupine caribou herd move slowly across a map of Alaska and Canada. The dots make sudden, jumpy movements, but for some reason she finds their presence incredibly comforting. For a long while, the herd was so threatened it almost dropped off the map completely. They've recovered a little, and are hanging on, but barely.

For the last couple of years in particular, the caribou's movements have been erratic. They've avoided roads being built and the changing weather—both early wildfires and late freezing rains. But all this has driven them miles off course from their calving grounds.

No migration is ever the same—not by timing or distance or route.

But somehow, Eila knows. When she looks at the pixelated topography on the screen, she doesn't see a picture of a place—she sees the place itself, as if she is there, feels her feet moving across the landscape, surrounded by caribou. To her, the dots are not computer code but the living ecosystem of her beloved animals.

Which is why it was so hard when the list of those selected to go on the next research trip was posted. The team started planning their annual summer trip to the Tumi Field Station, but it's Eila's turn to stay behind and run the lab. She considered begging Lucas, the team lead, to take her, to ask someone else to stay. If she could just see the caribou again, maybe she would also be able to help them. And perhaps it would also fill that hole that seems to be growing in her every day. But she couldn't bring herself to ask, so she just nodded quietly when they passed the list around, trying to stop the tears stinging her eyes.

Drew walks in, a coffee mug gripped in his fingertips and hanging by his side, an afterthought. He leans on the doorframe and says, "You ready to leave yet? Can I take you to Jack's for a beer?"

"You're heading out in a couple weeks, huh?" she says, ignoring the invitation.

He shrugs apologetically. "I know that you—"

"It's fine," she says. "I've got stuff here." Eila glances out the window, at a raven tiptoeing around a truck bed, an orange light climbing the blinds, and says, "Ugh, sometimes I wish it would stay winter. When the light comes back, I almost don't want it to. It's too much."

"It's hard to come out of hibernation," Drew says. He's always been kind to her, but ever since she lost her father, she gets the sense that he'll say anything to make her happy. "It's too much at first, but then somehow you always settle into the gentle light of spring, and then you can't imagine the dark. Cycles."

"Poetic. I think I'll stay here for now," she says. "I already know where they're going, but I want to see."

Drew's eyes narrow. He believes her, of course. She's always known where the caribou will go and when, almost down to the second. He crosses the room, places the coffee mug on the desk, and leans over her, eyes on the moving dots.

On the map, there's a road directly in the herd's path, one of the newer hunting access routes. The caribou usually don't go within a few miles of roads like this, partially because the dust makes vegetation scarce and partially because they see it as a danger. They could go north or south to avoid it. North makes the most sense because there's more food in the mountains, but they would have to take the ridges, which would also be risky.

"Where?" Drew says.

"Here." Eila points south, to where the road becomes a bridge that crosses the Chandalar River, a tributary of the Yukon. "They'll go under it. Cross the river."

"We'll see," Drew says. "They could just as easily go into the mountains."

"You know I'm right. Should we bet on it? If I win, I get to go on the research trip."

"Umm," he says. "How about if you win, you get to go home and wallow alone. If they head into the mountains, you have to come to Jack's with me. Either way, you're getting out of this freezing office."

"All right, fine. Thirty seconds."

Eila closes her eyes. She sees endless sky and greening tundra stretched out before her. She also sees human "progress" and flinches at the smell of diesel and the sight of gravel where shrubs should be. She counts to thirty, and when she opens her eyes again, the dots have already begun to turn south, miles from the road, headed for the twisting blue line of the river.

She looks at Drew, who rolls his eyes.

"I'll still go to Jack's with you," she says.

As they cross the parking lot, indigo clouds scattering across a dusky sky, Eila fishes around in her bag for her keys but can't find them. "Shit," she says, remembering that she left them in the ignition. She'd been searching for her water bottle before heading into the lab. She scratches ice from the window, cups her hands around her face, and peers into the dark car. "Yep. They're in there."

"Do you have a spare?"

"Yeah. In my cabin. Also locked."

"Hmm," Drew mumbles. He thinks for a moment. "There seems to be a flaw in your system. Any windows we can climb through?"

She shakes her head. "Only if we break them first."

"All right, well, let's go kick down a door then."

"What?" she laughs, before realizing he's serious.

"Come on," he says. "Can't be that hard, can it?"

On the drive to her cabin, Eila doesn't know what to do with her hands, so she wedges them between her knees and looks out the window, squinting into the dark. They pass the black stretch of frozen Ballaine Lake, the center of it glowing with the reflection of the moon, and she can't help her heart from going there. She imagines Jackson skiing across it. Then she pictures herself just behind him, and it feels like the state she's been in for the last five years. Trying to catch up, trying to reach the shape of him, but never getting there. Then the road is edged with the silhouettes of dense spruce, and they turn onto the quiet dirt road, and she closes her eyes and shakes it all away.

When they're standing in front of her locked cabin door, they realize it's much harder than either of them anticipated. They try heaving their shoulders against it first but learn quickly that this method will only cause them pain. They stand back, count to three, and thrust their feet in unison into the door.

"This must literally be the oldest, flimsiest door in history," Eila says. "This is ridiculous."

By their fifth attempt there's some movement. After ten perfectly choreographed kicks, the wood cracks around the doorknob, and they're able to push it the rest of the way. Drew wiggles the doorknob off and sets it on the counter. "All right," he says, "grab those keys and we'll go back for the car. You really owe me that beer now."

"I'll walk to get the car in the morning," Eila says. "There's beer in the fridge." She's not feeling like being around strangers, but she's grateful for his help and wouldn't mind a drink.

They sit on the front porch, the air too cool for mosquitoes. The spruce trees around her cabin are silhouettes, the sky almost fully dark.

"That's a first for me," Drew says, pressing the cold beer bottle against Eila's aching shoulder.

She laughs. "I had no idea how hard that would be. They always make it look so easy in movies."

"But hey, we did it. We can say that now—we've busted down a door. It's impressive. *We're* impressive."

She regrets it immediately, but inevitably, Eila feels a pang of sadness that he isn't Jackson. She's almost angry at the missed opportunity, this experience that she didn't share with him. It's not Drew's fault, and she's sick at allowing this thought to creep in after how kind he's been.

"I bet my dad could have done it with one kick," she says, looking down into the narrow mouth of the bottle.

"Sorry," Drew says.

"There's nothing to be sorry for."

"Well . . . ," he says. He grips the porch step and says, "This porch has held up nicely."

Drew only met her father once, right after Jackson had disappeared. Eila and Drew had just come back from a research trip to the news that Jackson Hyder had fallen—possibly jumped—into the Chena River. A few days after that, Drew came by Eila's cabin to make sure she was okay, and instead he found Stefan tearing down and replacing the porch. He put Drew to work immediately.

"Think it's because of you, or because of him?" Eila asks.

"I want to say both, but probably him. You sure you're okay?"

"I'm totally fine." She spends a long moment looking at his face—the creases around his eyes and the little curve of a scar on his chin that subtly catches the moonlight. He leans over, then hesitates, his nose an inch from hers.

She turns away, says, "Ah, dammit. I'm just . . . I'm not totally fine. I'm a mess actually, and I don't know what I'm doing. I need to figure out what life is supposed to look like now, without him—without *them*—but all I really want is to fly up to the Brooks Range and walk with caribou for the rest of the summer."

"Hey, no worries. That was stupid. Nothing to take seriously." He nudges her shoulder with his and they both wince and say, "Ow."

It wouldn't have been the first time they kissed. It's also not the first time Eila has turned away. And though he's the best friend she has now, he still isn't Jackson. And somehow, he's understanding enough to accept even that—that she's still in love with a man who is dead. They look at each other for a moment in the dark, then laugh off the awkwardness and clink their beers. They nod at the unspoken decision to just be happy that they're here, alive, strong enough to break down a door.

25

In the morning, Eila starts walking toward the lab to pick up her car, but instead, her feet take her across the main road onto Snowdrift. Maybe it's some kind of self-imposed penance, or a superstitious apology for sharing those moments with Drew. Maybe it's simpler—that raw feeling of missing someone and just needing to be close to their things. To be close to Jackson in some way.

She brings her father's journal in her backpack. At some point she needs to open it, and she suspects she'll be moved to do so spontaneously. With her hands in her pockets, her legs move fast, the air filling her chest too quickly. She passes through clouds of her own breath.

A stream of water runs down the road, carving a crevice into the packed dirt. Her father always graded and leveled the road each spring, and Eila wonders who is going to take up the task now. How long it will take for someone to realize the earth here is breaking apart.

It's strange, she thinks with a detached sense of curiosity, dealing with two losses. She was just learning to accept the first. Her brain seems incapable of separating them. Instead, they mix together, a thought of her father leading to Jackson and vice versa.

Something rustles the trees, and she can tell by the size and awkwardness of the fluttering that it's a grouse. *If it's not a grouse, I won't go. I'll turn around and go back for the car.* Then the wings, broad and speckled, flap madly in front of her as the bird makes a chaotic jump from the alder branches and scuttles across the road. Maybe Eila made the deal only because she was so sure she was right. The grouse leads to Jackson again—the time he killed one with an arrow and terrified them both—then to her father—who taught Jackson to clean and cook and take responsibility for the bird—and back to Jackson again and this damn road.

She can't count the number of times she's walked to his cabin, though that's not to say she hasn't tried. She's prone to counting; it's something she does when she's afraid she might forget. And because, inevitably, her mind is tirelessly drawn to numbers and statistics and calculation.

26

Their walks began in third grade, the year her father finally allowed her to go out walking on her own—Halley and Snowdrift only. She'd sneaked out and wandered plenty of times before that, but this year, she could head out the front door and say "Goodbye," and Stefan would wave without adding "Be careful." This delighted her beyond anything. At the time, Jackson's mother was still around, but she'd never had such rules for him anyway.

When Eila and Jackson met, Eila thought they might be a different species from the rest of the students—two pieces that completed their own puzzle, yet pieces that didn't have a place in the bigger puzzle of the world.

At eight, Jackson was a new student. He'd recently moved from Juneau, arriving on his first day of school with a thermos of black coffee. He sat in the last row of desks, twisted the cap from the thermos, and poured the dark steaming liquid until it nearly reached the brim. He sipped it without once glancing up at the curious eyes of the other students, as well as the teacher.

In the back of the classroom, his eyes scanned a book of poetry, Mary Oliver's *Owls and Other Fantasies*, while the teacher pointed to maps and drew sentence diagrams on the board. None of their teachers seemed to care that Jackson paid more attention to Oliver than their lessons or that he rarely participated in class activities. He was like a ghost with a side part in his hair, wearing a neatly ironed button-down shirt and observing politely from a distance. At times, even Eila forgot he was there.

When she took the bus home, Jackson stepped into the aisle without looking up, apparently unconcerned with seating arrangements. Inevitably, he landed in the empty seat next to Eila. That spot had been vacant ever since she'd declared veganism the previous year. She'd also begun wearing her mother's old concert T-shirts tucked into her baggy jeans and wasn't sure which of the two had the more repellant effect. Regardless, neither the tofu she brought for lunch nor the oversize Jefferson Airplane shirts awarded her any friends.

It wasn't until a few bus rides into the school year that Jackson invited her to his house at the end of Snowdrift Road. It was September. Eila is sure that was walk number one. She wants to remember them all. The only sounds she remembers are their water bottles sloshing around in their backpacks and the high-pitched double notes of kinglets flitting in the trees.

If she counted every school day for the rest of that year, it would have been about 185 days. During the summer, they started trading off. Half the time they'd go to Jackson's, which was fun because his mother was never home. Half the time they would go to Eila's, where Stefan would make pancakes or grill them hot dogs. If she took account of those summer months, that would add about thirty trips to her total.

But Eila realizes she hasn't counted weekends. She estimates another forty or so for those, realizing that her math is already becoming lazy and somewhat haphazard. She guesses there are more walks, because it's her story, so why not. She's at 235 when she remembers fourth grade— the year they found the hideout.

It was an old sauna that Stefan had built when he first became the carpenter and landlord for the cabins on Snowdrift. It was there for any of the tenants, but no one had used it in years. The sauna was tucked into the woods off Snowdrift, facing the valley between their cabins and the town. It was shaped like a barrel keeled over, and inside there were two tiered benches and a woodstove that pumped heat into the tight cedar-lined room, though they never turned it on.

That year, they walked to the sauna most days instead of to either of their houses. Eila brought neighborhood dogs with her, feeding them treats and teaching them commands their owners probably weren't aware they knew. Jackson would lie on his stomach on the top bench, reading and repeating words from whichever language he was teaching himself at the time. He liked making his mouth form new shapes and sounds. It never seemed hard for him either. He just opened his mind and allowed things to pour in. And he retained them too. Fourth grade, Eila remembers, was the year of language.

It was also the year that once, climbing down from the top bench to get to the door, he stumbled and his hand fell onto her shoulder. She froze, a chill running through her. The kind of chill she'd never actually felt in winter. The kind that lingered long after, when she was home that night, reading in the loft. She had to read each sentence at least two or three times because her mind was somewhere else, back to that touch.

Eila feels the tingling now as she calculates the at least 250 times they traversed Snowdrift to the sauna. Almost 500 total walks already, and she's just getting to her fifth grade memories. The year of Jackson's handstands.

She watched him, hands on the ground, legs above his head. There was something unsettling about seeing him upside down, so she taught herself handstands too. Her father had removed the sauna to build a better one, and they'd lost their hideout. That was fine with Eila. She was happier doing handstands in the woods anyway. She remembers facing each other while inverted, the way he looked shockingly unfamiliar. She remembers Jackson saying "Chapter 107, in which the world suddenly makes more sense upside down." He recited variations of this phrase frequently, choosing a random chapter number each time.

And now, as she's calculating fifth grade, she wonders if a walk still counts as a walk when you're on your hands for most of it. And could she count the times they just lay on their backs in the middle of the dirt road, laughing and stretching their sore wrists?

She's past 700 now. Of course, her math, which comes out to an average of about 240 road traverses per year, must be adjusted for sixth grade. The numbers are hard to estimate that year. There were quite a few days when she walked the road twice in less than twenty-four hours—because Jackson began calling her house whenever the northern lights were out. He'd let the phone ring once before hanging up, and Eila knew that was the signal to head outside. They found their way to one another, thermoses full of hot chocolate, heads tilted up to the sky.

But Eila also had pneumonia that year. Weeks were lost to the sickness—weeks that Eila imagined him out walking with some other girl. And just as Eila is about to land on how many weeks that is, she reaches Jackson's cabin.

She's done these calculations before—many times, in fact—though she's never gotten to a final count, and she's okay with that. It's a distraction exercise. If she ever found the answer, it would only serve as another goodbye.

27

After five years—*five years*—without Jackson, still almost nothing has changed.

The path from the road to the front porch is still as firmly packed and bare as it was before Jackson disappeared, like the constant tread of his feet had worn the earth down to the bone forever. Nothing will ever grow there again. There's the firepit in the front yard and the small square of mounded dirt that never really was a garden anyway—all the same except overgrown with weeds. The dark-blue fabric, not exactly a curtain, hangs in the small kitchen window.

The row of little plants on the windowsill that Eila still waters.

She decides not to go inside today. She doesn't want to care for an empty cabin or wander among Jackson's space. She just wants to hold something that belonged to him. To them.

In a corner of the porch rests the elaborate shrine she and Jackson built to all the wild creatures: mouse skulls, bird bones, snake skins, and porcupine quills that they'd found. A precious collection of dead wild things—artifacts of an entire childhood, relationship, life they'd accumulated over the years.

She chooses carefully: the delicate yellow-white skull of a fox sparrow they found. One mid-June evening, full of light—when they'd watched the sun complete the whole of its shallow solstice arc—they were at a cabin her father had just finished building. The cabin was still vacant, and they'd used the kitchen to make halibut melt sandwiches and climbed to the roof to eat while the sun considered the horizon. Jackson had done handstands on the roof peak that nearly stopped Eila's heart. Eila had wished her heart *would* stop so they could stay frozen in that moment. They licked melted cheese from their fingers and lay on their backs and said absolutely nothing, even though she imagined saying so many things.

Under the midnight sun, they witnessed a hawk dive and snatch the sparrow from a tree branch, and a few days later, Jackson went out looking for remnants of the little bird to add to their shrine. It seemed like a terribly important addition, perhaps because of the eerie solstice light, or because he'd searched so tirelessly. Eila was crushed by its translucent beauty when he finally placed it in her palm.

28

When Eila reaches her office at the station, there's a new doorknob on her desk, and she can't help but laugh. She turns on the computer to check the herd's movements and finish typing the notes from her field spreadsheets. The caribou are still moving, always moving, southeast of the Brooks Range. Eila would give anything to follow them right now, to see them up close, to reach out and touch the same plants, to feel the same breeze on the tundra, even—though it would get old quickly—to endure the torment of the same insects.

There are far fewer trackers on screen than yesterday. She calculates that another four of the collars have gone dark, which is a lot for one day. It doesn't necessarily mean that those caribou have died, but it's the most likely scenario, which means proportionally, many more of them are gone.

On a hunch, Eila pulls up the vegetation spreadsheets they've gathered over years of fieldwork. Right away, a column stands out. She scans the numbers, blinks to be sure she's seeing correctly. At first, she thinks someone must have transposed something, pulled the wrong numbers from the data on her spreadsheets—site locations, type of biomass found in each of the quadrats. There's a clear trend, as the locations move farther northeast, where the recorded quantities of reindeer lichen notably decrease.

She compares the data across years past. The numbers dwindle as she traces her fingers across the screen, noting that the density and land cover of the lichen are also diminished from what they used to be. The further back she goes, the clearer the picture becomes. Over the last five years, the lichen has been slowly dying out. All the other plant types either remain static or are thriving.

Even with a generous allowance for the greening that's happening on the tundra, this is a significant finding. As the primary winter food source for the caribou, the declining lichens must have at least some correlation to the decreased caribou population. This, she surmises, likely accounts for why the caribou have been later each year to their calving grounds—they're spending more time searching for food to sustain them.

She prints a map of the Brooks Range and uses a highlighter to draw a line across it, showing the path where the lichen is disappearing. This will change things. Her mind runs through various ways she can convince the research team to at least look into this anomaly, if not completely change their entire mission.

She doesn't allow herself to consider begging Lucas to take her again.

But when she opens her inbox, there's an email from him with the subject line "The Trip." Eila holds her breath, opens it. Not sure what she's reading is real. Her chest begins to buzz with a mix of excitement, relief, and guilt. Drew backed out of the trip to the research station, and they have room for her now, if she can swing it. "I can swing it," she types immediately before hitting send.

She wants to call Drew and promise him a lifetime of beers at Jack's. She wants to thank him for so much more than just giving up his spot for her, but she knows him well enough to know he'd only get shy about the recognition. Instead, she reaches into her bag for a sticky note and writes:

> Thank you for:
> Breaking my door.
> Fixing my door.
> The closeness of caribou.

It's a bit ridiculous and feels like not enough, but she leaves it on a stack of books by his computer. When she returns to her desk, she sees her father's notebook sticking out of her bag, and she remembers her promise. A promise she so far has been too scared to keep.

I can do this, she thinks, the spontaneous moment presenting itself. *Just one page.*

A Road Called Halley

Eila was only four when I arrived in Alaska. She was babbling in the back seat of the station wagon the whole drive, asking where we were going, and I had no idea where we were going—only that, after Maisie left, I needed to go far from where I was. I didn't know what I was going to do. Using my hands was the only thing I was really good at. In my old life, I was a farmer. In this new one, I figured I'd just have to learn to do something else.

It took ten days to drive from New Hampshire through Canada. I mostly kept to myself. Not because I wasn't interested in meeting people, in learning things. Just because I was sure it was so obvious how inexperienced I was with parenting, adulthood, life. Backward thinking, maybe.

Then, after crossing the border into Alaska, a man at a roadside diner in Tok asked where I was headed and why. The man wore a blue trucker hat and a white T-shirt and had rough two-day scruff on his square jaw. Since I couldn't answer either question, the man said, "Well you sure won't be leaving anytime soon. I can tell. You look like you were made for this."

Back then, I still had a full head of shoulder-length hair. My shirts were all crisp button-downs. The beard was a few years away. I was skinny. My shoulders were small and my pants always hung loose around my hips, even with a belt.

I didn't have the first clue what I was made for, other than protecting this tiny but growing human.

"You'll figure it out," the man said. "You'll have to."

The man wiped the corners of his mouth with his thumb. He took a pen from the pocket of his T-shirt and wrote the address for the land management district office in Fairbanks on a napkin. "They always need help cleaning and building and whatever else," he said. "It's where I spent my first few years here."

I mumbled thanks, which apparently encouraged the man, because he quickly came forth with recommendations about where to find cabins for rent—small, cheap places, but they required four-wheel drive to access and hauling your own water.

I drove on to Fairbanks, up a highway that cut through hills of endless spruce and followed the silver conduit of pipeline. The road broke to gravel and then became rough, pitted dirt. Toward the valley, there was some kind of pontoon boat marooned on a pond not much bigger than the vessel itself. A crumbling shed sat next to it. I wondered how long it had been tethered there, how it had gotten there in the first place. If anyone was ever coming back for it. I remember thinking that it could happen so easily—settling yourself down without intention.

Another two miles and we were at our destination—a cabin I found in the paper, on a road called Halley. The road was all lined with purple fireweed and thin white birch. The cabins were sparse, tucked within the trees at the end of curved dirt paths. Their roofs extended out over doorways like they were wearing hoods.

Eila giggled as I drove over each bump and pothole. The slower I went, the worse the bouncing seemed to get. She liked it, though. I think she smiled more than she had in the previous two weeks of driving.

I did go to the land management office and was offered a job, my first task to build a public-use cabin in the White Mountains north of town. I'd never built a cabin before, and I didn't know why they trusted me to do such a thing, but I found the act of creating something from nothing was not a singular skill. It was something I could transfer from one venture to the next.

This will be the place, I thought. The place where I will settle and my daughter will grow. The kind of landscape that could act as a foundation for whatever I want to build. Anything was possible and it would all be new and genuine, from the ground up.

After putting it off for so long, Eila is surprised that she's tempted to keep reading. For all the time it took her to start, now she's hungry for more. To claim more of her father's past, the parts she was too small to remember. She allows herself just one more entry so she doesn't risk dwelling too long in history, and so there's still more of her father to discover.

Architecture

I'd been building those public-use cabins and clearing trails for a couple of weeks when I met Vern. I was in the mountains every day—Eila scampering in the moss, grasping at twigs and leaves, climbing boulders. Sometimes I couldn't help getting swept up in the great expanse of this place. It was so vast.

So unbelievably vast.

We were alone, the stunted black spruce so sparse over the open, rocky terrain that the world seemed much larger there than anywhere else I'd ever been. I could see for miles. The cloud's shadows darkened patches of land, creeping up and over jade hills like spreading liquid. The Alaska Range was small but stark white in the distance.

Vern was young—in his late twenties like me, I guessed—yet already silver-haired, and he came up behind me out of nowhere. Eila and I were crouching over a fully intact moose skeleton she'd found. It was laid out in the burnt grass with all four legs crossed over one another like a sleeping dog. The position made it look so innocent and vulnerable. If it had antlers, they'd been taken.

I bent down and traced my fingers over the rows of moose teeth. Vern took a couple steps back when I turned around. He clearly hadn't expected—or wished—to run into anyone else on the trail. I said hello, but I didn't even think to introduce myself. The social aspect of my brain seemed to have switched off with the mountain air. I showed him the moose, explaining that I was just telling Eila that we could be the first and last ones to ever see this.

I stared at Vern's canvas bag, spilling over with garden tools and gloves and clustered fuchsia flowers. And then my manners came back to me and I told him my name. I couldn't help myself—I had to ask about the flowers.

Northern yarrow, he said. Nothing terribly special. He opened the top flap of the bag. And he explained that he was wandering, trying to get a little lost.

It seemed like such a miracle that anything actually grew here.

"It's all about adaptability," Vern said, revealing a little excitement. I didn't yet know he'd been a teacher, but he was a natural, explaining all the modifications plants made in the Arctic. He bent over, waving his palms over a swath of white flowering labrador tea. Some of these adaptations:

They survive such a short growing season.

They sprout up close together and stay low to the earth.

They've learned to thrive on the little sun they get, and for such a short time—their new buds emerge in the fall so they are ready to open right away come spring, as soon as it's warm enough.

Their leaves are smaller so they can better retain moisture. They conserve.

His gaze passed over a whole hillside of fireweed that I swear was the color of amethyst and just as brilliant. He seemed very pleased by the view, but then a darker look came over him. He looked down at the bag in his lap, the yarrow bursting out.

"But don't be fooled. That's not to say it's an easy life. They've altered their entire being to simply live. Can you imagine? It tells me that anything is achievable. Or, to put it another way, that nothing is impossible. I'm telling you this because I suspect we'll never see each other again. You see, I think we can have it all. Anything we want this life to be, we only have to change our way of thinking and being, and then design it, and then build it."

He had no idea then, and neither did I, that we actually lived so close. That he would, indeed, see me—see us—many times again.

29

It feels important to increase socializing, since she'll be isolated with her colleagues for a couple of months. And she's out of practice. Though she doesn't need it, she asks for advice about the computer code she's writing to analyze data. She drinks more coffee than usual just for a reason to go into the kitchen. There her colleagues often run through research and paper ideas. She purposely buys breakfast from the bagel shop on the way in so she has to eat with the others. She lingers in the hallway, pretending to peruse maps, until someone inevitably walks by. And she goes out to Jack's with the group after work, forgoing her usual vodka soda for a single beer so she can maintain coherent conversation.

Four others are going on the trip, each with their own area of expertise. Lucas, the team lead, focuses on weather—the increase in rainfall, snow, the length of seasons. Wes is the bug guy, recording stats on the biting insects and parasites, and the new diseases they may bring to the herd. Gabe looks at the impacts of new roads on migration routes. Katy, a recent graduate from the biology program, is working with Eila, flying drones and taking vegetation samples so they can analyze what the caribou graze on. The pair will study particular effects of the tundra's warming: longer growing seasons, taller shrubs farther north, and the decline of the lichen—the main food source for the herd this time of year.

Eila brushes up on flying the drones so she doesn't look inexperienced in front of Katy. The silhouette of the tiny machine soars over the trees behind her house, blinking in the glowing night sky.

The team will leave at the beginning of July. The tundra will be greener, more alive with vegetation and animals and, yes, insects at that time. It seems such a long way, but *she is going*. She repeats it to herself over and over.

I am going.

When the end of June comes, buzzing sounds take over the valley, extending long past midnight. Eila has been patient, but her heart is already out on the tundra. There's still a week to go, but she can't keep herself from packing. There are dozens of items to bring for her research, mostly things she'll have to get from the station, but she begins at home.

She starts with the basics. A sleeping bag, water bottles and filters, collapsible water jugs, lighters, a first aid kit, bear spray, zip ties, glue, duct tape, camera, chargers and extra batteries, and a list of emergency contacts.

After searching for her mosquito net, she remembers leaving it at her father's cabin after a hike last summer, before he was diagnosed. She walks up Halley Road, halfway to the main road, where Stefan's now-empty cabin is tucked behind overgrown knotweed and vetch. When she opens the door, the smells of damp firewood and ground coffee waft over her.

She's left the place much as it was, afraid to break the spell of memories contained there. Stefan's guitar still leans against the bookshelf; his flannel shirts still hang in the closet. There's a sprinkling of cold ash in front of the woodstove. It all looks the way she remembers before— before everything—and she can almost linger here, pretend he might come through the front door. Until she turns and sees months' worth of empty medicine bottles gathered on the counter, shoved together between the toaster and the coffee maker. She sees the wheelchair, folded in the corner by the small pile of unused firewood. She sees the crutches he used to get to the outhouse, reminding her how insane it had suddenly seemed to live without running water. Before it had been the houses with indoor bathrooms that struck her as ridiculous.

In his office, the mosquito net is lying right there on the desk, but Eila's distracted by the framed photos on the wall. They form a constellation of her father's life—some moments that Eila was a part of and others that she wasn't. In one, she's about five, sitting on a half-built porch with a hammer clutched in her hand. The sun is behind her, and its rays spill over her shoulders and around her face, exaggerated prisms of light caught by the camera.

In another, her father and his younger brother are standing at the top of a mountain. They're just kids—fifteen or sixteen maybe? The sign between them reads CRAWFORD PATH – MOUNT WASHINGTON. They're dressed in jeans and puffy vests, bandannas tied around their long, late-seventies hair. Her father has a round tin canteen hanging from his hip. He told Eila stories about his brother, Anton, who'd died in a rock climbing accident when he was twenty-two. In some ways, Eila knows more about Anton—both in personality and appearance—than she does about her own mother. And this isn't because Stefan intentionally withheld information from Eila. It was because he didn't have many memories of her mother, Maisie, to share. And he had only one photograph. She'd danced in and out of his life so quickly, he used to say.

It wasn't how I ever imagined parenthood. But it's what had to be for you to be here, so I wouldn't trade it for anything.

She scans the rest of the photos, which she knows one day she'll have to take down and pack away. Her eyes pause on another photo, one she doesn't remember. She's wearing the same outfit as the one with the hammer. Her pigtails are tied with the same yellow bows. And she's sitting on the same porch in her father's lap. He has her in a bear hug, his nose pressed into her cheek. On one side of him is Vern, on the other is Sadie. Vern looks rigid, eyes focused directly at the camera in an unnerving way, as if he has a bone to pick with it. But Sadie radiates warmth. She's in a baseball hat, squinting into the sun, her shoulder touching Stefan's—her cheeks smiling and sunburned.

Eila is overwhelmed by the fullness of his life. The breadth and the depth of it.

Her hands shake as she pulls hard to loosen a desk drawer. Inside, she finds an illustrated book of Arctic animal myths that she remembers from childhood. It's a book her father brought back from a visit to Anaktuvuk Pass, and it's where the idea solidified for her that the caribou's spirits continue on over centuries. Her father read stories from this book nightly for years, and to her, they are as real as any facts about the Arctic's ecology.

Beneath the book, there's a stack of her papers and old art projects. She sees a spiral-bound notebook she's had since she was eight—one of her first attempts at tracking and recording data on animals, something she's been drawn to since she could hold a pencil. The cover reads: *My Wildlife Journal.* There are notes on every page about the predators of the Arctic ground squirrel, the diet of the snowshoe hare, the unusually daring behavior of the American marten. The lifespan of the red-tailed hawk. Her breath catches when she sees another artifact, yet another piece of her own mythology—a study she started on the Arctic fox when she was twelve.

For weeks, she was in the woods every day. She'd found the fox den, dug out beneath a rock wall at the edge of the neighbor's property. She watched them constantly, taking notes about what time the mother left the den, how many kits there were, when they came out to play, at what times of day, and what they ate. Eila became so good at hiding that she could stay out there from morning to night, from the solstice, when the foxes blended in with their mottled gray-and-brown fur, to the fall, when the daylight hours shortened and their color began changing to its winter white. Whole pages of the notebook are taken up with her columns, filled with numbers and meticulous notes.

Until October, when she woke up at two in the morning unable to breathe. She spent three days at the Fairbanks hospital with pneumonia.

She was bedridden for two more weeks after that with an oxygen tube stuck up her nose, during which time, the only reason she cried—other than the guilt she felt when she saw how scared her father was—came when she realized how much the lost time had cost her research.

When the doctors said she was free to remove the oxygen and go for walks again, she wondered if it was even worth it. Foxes tend to move their dens periodically, and even if they were still there, there was such a gap in her data that she'd have to begin again next summer anyway.

Through it all, she hardly saw Jackson, which only added to the torture of being stuck in the house. She mulled over what he might be doing without her. But when she was well enough again, and they could hang out on the back porch together, he presented her with pages of data he'd recorded while she was stuck in the cabin—exactly as she'd been doing it, down to the cloud shapes she used to dot her i's.

She looks at it now, the handwriting that looks so remarkably like hers, the extra pages shuffled in, and she remembers how Jackson had been so determined, not simply to please her, but to collaborate. How he'd always been so invested in what she cared about, whether she told him about it or not.

Somehow, he always knew.

30

She'd knocked on Jackson's cabin door and found him reading a book on anatomy. It was one of those oversize doorstops that they have to put on the top shelf of the library, and he had it open to a diagram of the male torso. He was taking notes in fast, messy scribbles.

Jackson had told her once that it was unfathomable that people lived every day with their bodies but barely understood how they worked. They couldn't name most bones or muscles. Most couldn't even tell how many bones or muscles they had. It was a complex system, and yet people just went about thinking all they needed to know was "food in, food out, drink water, exercise." They relied on someone else who had studied the body. But not all of it, of course. No. They were *specialists*.

He needed to know everything.

Eila stood on the doormat in snow-covered boots. He kept writing, whispering to himself: "The fiber composition of the vastus lateralis, also the latissimus dorsi, deltoids, and triceps groups. Normally around fifty percent or so. But in the elite, maybe up to seventy-five percent."

"What are you mumbling about?" she asked.

"Muscle fibers," he answered, as if that should have been clear. "I'm almost done."

She looked around the cabin. His mother's plants hung in every window, their long tendrils draped over bookshelves and doorframes. Jackson was wearing shorts and a T-shirt, his legs crossed on the couch, his feet bare. They both had an incredibly high tolerance for the cold, but for different reasons. Jackson simply wanted to feel everything, no filters. He didn't believe in changing clothing based on the seasons. When it was hot, people were meant to feel hot. When it was cold, they were meant to feel cold. Why alter the experience?

But Eila, well, she just wasn't cold.

Jackson pushed a hand through his hair and scratched his head, and Eila got tired of waiting, so she asked, "Want to go skiing?"

"All the gods and goddesses!" he yelled, closing the book with force and slamming his pen down hard enough to startle her. "How are you always reading my mind? I was literally just cataloging the muscles used by elite cross-country skiers. Mainly because next winter, probably, I'm going to work on my endurance."

"Aren't you already working on your endurance? Don't you do that every day?"

"In other areas, obviously, but not as a skier. It's a completely different kind of movement, a totally unique set of muscles."

"Well, should we go do some research then?"

They skied across the frozen lake. Eila blinked the frost from her eyelashes, watching as Jackson took off with smooth strides. Sometimes, she wished he'd just slow the hell down and try to enjoy not moving.

The lake was edged with spruce, all glistening and encased in ice. Eila and Jackson moved soundlessly under the dusky sky, cornflower blue in the middle of the day. Jackson was working on rhythm, syncing his movements to some earthly measure. And Eila saw lynx tracks along the edge of the lake and veered off the path to follow them.

As they disappeared, she turned to find that Jackson had followed her.

"What?" she asked. "What is it?"

He looked at her through his sparkling ice-flecked eyes and said, "I don't know."

She put her hands on her hips, her wrists still in the pole loops. "Aren't you supposed to know everything?"

"I know that I felt you weren't behind me without looking. I know that my need to count and my rhythm were overtaken by the desire to be closer to you. And that's all. Well, I know—"

She pulled her scarf down from her nose, then pulled his down, too, and kissed him. For the first time. How many times over the years had this *almost* happened? And then somehow, they were in the snow together, and he was tracing his fingertips over the freckle beneath her belly button. The *north star*, he called it. He held his hand there, as if feeling for a pulse, directing the flow of energy that traveled through her center into his body and vice versa.

Back and forth. Back and forth. An equal exchange.

Then he moved his hands to other places, examining and calculating every inch of her, trying to learn her body as completely as he'd studied his own. As if there was great purpose in his understanding of her, something far beyond simple desire. They lay with the frozen ground beneath them, the spiny ice-covered treetops spinning above. The temperature dropped as the brief sunlight softened and then disappeared altogether.

Afterward, Jackson leaned back against a tree trunk, and she wedged herself between his legs and leaned against him, the tip of his nose brushing her ear. She wondered how long it would last, this stillness. How long before he was fidgeting, gliding once more across the smooth snow of the lake.

"This feels good," he said.

Eila had just finished her master's in ecoinformatics, and Jackson was still trying to decide between becoming an endurance athlete or a personal trainer, or going back for more schooling to become a physician. He'd studied nutrition and had been helping people in town find healthy lifestyles. But he had a hard time asking for money, and found it harder and harder to stop moving his body to do the job. He claimed he just wasn't a businessperson.

But Eila had always known what she would end up doing in one form or another.

"In the spring," she said, "they've offered me a job on a research trip up north. To gather data on the vegetation and the effects of environmental changes on the caribou."

"When is it?"

"May. We'll only be gone for a month." It felt like an apology, but she wasn't sure why. She wondered if he'd want her to go, or wish she would stay. Nothing between them had ever felt fragile before, but it did now.

"Take notes for me," he said.

"About what?"

"About all the things you see, and what the air feels like in your lungs, and how your legs feel walking across the tundra. And everything your heart does."

This new thing between them did feel good. It didn't feel weird or difficult. It felt exactly as it should—wild and predictable at the same time. And yet, after they'd spent their whole lives together, after knowing so much about each other, she never expected what came next.

For the next two months, she barely saw him, which wasn't all that unusual. They had their own lives, and there was always a casualness to their meetings. But now—why was something so different? When she did find him, he was running the long, empty roads that linked their cabins to town. He looked down and didn't wave. Once, she swore she saw him turn the other way to avoid her. He didn't come by with rocks or bird bones or twigs from interesting trees he'd found. He didn't call and let her phone ring just once to let her know that the northern lights were out.

Everywhere she tried to catch him, he eluded her.

He was a ghost. Until finally, winter ended and the research trip was upon her. When she still couldn't pin him down, she had no choice but to leave without saying goodbye.

She spent the month collecting data, following the caribou's movements. The tundra was so vast and empty, a void she could fill with the thousands of emotions she was wrestling with—the relief that the connection she'd always felt was not something she imagined, and the acute pain of not knowing why he'd become so distant immediately after. She was also overwhelmed with the beauty of the mountains, and frustrated by the impact environmental changes were having on the caribou and, by extension, the Indigenous communities that have always relied on the herd not just for survival but for their spiritual traditions and cultural way of life. She struggled with feeling inferior and small compared to the size of the problems the Arctic was facing, while at the same time becoming ever more determined to do something to help.

What would happen, she wondered, when she came back ready to tell Jackson everything her heart had done? It's what he'd asked for. Somehow, the equation always worked out to the same result no matter how she got there—the joy and the heartache still added up to nervous anticipation. To get back, to see him, to sort out whatever misunderstanding had occurred before she left.

But when Eila returned after her month in the Brooks Range, Jackson was gone. Disappeared, dead, no one knew or even had a definitive story yet, though a rumor was circulating that he was last seen standing on the bridge over the Chena River. While there were a few quiet inquiries about suicide, that theory had been thrown out quickly, in part because Eila and Stefan had been so insistent that it was impossible. They knew him better than anyone—his immense joy at the prospect of the future—and they knew, too, he was nowhere near done. What seemed very likely, however, was that he was attempting to feel something new, perhaps test himself, and it had gone terribly wrong. It might have been a too-optimistic, too-wild assumption for anyone else. But not for Jackson. Nothing had ever been too wild for him.

31

Vern Graves

The holes have been popping up all over the backyard. When Vern moved into this cabin, no one could have predicted exactly where the permafrost lay underground, or how close it was to the surface, or how soon it might thaw. But here he is, twenty-five years later, knee deep in a sinkhole, staring at a crusty layer of ice beneath the muddy surface.

He started filling the holes with extra dirt from the compost, but each time it rained, new depressions appeared. The firepit has turned into a swamp. Spring breakup has been longer and wetter than usual. Today it's sunny, and the snow buntings are back, and he thought he might go out and attempt to fill in the holes again. But it's backbreaking work and he's already tired, even though it's barely ten in the morning.

Vern goes inside for some water and promptly drops a full glass on the counter. His hands are blistered from the shovel and his knuckles ache, making his grip unsteady. Rather than pooling, the puddle immediately travels in a steady stream from one end of the counter to the other. Now he knows for sure that the permafrost beneath the cabin is also thawing, at least on one side.

He knows what he needs to do; he just doesn't have the means to do it. He needs to jack up the house and wedge boards into the gap to level it again. He doesn't own a jack, nor does he know how to use one, nor is he convinced he possesses the strength.

This would have been such an easy fix before. If this were last spring, Vern would have picked up the phone, or walked down the street, and asked Stefan for advice. And Stefan would have told Vern to just hang on; he'd be over soon. And then a problem that would have taken Vern days and dollars to solve would have been fixed in half an hour for free.

But Stefan is gone.

Vern thinks of that drive home, when, after a great deal of debate, he turned toward Stefan's house and revealed—uselessly—the truth about the bees at the old homestead. How Vern begged, and how Stefan refused to even entertain the idea of using whatever was in those bees to heal his disease.

Stefan's laugh was so deep, so full, that his eyes began to water. "What, then live forever?"

Vern wondered if Stefan even believed him. Perhaps he thought Vern was joking. But Vern continued, nearly begging, as if they both knew the truth and how it all worked.

Admittedly, Vern had never known *exactly* how it would work, but he made a point of adding that it was only because Sadie had forced him to walk away. He just needed to study it more.

"This is nature, Vern," Stefan said. "This is how it has to be."

Vern soaks the water up with a towel. The phone rings, but he only turns around to glare at it. After a month of ignoring him, suddenly Sadie's begun calling almost every day, asking him to go for trail walks at Creamer's Field, where she works at the visitors' center. He's been trying not to read into it, her sudden revived interest in his presence. They were friends before and they're friends now. He knows he's no replacement for what she had with Stefan, and it's not like he's some rebound. Still, she's gripping again, and he's been getting used to distance. Usually, he tries to avoid meeting because they always end up talking about the past, which makes Vern squirmy—but she's never been so persistent.

The cranes are beginning to arrive at the refuge. He and Stefan used to find it relaxing to watch them tiptoe across the field with their slow grace. In the past, Vern might have accepted Sadie's invitation, but what happens when the birds go on dancing, except half the company is missing?

He pictures walking with Sadie through the woods, the unspoken presence of Stefan floating along the path between them, the silence excruciating. Then she'd ask him something, like, *Do you remember that time?* And Vern would shrink into that old version of himself—the one that abandoned life in the Lower 48, the one that wasn't ready to just pick up and start again, despite the insistence of these two friends that he move on already.

Start over.

32

It's the second time this week that Vern's had to drive into town, which annoys him. If he'd known his house was sinking a few days ago, he could have killed two birds with one stone, but here he is, pulling into the lot of the hardware store.

He's about to shut the car door when he looks up and sees her. The woman walking across the parking lot with a roll of wire netting under her arm and a thermos in the other. Her hair is blond, twisted up like two horns on top of her head. She has a long nose—Vern thinks *owl*—and for a moment, he forgets everything and his body goes numb and he slams the car door on his finger.

The shout that escapes his mouth startles even him. He makes a fist, so angry he might punch the car window in. Vern shoots a glance back to where the woman was—the one he was positive was his wife, despite knowing Lenora had died years ago. He spots her in the passenger seat of a pickup. The driver is backing away, and Vern can no longer see her face.

But he doesn't need to see it. He remembers it so clearly from that long-ago moment on the beach, the sunshine-blond hair and the scrunched nose. The freckles. As the truck drives away, Vern squeezes his throbbing finger, if only to remind him that reality is still here.

He wanders the store's aisles, looking for cheap but sturdy pieces of wood that he can use to prop up the cabin. Then he asks an employee to help him find a jack, and the kid asks why he doesn't just use the one in his car, to which Vern scoffs and says it's broken. He's forced to buy the jack then, because he can't reveal that he's lying, that he hadn't considered the car jack would do the job just as easily. He purchases some extra cleaning supplies and paper towels, because everything is still so muddy, and the house needs a good spring cleaning anyway. He grabs nails and screws, a new tarp for the stacks of firewood in the backyard—things he isn't sure he needs but may save him another trip to town.

Back in the car, he looks at his finger, still hot and red and swollen. He can't shake the image of her, the blond girl with the angular nose. The twisted buns at the top of her head. It's like she was carved from an old photograph, dangled there in front of him, as if to say *You can't run forever.*

Perhaps the past was always meant to catch him. Vern says his wife's name out loud, something he hasn't done in a long time, like it could transport her there to hold his aching hand, soothe his raw heart. Or perhaps transport them both, back to a time when hearts needed no soothing at all.

This time, when his mind wanders, he allows it.

"Lenora."

33

They met on a beach in Maine, after sunset. Lenora sat with two other girls on rocks that jutted out into the water, a bottle of Salty Darling bourbon passed between them. Vern was less focused on his life goals at the time, just trying to get by. To survive another day. But that night everything changed—the night terror and beauty collided.

He was twenty years old. She was just about to turn forty.

He almost didn't notice Lenora at all. He was busy watching crabs amble back and forth from the water, clicking their claws at the darkness. Their black shapes moved with such an awkward grace that he found himself wanting to get closer and closer.

He heard a voice. And a tiny laugh. When he turned around, she was behind him. She was wearing a striped dress—in the dark he couldn't tell what color—and her thighs were exposed, knees half-dug into the sand. She held out the bottle of bourbon, and when he reached for it, her grasp lingered a few seconds, a tease, then let go.

Vern looked over his shoulder. The other women leaned into one another, their cheeks touching as they watched and whispered. He took a swig and said, "Makes you want to sing and dance," then silently cringed as he twisted the bottle into the sand.

"What are you doing?" she asked. "Sitting here alone, staring into the darkness." She wiggled her fingers to imply some sort of magic was taking place. Something mystical.

The moon reflected in the water like flickering white flames. Vern thought he could see the same pattern in her long hair.

"You don't see them, do you?" he said.

"See who?"

"Them."

She squinted, and when she saw the creatures, some the size of her hand and others bigger, she jumped onto all fours. Lenora prowled toward the crabs, slapping her hands on the sand and laughing when they didn't scuttle away. Instead, they defended their ground, moved closer, and snapped their claws in her direction.

Vern never told her why he'd come out to the beach in the first place. It was an inconsequential secret; it just never came up. But it wasn't because of the crabs or the moonlight or the sea air that always left his lungs feeling damp long after he'd returned home. He'd come because he thought it would be his last night on Earth. He couldn't pinpoint a specific reason. It was just a feeling. He was sure something terrible was going to happen.

His army service had come to an end. He'd returned to his hometown like a stranger, his own mother barely recognizing him. She'd opened the door and said, "Yes?" as if he were selling vacuum cleaners or handing out religious tracts. And he'd been self-absorbed enough to worry that there was something wrong with him, not her.

Some endless well of anxiety had been tapped within him, and he couldn't turn it off. It ran through every part of his body, like a series of tiny needles beneath his skin that touched different parts of him, moved on, and cycled back again, only with a more familiar terror the second time around.

He hadn't told Lenora this because she was the most perfect thing he'd ever seen. How could he say that their introduction had coincided with inexplicably terrifying premonitions?

She was one of those girls, the one out of three who took leaps, went out and slapped strangers on the back. Not one of the shy ones who hung in the wings, watching and wishing, giggling but knowing she'd never follow through.

Lenora had guts. She was wild with joy when those crabs fought back.

He didn't know what had made him do it. Perhaps he was feeding off her playfulness. Perhaps he was acting against the fear that tormented him. Vern reached out and grabbed her ankle, tugged on it gently. Lenora spun around and sat down, the heels of her hands pressed into the fine sand. Her eyes glowed like a hidden animal's, flecks of moonlight flashing in their corners.

Vern froze.

She picked up one of the crabs and ran toward him, pincers flying. "You're going to pay for that," she said.

"I'm sorry," Vern said, holding his palms up. "I don't know why I did that. I am so sorry."

Her shoulders sagged. She knelt down and dropped the crab lightly onto the sand.

"Well," she said, shrugging. "There are worse things than being afraid of a crab, I guess. Though honestly, I can't think of any at the moment."

"Being forgotten," Vern mumbled.

"What's that?"

"Nothing."

"No, I heard you. It's okay. It's going to happen eventually, to all of us. We're just little flickers on the big movie screen anyway."

"What?" Vern said, standing up and brushing sand from his khakis. "That's even more terrifying."

"Oh, sweetheart. Don't worry. I have the cure for everything. Come with me."

And Vern followed Lenora back to her apartment, where they spent two hours in the kitchen, drinking more bourbon, and then a little beer, then water. Vern rambled about who knew what. Lenora half listened while making the most delicious peach pie Vern had ever tasted. Flour dotted her face and her yellow-striped dress.

Lenora was right. She did have the cure for everything. Just about every fear he had dissolved on his tongue along with that sticky, sweet peach filling.

But Lenora is gone now—another thin, fading thread woven into Vern's history. Vern opens and closes his throbbing hand. He wonders how long the pain could possibly last from something so brief. And where is the pie now to comfort him?

PART 3

34

Eila Jacobsen

This is where she goes to listen.

Eila sits on a bench in a small room with white walls, five rectangular panels hanging in front of her. She's in the middle of an installation, an art exhibit in the Museum of the North in Fairbanks. The artist named it after an Iñupiaq word that describes a place on the Arctic coast where a woman, according to legend, would go to hear the language of the plants and animals that surrounded her. The sounds, the silence, the invisible heartbeat of nature, all part of this place—*Naalagiagvik*.

The panels speak to a computer that transmits raw data from the atmosphere—seismological, meteorological, geomagnetic—and translates them into color and sound. The light display changes constantly, moving with the rhythms of the earth, shifting in waves from orange to yellow to purple. Right now, a faint humming means little seismic activity.

There are footsteps outside, and someone grabs hold of the door handle. Eila bites her lip, holds her breath, clutches her father's journal in her lap. She's been told before not to come in after working in the barn. This place is about sight and sound, *not* smell, was the delicate way the museum manager put it. She slides her muddy boots beneath the bench, exhaling when the person apparently changes their mind about coming in.

Bells chime overhead, a sign that the northern lights will appear. Scientifically speaking, their sound is linked to geomagnetic activity, the particles responsible for the aurora borealis. But for Eila, they're linked to her sense of longing—always for Jackson, but now also for everything. For things to be the way they used to be.

But this isn't how things work, she reminds herself. For all the science she is surrounded by—echoes of the universe's complex and miraculous systems—none of it is capable of reversing time. Eila releases her tight grip on the journal and opens to the next entry, the sounds of the bells fading.

The Age of Forests

Right after Sadie's house burned, Vern came knocking at my door, needing help. We'd all been spending most weekends together, hanging out on Sadie's back deck, eating and drinking and watching Eila play. I kept thinking she needed to spend more time with other kids. But she always found toads—once even a fox—to play with.

But the problem that day: Vern had apparently lost his glasses in Sadie's field just before the fire. He begged me not to ask questions the whole way to her house, which was suspicious enough, but he also kept saying it was an accident—he'd just been looking at the wildflowers in her back field. He didn't exactly admit anything. His nervousness made me nervous. I kept my eyes on the road, hoping he wouldn't see the anxiety in them. Hoping he would just stop talking and that we'd find his glasses. I couldn't begin to imagine how one shifts from friend to trespasser to arsonist so quickly.

We climbed the burned hill while Sadie wasn't home. We searched everywhere, but we didn't find the glasses. Just acres of dead grass and a reminder of that night when the whole place had gone up in flames.

Eila and I were there when it happened. Neighbors gathered too. Everyone stood in front of Sadie's cabin while the fire spread across the field to the house in what seemed no time at all. Sadie's cheeks glowed amber as she watched the flames slither up the walls. She kept blinking, her eyes shining. A whole section of the house collapsed, bursts of flame surging outward as the pieces crashed into one another. Eila reached out and grabbed Sadie's hand. I'd never seen her do anything quite so independent or sympathetic. Suddenly, I glimpsed who she might become. I knew she was kind and compassionate. But it was the first time she'd taken initiative that way, doing what she thought was right or helpful without asking my opinion.

Or, maybe it was just the first time I was paying attention.

I made a promise to do it more.

He didn't say it, but the truth is that Vern just added one more fire to a world already on fire. One more blazing forest that did nothing but steal food and habitats. One more obstacle put in the way of Earth's potential for healing.

A fire can be good, though, too. Sometimes necessary.

In the middle of that summer, I was working on a new cabin on Sheep Creek Road. It had a nice long porch out front, and out the back you could easily walk straight to Goldstream Creek.

Sadie found me there, pulled the charred glasses from an envelope.

"What was he doing out in the field, you think?" she asked.

I stumbled to answer. I'd been wondering if he'd seen us too.

"Huh," she said. "Well, either way, he was out in my field before the fire. But is he a dummy who just dropped his glasses and forgot to pick them up, or was he up to no good?"

"I . . ." There seemed to be no clean way out of this.

"Do you think he saw us?"

She looked at me hard, and I crumbled. I nodded. It felt involuntary.

"Probably. He said he was just looking at the flowers. It could be true. But I doubt it. He was acting pretty guilty."

"Huh," she said again. "Also, there was this." From the envelope, she pulled out a scrap of paper, the edges black and curling. It had half of her name on it and the beginnings of the words "Tanana" and "Fairbanks."

"I found this myself," she said. "I remember now. He was someone I met in passing last year when I traveled to Maine. I told him about this place. I feel bad that I didn't recognize him."

I don't know why I thought to defend him. I didn't know him any better than she did, but somehow, I felt the three of us were meant to be here together. "I don't think he's a bad guy, really. What are you going to do?"

"We're going to keep all of this between me and you, okay?"

I asked her why—why wouldn't she just want the truth out in the open? Let Vern pay for what he did. At least let him know that his one bad deed had led to an even worse one.

She crossed her arms over her chest and turned away from me. "I've been needing to move on anyway," she said. "That house, well, there are bad feelings stored up in it, you know? And I've been stuck for a while, and now I'm being forced to start over. It's like something out there is pushing me to change."

I stood next to her in my heavy work pants and steel-toe boots, sweating through my T-shirt. I held a socket wrench in one hand and Vern's glasses in the other.

Sadie kept shifting from one foot to the other. She put her hands on her hips, and then in the pockets of her jeans. She lifted one foot and examined the underside of her boot, pulling a stone from the sole.

I waited. I could tell there was more. She shrugged and said, "Sometimes a forest has to burn so it has the chance to regrow. Anyway, I found something else. After the fire. In the ash."

That's when she told me about the flower, impossibly blooming. "I think this is my purpose," she said. "If I ever had one, I think it might be figuring out where this flower came from. How it exists. How it was born. Create another one."

I remember more about that summer than I do any season of my life.

Eila in the grass, by the river, in the river.

Eila testing her boundaries and mine. Wandering toward the tree line. Staring down an Arctic fox kit the color of wet earth.

A child's hand wrapped around a hammer. A crooked nail.

A mud pie. Eila, filling the inside of a pie tin with river mud, decorating the pie with stones, dandelions, golden aspen leaves, pine needles.

Eila, holding a wood frog in her palm. Eila, putting the wood frog on Vern's head when he complained of migraines because he could never sleep in the summer with all that sunlight. And because Sadie had told Eila an old Koyukon story that the ballooning of the frog's throat could cure headaches.

That night we sat on the unpainted front porch with wine in ceramic mugs, listening to all the wood frogs rattling and calling out. Eila, half asleep, thought they were talking to her. A sound like laughter. The sun was hot orange, dipping to kiss the river before inching upward again.

It was a luminous end to the summer.

We all returned to Fairbanks together. Me and Eila to our cabin. Sadie to the neighboring one. Vern just one road over. And we all disappeared into our respective winters, until the seasons changed, and changed again, and it was time for Sadie to go back north, and Vern with her, so they could experiment with the flowers in the vast solitude of wide-open Alaska.

After the first couple of years passed this way, I finally approached Sadie about why she'd asked for Vern's help. It's one thing to forgive someone and move on. It's another to pursue that person's presence intentionally, frequently. Second chances—that might have been one explanation, but Sadie told me it was more complex than that. When she was a kid, she told me, she loved to climb trees. Once, she'd climbed into one of her neighbor's fruit trees and broken a vital branch. Her neighbor—an eighty-year-old woman—was heartbroken because her own mother had planted it before she died. The tree died the next year, but instead of remaining upset, the woman asked Sadie if she would like to plant a new tree in its place, and on top of that, if she'd take care of all her trees for the foreseeable future. The woman doubled down on kindness and love, and she gave Sadie a purpose that rebuilt what had been destroyed. That's what Sadie wanted to give Vern. Not just forgiveness. Kindness, love, and purpose. You have to believe in people, Sadie said, no matter what. There's no moving forward for humanity otherwise. Not everyone will feel this way, and too many will work against you, trying to tear it all down in your wake, which is why it's so important that those of us who have the capacity to restore, do it.

I think a lot about that now. Sometimes a forest has to burn so it has the chance to renew. Eila, smart as she is, tells me the same. The forests are younger now, she says. Wildland fires have broken out more in recent years, and the forests are regrowing, but the caribou are starting to avoid stands of the younger black spruce because their usual winter foods—the lichen—can't be found there. They use their broad hooves like shovels, digging into the snow, searching. The caribou suffer when they linger in these newer forests and so they must travel farther to find older woods with richer food. A quick-moving caribou is a healthy caribou. A hungry, insect-pestered one is slow and lost. When they avoid the burned areas, their routes change and their migrations can take longer. If they arrive at their calving grounds later in the spring, the calves have less time to fatten up for their journey to the wintering grounds. Smaller and weaker calves are easier to prey on.

Eila is studying this cycle so she can make some sense of how this Earth is changing, how the creatures and plants—all so carefully woven—are far less predictable, but also evolving and rebalancing.

I've held on to so many things, from so long ago, and yet, I don't remember why I started writing this. I can't remember where this was going. How I got here, to the caribou.

Perhaps it was new growth. Or cyclical patterns. Neither are available to me anymore. But they are for Eila. She still has time for both.

Eila doesn't remember telling her father about the caribou and the age of the forests. She doesn't remember describing the way they shovel through the snow with their hooves to find lichen, or how their knees click and clack as they walk, the way Stefan's sometimes did in the mornings or when he crouched to pick up something. If her father were here now, she would tell him that her joints have become creaky as well. That she is feeling older faster than she expected. That the cycles are harder to pinpoint every year, but there is always new growth.

She leaves the museum, passing beneath a massive whale skeleton suspended from the ceiling. In a few hours, she'll be loading research gear into the belly of a plane and heading in what she hopes is the right direction.

35

The small plane shakes like it might break apart, its propellers grinding and vibrating, and Eila isn't sure if her heart is frantic from fear or her proximity to the wild. The rest of the team sits on either side of her, their hands pressed against windows, straining to see a little farther, a little more. The excitement never ceases. The landscape below changes from thick boreal forest to wide-open tundra. It is continuous, studded only occasionally with small, but very old, trees. Darker, taller trees edge the rivers. There are pockets of lakes and a sky that telescopes in never-ending ripples of clouds.

After they land, a Scottish man named Isaac is leaning against the garage door near the airstrip. He walks them through the station, pointing to a line of bicycles near the main building. "Fer gettin' from one place t'the next," he says. The Tumi Field Station, which they call simply TFS, is an arrangement of weatherproof tents for housing and trailers for research. Each of the domed tents has two dorm-style beds and a small desk. There's a recreation building with a Ping-Pong table and a movie theater that consists of four couches, a television, and a wall of VHS tapes.

There are already five other teams there, the head count totaling forty-two after the Fairbanks team arrives. Everyone is working on a different aspect of climate research.

Eila's team crowds into the boot room, where they take off their boots and shed their jackets. Isaac waits in the hallway. He has a thick beard and wears a blue glass bead on a cord around his neck. He points to a small table with an open logbook and rows of two-way radios. "Don't forget to log in," he says. "Then I'll show you the dining hall. Chef cooks the most elaborate meals from the most boring ingredients. He's a magician."

Isaac studies how the temperature of Arctic stream water is changing due to thawing permafrost. He rambles about headwater catchment hydrology and stream discharge trends as they follow him down a long hall. Every inch of the walls is covered by tacked-up paper—maps, data sheets, first aid warnings, photographs, sticky-note drawings, and jokes.

Parallel lines have so much in common. It's a shame they'll never meet.

When Eila and Katy find their tents, Eila unpacks, sits on the bed, and opens her laptop, navigating to the caribou cameras. She changes the view so she can see from the caribou's point of view. For the next few hours, Eila watches from the camera on the caribou's neck—the shrubs shaking as the cow nibbles on the branches, her jaw muscles churning as she eats, the other herd members as they amble past.

There's a rainbow against a bruised purple sky.

Eila hears Katy say something, but the words are distant. When she arrives late for dinner, there's a handwritten sign taped to the door that says: **NERDS WELCOME. COME ON IN. WE HAVE ⬚.** She feels strangely at home.

In the morning, Eila and the team drink coffee on the airstrip, waiting for the helicopter to take them to their first field site. Because they each have separate areas of research, they'll be going to different places. But since Eila and Katy are both surveying vegetation across multiple areas, they'll stick together. Eila spots Katy sitting in the grass with a steaming mug and a map in front of her. Wes is taking water samples at a nearby lake, and Lucas and Gabe are hiking to where a new road has been proposed.

"What do you think Drew is doing right now?" Gabe says, elbowing Wes.

"Drinking coffee, same as us," Katy says over her shoulder.

"Yeah, but not enjoying a view this good, that's for sure." Gabe raises his mug to the mountains. "I bet he was just too scared of the plane ride. Not everyone has the stomach for it."

"He's been up here more than you have," Katy says. "Don't be a jackass."

Eila feels nauseated and crouches to light her stove and get some water boiling. She glances at Gabe out of the corner of her eye, on the verge of telling him—telling them all—that Drew didn't just flake out. That there's sneaky generosity behind his staying behind. But her voice feels hoarse and scratchy and she can't bring herself to speak up.

Katy leans over to show Eila pictures of her kids on her phone. "I really shouldn't use the battery up for this, but they're just so cute. I can't help it." Katy has a seven-year-old and a five-year-old, and she gets a little teary eyed when she tells Eila about what they're planning to do with the remaining few weeks of summer vacation. Weeks she is going to miss. Fishing and kayaking and a trip to the Museum of the North. Her husband runs a dog mushing tour company, and in the summers, when he's not taking groups out, he takes the kids, and Katy does the bulk of her research.

"We've got a system. These kids, man, they have such a different relationship with nature than I did," she says as the helicopter approaches. She raises her voice to match the sound of whirring propellers. "They're so lucky."

Katy didn't grow up in Alaska, but that doesn't really explain her comment. Eila finds herself thinking about luck and nature—two words she's never put in the same sentence, the latter something she's probably taken for granted.

When they get to the site, they jot their names at the top of the data sheet and get to work. Eila takes notes while Katy describes the terrain in a lilting dramatic voice, then the current weather in a more serious tone. They note the prominent vegetation they find. Eila writes: *Murphy. Sedgy-dryas tundra.* Eila lays out a long measuring tape across the ground, and along the length of it, she sets down the quadrats they built before they came—a one-meter square made of PVC pipe.

Katy positions ground control points—large X's that the drone can see from the air—and then fiddles with the drone to get it working properly. Eila overhears her cursing a few times and giggles quietly to herself, thankful she doesn't often have to fly the seemingly possessed equipment. Katy walks around with the controller in her hands, her eyes flicking up to the drone and then back down again. Eila sits next to the quadrats and estimates the type of ground cover in each, taking samples of each plant type within the quadrats: Arctic willow, white heather, dwarf birch, Labrador tea.

"What did you mean earlier?" Eila asks, snipping a section of Arctic willow. "About your kids having a different relationship with nature."

Katy holds a bag open for the sample. "I grew up in a city, for one. But I don't know, they just get to see and do things that I never did. The day before I left, they took off in the woods, and didn't come back until dinner, both with buckets of blueberries. I don't think I had any concept that a life like that even existed when I was a kid."

Eila mumbles a *hmm*, realizing she's always had that kind of connection with nature, and she can't imagine not having it.

"They're so much smarter than I was," Katy goes on. "So much more aware of the world. So much more in tune with the way things work. I don't remember being like that. I feel like they have so much more potential." She laughs self-consciously. "Honestly, I can't wait to see what they become."

"But you still found your way here," Eila says. She snips more shrubs and drops the stubby branches into a bag. "Even if you didn't start out with a love of nature, you ended up with one."

"I guess that's true enough," Katy says. "They just have so much *wonder* in them still."

Eila isn't sure she remembers wonder like she used to either. Her father seemed to be trying to capture it in his journal. Eila isn't sure if he managed to hang on to it his whole life, or if it was a gift that returned when the end was in sight.

"When was the last time you felt that childish wonder?" Katy asks.

Eila thinks of the sound of sandhill cranes, the changing color of snowshoe hares in winter, the symmetry of sun dogs. Before she can answer, Katy says, "I remember the first time I touched permafrost. That was probably the last time I really felt wonder. It was so cool, being able to just dig down, not even that far, and feel ice, even in summer. It kind of just made the earth feel so unknown and magical."

Eila laughs. "When I was a kid, we had this really hot summer, and all my dad's cabins started sinking on the south side. He spent days running around with a car jack, propping up cabins, wedging boards beneath them."

"Oh god, that sounds insane."

"Yeah. It's really not funny, I know, the implications. It was kind of hilarious watching him, though—he was like a cartoon character bouncing around from house to house. I would have helped more, but he wouldn't let me."

Eila is smiling so hard she has tears in her eyes. See, she thinks, there is wonder in chaos and in memory too. "Of course," she says, "that kind of thing happens every year now."

She's working on their twelfth quadrat when it hits her—she hasn't written the word *lichen* even once. Eila pulls notes from previous years at the same location. Over the last ten years, the ground cover of lichen has decreased by almost 75 percent—a huge drop.

"Maybe it's pollution?" Eila says.

Katy shrugs. "Has it really gotten *that* much worse in the last couple of years?"

Eila holds up a bag of sedge, the light filtering through the plastic. She looks at the bags on the ground, filled with microscopic pieces of information, the answers to her questions once she returns to a laboratory.

"I mean, yeah, it has," she says. "It's gotten a lot worse. But you're right. It shouldn't be enough to wipe out the lichen. It doesn't make sense."

"But the lichens would be the first to go. They're so susceptible to chemicals and pollution."

"There's the new road," Eila says. "But that's west of here, and the issue is clearly moving east."

"Holy shit, look." Katy crouches and points to a moose and her calf wandering between the short trees like curious tourists. Moose have been traveling farther north, as the trees have—skipping out of the boreal forest over the mountains. The moose are appearing in places that alarm researchers and, seemingly, the moose themselves. They search the terrain for something to nibble on, their steps tentative. Eila sees moose so frequently in Fairbanks, but there is something hypnotizing about them in the wild. When did she stop looking at them with that childish wonder?

In her bunk that night, she thinks about the moose again, pushing their boundaries, instinct drawing them to places unknown. Is she losing her sense of connection to the wild? What she had as a child, tracking and recording animal data just for the fun of it. Chasing them through the woods. She closes her eyes and tries to imagine where the caribou are right now. For the first time, she has the acute feeling that they aren't going to make it, when she's always been sure that they somehow would. She's always believed in nature, in its power to adapt, adjust, and right itself. She's always perceived her role in that balance as well. That kind of connection doesn't just disappear. Does it?

From the bed beneath her, Katy whispers, "At dinner, they were talking about taking tomorrow off. Doing something for fun."

"I'd rather keep working," Eila says.

"No helicopters. The pilot is taking off too. It's okay to have fun, you know."

Eila grumbles. "What are you going to do?" she asks.

"Most of them are going to hike to the lake for a swim. I heard some of the Swedish team say they wanted to play field hockey on the airstrip, though."

Eila pauses, then says, "I could work in the lab, I guess. I've also got reading to do. Don't worry—that *is* me having fun."

In the morning, Eila waves Katy off when she tries once more to rope her into a morning swim followed by team-building games. Eila puts on headphones and points to her father's journal in her lap. "Important reading," she says.

Dreamer

Eila. Pink hair. Dreams.

Eila came home from school with pink hair and stood in the doorway, her backpack dangling from her hand. She was wearing a huge sweater with jeans underneath, the hems of the pants tucked into fur-lined boots. Her eyes widened, as if she was the one taken aback, instead of me.

Pink reflected and bounced off every surface in the cabin. In the window behind her, on the refrigerator door, on the ceiling fan blades. She radiated neon.

I didn't think to comment on the style. Instead, I found myself wondering how she managed to do it without my knowledge. What were the logistics? And why? More curiosity than distress.

"There was a fight," she said, which only confused me more. The two things didn't seem connected.

"And," I said.

"Well, I was about to stop it."

She dropped her bag on the doormat and slumped down on the couch.

I chose my words carefully, not wanting to say the obvious—what did you do to yourself? But I also wanted to acknowledge her shockingly bright hair somehow. "Did you have to dye your hair to end the fighting? Give everyone something else to talk about?"

"Oh," she said. "That." Eila pulled at a strand and eyed it, twisted it in her fingers. "No, that was something else." She never actually told me why she dyed her hair, I just realized.

"Well," I said, sitting at the kitchen table. "I like it. So, what happened?"

Eila pulled off her boots and placed them next to the couch. She sighed heavily and shook her head.

That morning, they'd had school pictures, she told me. Jackson didn't have any money. He wouldn't have cared—he wasn't the type who wanted a school picture anyway—but one of the other kids at school started teasing him, which eventually led to the first real fist fight Eila had ever seen.

Eila hadn't intended on taking a school picture either. But since they started fighting, and since she wanted to make sure Jackson and this other boy became—and stayed—friends, she snuck out of school, ran all the way home, and returned with most of the cash she'd saved from her allowance over the past year.

"Didn't you want to spend that on something else?" I asked.

She shrugged. "I couldn't think of anything else at the time."

Eila paid the cameraman and filled out the form and convinced him to take a photo of all three of them. In a couple of weeks, she told me, there'd be an envelope of photos arriving at our door, one of those backdrops that looks like a poorly erased chalkboard. The three of them would be in front: Eila, Jackson, and the twerp, Lawrence Keeler.

"They're giving me the Peacekeeper Award at school," Eila said, looking at the floor. "Whatever that is."

Jackson was the only real friend Eila ever had. Maybe because they were both awkward with the other kids. Maybe because they didn't need anyone else. I still have the picture. It's been pinned to the visor of my truck all these years. Jackson has a bruise under his left eye. The Keeler kid has a fat lip and a smear of blood on the side of his nose. Both of them are staring deadpan at the camera. Between them, Eila has a hand on each of their shoulders, a smile so big her eyes are hardly open, with hair the color of cotton candy.

This is not a memory. I don't need to write it down so I won't forget it. It's the image of someone right outside.

It's a character sketch.

Eila the peacekeeper. Eila the idealist. Eila the dreamer.

She could never be persuaded that the world is sometimes a cruel place, a sad and ugly place. Not even sometimes. There was always a sense of hope, as if she had a book of answers the rest of the world did not.

For example: she still does not believe Jackson is really gone. His disappearance was disturbing, but not exactly puzzling or surprising to anyone else, not really, when we thought about it. Accidents happen. He was a wild person, always pushing.

I remember Jackson and Eila when they were younger. The smallest of details, but an extraordinary number of them—scraped bicycle paint, a dead bird, heavy books on human anatomy. I spotted the two of them so many times out of the corner of my eye, following me, hiding in the woods, watching me work. I remember the spring he took off running and never seemed to stop, dizzying the whole town with his repetitive laps. The tracks he left everywhere in the dirt.

These pieces are clear. But there are aspects closer to this moment that are blurred, but important. Like something Vern told me, a conversation he had with Jackson just before he disappeared. I can't remember, but I wish I could. So many things I'm desperate to reach back and bring forward in my mind again.

Eila's holding her breath.

She reads the line over and over—*a conversation he had with Jackson*—then flips through every page of the notebook, scanning for Jackson's name, hoping Stefan finally remembered and completed the thought.

But she finds nothing. And since her father and Jackson are both gone, she knows she will never learn more about that conversation, unless she gets it out of Vern. And since she can't do that, she's struck with complete lack of control, panic. Like she's being held underwater.

When the wave passes, Eila assures herself that she must be projecting, seeing what she wants to see. Making more of this than is rational. What else could there possibly be to know anyway? If she and Jackson were as close as two people could be, then reason tells her she knows everything. What she needs now is to refocus, to get back out there and solve real problems with real science. Recenter. Find the caribou.

Yes, she used to be a dreamer. But it seems less and less true lately that she couldn't be persuaded of the world's cruelty. What she never did tell her father was that she does accept Jackson's death. That she gave in, or gave up, a long time ago.

Eila walks outside to the reindeer pens. The only caribou she's seen so far are the domestic reindeer that have been living at TFS for generations now.

She watches two brothers sparring—Bo and Vigo. Against the odds, they were born as twins. They're not trying to kill each other. That isn't the goal. But the two reindeer lock antlers with stubbornness, a violent dance of thrusting and retreating, back and forth. They snort with their muzzles close to the ground, breath steaming, necks craning in one direction and then the other.

Then Eila hears a crack and sees that Bo has broken one of his antlers in the spar. He backs away, snorting puffs of steam from his nostrils, bowing. The piece of antler lies in the dirt between them. Bo ends the spar, and Vigo backs away too. Then Bo seems to change his mind and runs again at Vigo, head down, broken antler leading.

Even from a distance, Eila notices a change—a decision in Vigo's eyes to not engage again, but also to go one step further, even if he doesn't yet know what that entails. Vigo looks to the fence and then runs. He leaps where some of the wire has been pulled down, catching his chest on the exposed, jagged edge. He stumbles but gathers himself on the other side and takes off, bounding into the sun-streaked snow beyond the pen.

None of the reindeer at the Fairbanks station have ever done anything like this.

Eila's already running after him before she realizes it. Her lungs feel like they might burst, but she can't stop her legs. Some element of spirit propels her forward. She can barely see Vigo ahead, hurtling on like a force unbound and free across the tundra.

She blinks through the snow, wondering where he's headed, if he still has the instinct to find the herd even though his parents and grandparents were all born in a barn. Wondering, too, if she's trying to catch and secure him, or if she's escaping too.

Vigo bolts down the airstrip, empty now that everyone decided to swim, and then he veers toward the mountains, running across the open tundra. Eila follows, her field training kicking in, her brain noting that she hasn't signed out or taken a radio. But she doesn't have time for formalities or procedures.

She loses sight of him, her heart knocking against her ribs, but she's afraid that if she stops, she won't be able to start again and she'll have lost him for good. She's about to scream his name, though she knows what little good it would do, when she hears the low grunting.

"You had to try it, didn't you?" she whispers, crouching and slowly inching toward him. He's standing next to a spruce the height of his chest—not much of a hiding spot—and he's still, watching her from the corner of his eye. He seems to consider his options, then allows her to crisscross the rope around his body.

Eila forgets, though, that he was hurt by the metal fence. When the rope pulls tighter on his chest, Vigo flinches and bucks her off, throwing her to the ground. She hits the earth hard, shoulder first, her breath forced out of her.

"I guess I deserved that," she says, trying to catch Vigo's eye so they can share this moment, an unspoken nod to their injuries, as if they are not of different species. He looks away, suggesting the event never happened, and she isn't offended. It's nothing personal. She's seen how animals treat their brothers and sisters with a fierce kind of respect, and this makes her want to stand up and hug him all the more.

Something breaks inside her. A child version of Eila would have dreamed about this moment—alone on the tundra with this massive, gentle-yet-powerful creature. If she turns her back to the station and squints her eyes, she can transform the scene into something else—a fairy tale maybe. The kind she's longed for her whole life.

The snow turns to rain, heavy drops splattering on her coat, a curling fog rolling over the mountains toward them. Eila's knees sink into the slush and tangles of wet grass. She isn't sure she can bring herself to move.

But it's here, holding the rope, her shoulder throbbing, that she notices the lichen on the ground around her. Except it looks like something else—a plant she doesn't recognize. She plucks a piece of it and holds it in her palm, seeing immediately that something is wrong.

It *is* reindeer lichen—the caribou's food source for the winter. But there's some kind of foreign growth that seems to be choking the lichen, breaking it down. Eila is short of breath, realizing that she's found it—at least the beginning. What she uncovered in the data in Fairbanks. She'll have to take more samples, a lot more, and run tests back at the field station to determine if it's also directly harming the caribou. But this is it. It has to be.

She finds another patch of the same affected lichen a few feet from the first. There's a trail of it, all leading east away from the TFS. It occurs to her that it might be dangerous to even touch it, but it's too late and her eyes follow a sporadic trail until it disappears over a distant hill. She'll need to go farther to get more.

Stranded with a rogue reindeer and an infected plant, Eila doesn't know what to do. She doesn't have a radio to call for someone at the station. She doesn't have a tranquilizer to sedate Vigo so the animal handlers can carry him back in the helicopter. But after tucking the lichen sample into the pocket of her work pants, she finds that he's willing to walk with her, and this breaks her again, even more.

He doesn't resist at all, as if the whole thing had been merely an experiment. Just to see what it felt like. But Eila knows these animals better. She knows he must feel the pull to run and migrate like all caribou. Like thousands of his ancestors. A few generations couldn't possibly erase that instinct.

36

The late-summer rain and snow continue to come and go in unpredictable waves, which prevents the Fairbanks team from flying out when they originally planned. The other researchers are antsy, but they find ways to entertain themselves. They play foosball in the rec room and hockey on the airstrip. Katy takes a video, which she later shows Eila, shaking her head. "Ice hockey in August," she says. "It took five minutes before one of the Canadians smacked the puck into a pavement divot and it flew into Gabe's face. Black eye. Personally, I think he's wearing it a little too proudly."

Since bringing Vigo back, Eila has spent all her time in the lab, analyzing the lichen sample. She closes one eye, presses the other into the eyepiece.

"See anything notable?" Katy asks with what sounds like genuine interest, though she's picking up other slides and holding them to the light. Eila suspects she'll find interest in anything that doesn't involve endless charts and data at this point.

"Um, yeah," Eila says, biting her lip. "It's definitely a new compound, not part of the normal symbiosis."

"Maybe another fungus?" Katy asks, pausing to consider the idea. "But more than one fungus can be part of the lichen. That's not abnormal. A parasite then? What about it is so deadly to the whole relationship?"

"It's not another fungus. It might be a parasite attacking the algae components of the lichen, and the algae can't regenerate fast enough. What I don't understand is its pattern across the tundra. It's like a river of infected lichen, flowing east. Why isn't it everywhere?"

Eila looks away from the microscope to see that Katy has been distracted by a poster of mushrooms on the wall. "Hey," Eila says. "You should go have dinner or something. I'll do more analysis and let you know what I find later."

"Sure," Katy says. "I do need to call my kids. They've apparently grown nasturtiums, and I need them to describe every color in detail or I might go crazy here. If I see another goddamn summer snowflake, I swear . . ."

The next morning, Eila gets a call from Geneveive, a medical researcher from France whose expertise is mental health. Seizing the unexpected weather opportunity to further her research, she's assessing the various teams' psychological states, now that they're stranded in a remote research station with mostly strangers, far from home and family, with no particular end date on the horizon. She's called each person in to discuss the stress of living there, in addition to the disruption of day-night cycles in the Arctic. The sun is finally beginning to set for a few hours at night, but most of them are still sleeping with masks to block the sunlight.

Katy tells Eila not to worry—the word she uses to describe her own conversation with Genevieve is *pleasant*.

"Do we have to?" Eila asks.

"No," Katy says. "But everyone is doing it for the sake of research. Well, except Magnus, the Icelandic pilot. Although he probably needs it the most. Apparently he's going nuts here. Claustrophobia, social anxiety. What's the phobia of being around a lot of people? I'm not sure."

If it's for the sake of research, Eila will do it. She doesn't want to be unsupportive.

She meets Genevieve in her office, sits in a folding chair by the window, and Genevieve asks how she is dealing with being away from family. Eila lets out an unintentional laugh, then tries to disguise it as a cough, hoping she doesn't sound too sarcastic or uncooperative, but she doesn't know how to answer that question.

How does she say "I have none"? She thinks for a moment about Sadie and Vern—friends of her father's, yes, but they've also been in her life for as long as she can remember. Vern was there when she learned to ride a bike, and Sadie made every one of her birthday cakes growing up. Isn't that family? She thinks of Drew, the two of them bracing each other as they rammed their heels into a door, sharing a beer after. Drew, holding down the fort so she can be here, staying because he knows how much this trip means to her.

She says, "I'm doing okay."

Home is an easier topic.

"I'm home out here," Eila says. "Well, not *right* here. I guess I should say *out there*." The thought completes itself in her head—*with the caribou*—but she doesn't say any more.

"How are you feeling physically? Are you sleeping enough? Eating enough?"

Eila shrugs. "I assume so. I'm pretty used to these daylight cycles. I've lived here all my life, almost. Made for a frozen world, I was told."

Genevieve smiles and writes something down. "That's beautiful. Who told you that?"

"My father," she says, and before Genevieve can ask about him, she adds, "He died a few months ago. Brain tumor."

"I'm so sorry," Genevieve says. "How are you doing?"

"Honestly, it feels like I'm drowning. I want him back—I want them both back—but that's not possible. I just want to kick and scream, but I know that will only make me sink even further."

Genevieve's shoulders sag a little, and she tips her head to one side, perhaps at the unexplained use of the word *both*. "You know, I'm obviously conducting research here, but I'm also just another colleague when it comes down to it. So if you ever want to talk more, or just hang out, let me know. Off the record and all that."

"Thanks," Eila says, fidgeting in her seat.

"Is there anyone else, though? Do you have a partner or close friend back in Fairbanks?"

Eila sighs. Why does she even think of Jackson when he's even more unreachable than her father? She's unable to conjure Jackson's name on her lips. Unable to even think of a word to describe him. *Soulmate* is cheesy. *Partner* seems far less romantic than it should. *Fated kindred companion of the wild*, that could work, perhaps.

She chooses not to say his name at all. Just, "He's gone too. We were like two versions of the same person. Except for one thing. He moved all the time, and I liked stillness."

"Liked?"

"I guess I still do. I like being in one place, as long as it's the right place. I'm not a big fan of change."

"Do you know what the word *bereavement* really means?" Genevieve asks her. "It's actually slightly different from grief or mourning. It's the process of adapting to a new situation—without the person, or persons, that you lost. In my opinion, one of the best ways to do that is to explore your surroundings. Take it all in and stay open to everything. Let yourself learn. And that's what you're here to do, right? At least, in part?"

"Yeah," Eila says, trying to sound thankful. "That's exactly what I'm here to do."

"Adaptability," Genevieve repeats. "It's the best chance we have at surviving."

Eila feels dizzy, thinking about her father and Vern's talk about the Arctic plants and what they do to survive.

37

In seventh grade, their science teacher announced, "Fungi create life as they eat death."

The class stared blankly, waiting for him to go on, to explain this end-of-days science fiction movie he was clearly inventing. It sounded nuclear.

"You remember the asteroid that wiped out almost all life on the planet, roughly sixty-six million years ago, right?"

The entire class shook their heads in unison. They did not remember this event.

Their teacher laughed. "You're being funny. No, of course you don't remember it. But you've heard about it, or at least you should have. In any case, when that asteroid hit Earth, what was left were some reptiles, some mammals, and, you guessed it, fungi. Mammals being warm, and fungi needing warmth to thrive, life began rebuilding. The fungi ate all the decomposing plants and animals killed by the asteroid and turned it into new life. Like a great big, Earth-size compost heap."

Jackson caught Eila's eye from across the room. A few days before, he'd eaten a mushroom loaf that his mother had made for lunch, and Eila had teased him endlessly about the revolting consistency, noting that he was eating fungi. Having given up veganism, she'd had a bowl of leftover chicken soup. Jackson gave her a smug look and gestured toward the teacher, and she knew exactly what he was implying.

Chapter 371, in which I eat life-creating fungi for lunch and you eat dead birds.

"Fungi take dead organic matter and break it down. As they do this, nutrients release and plants use them to grow."

He told them that even beer had medicinal properties—yeast being a single-cell fungus. Centuries ago, people drank beer not for fun, but because the yeast killed bacteria in water and made it safe to drink.

That night, Eila and Jackson stole a can of beer from Stefan's fridge. They tiptoed past him, where he sat on the couch, sleeping. His legs were propped on the coffee table, his head tilted back, a cup of tea in his lap. As they crept out of the house, Eila turned back.

"I have to get the tea," she said.

Jackson shook his head. "Too risky."

"Yeah, but if the tea spills, then he'll definitely wake up. I think it's worth it. Also, I'd feel way too guilty if he spilled tea all over himself."

Jackson pondered, then agreed. Eila slinked back to the couch, slipping the teacup from her father's grasp ever so gently. She placed it on the table and backed away.

They walked in the late-summer sunlight to the tree house. Sitting on the floor, they popped open the can, passing it back and forth while they played gin rummy. That was when Jackson showed her the travel books about Blackstone Bay and told her about the kayaking trip his mother was taking him on. There were islands where you could camp, where you could see bald eagles and hear the glaciers breaking apart.

"Maybe you can come," he said.

Of course, the trip his mother promised never materialized. At least not the way Jackson had imagined it, or in any way that involved his mother. But that night, he beamed as he looked over a map of the bay spread on the cedar floor between them. He pointed to where the innermost part of the bay curved into what looked like a great white mouth—the cluster of glaciers.

"Does this taste good to you?" he asked.

Eila shrugged. "Not really. It definitely doesn't taste healthy. Or like any kind of fungi."

"No," Jackson said, handing her the beer, one finger still pressed to the map. "I think whatever it was they were brewing back then was something very different from this. But—it probably sounds stupid—I do feel more alive."

38

The lichen sample begins to break down under the microscope, and Eila feels time slipping. But even as it deteriorates, it reveals new findings. Magnified through the lens is an entire tiny ecosystem captured in a single organism. It looks like branching, crusted coral. The fungal and algal compounds of the lichen, as they break apart, appear covered with microscopic splotches of turquoise, so luminous they look unnatural.

Katy immediately backs away when Eila shows her the reaction.

"What if it's radioactive?" she says, suggesting they grab hazmat suits from storage.

"This isn't the first brightly colored parasite," Eila reminds her. "There are plenty of neon yellows and pinks on lichens out there."

"True. But I've seen a lot of specimens, and I've never seen anything like this . . . in person."

Eila shows the sample to some of the other biologists. Isaac is convinced that it could lead to some new great medical discovery. The next penicillin. Eila reminds him that it's destroying the lichen, and possibly the caribou, not curing anything, as far as she can tell.

"It's all about perspective," he says.

"Why isn't it everywhere? All over the tundra?"

Isaac shrugs. "Maybe it has something to do with the caribou's migration path," he says in his thick accent. "Maybe they spread it in that direction. Like a kind of pollination, but of death."

As they analyze the components, they find all the biogenic elements necessary for new life. Carbon, hydrogen, oxygen, nitrogen, sulfur, and phosphorous. Their tests all reveal that this new compound could basically create life from nothing. Except for one thing. There is a distinct lack of calcium in the lichen makeup. This one missing mineral could be responsible for the deterioration of the whole symbiotic relationship, its inability to remain bonded.

Eila contacts other scientists, but no one has seen this type of compound before, on any plant, let alone lichens. She reads books from the lab and scours online articles, and she's left feeling that the only way to get to the bottom of it is to collect more samples. But their time is up; they're simply waiting for the weather to clear so they can return to Fairbanks.

She finds Lucas, the team lead, in the dining hall and explains everything she's found, everything Katy and Isaac have confirmed—that furthering this research is incredibly important to the caribou's survival.

"What's miraculous," she says, sliding onto the bench with a cup of yogurt and granola in her fist, "is that these compounds have everything needed to potentially *create* life, and yet for some reason it's killing this plant. It's sucking the life from the lichen. Why isn't it doing the opposite?"

Lucas blinks multiple times, and she isn't sure if he's trying to process what she said or if there's something in his eye. His forehead crinkles, and he says, "I promise we will get back out there for more samples, *next spring*. But we don't have the funding to stay any longer in the field."

"No," she says, a little too loudly, a little too forcefully. "That's not good enough. I can go out there myself. We have to find out what this is. It's only going to keep spreading."

"It's not my decision. We'll get you back out there, though, I promise. And you're smart, by the way. I happen to think you're brilliant. Which is how I know you can figure it out with whatever you've got now. Just have some faith. And also"—he grabs her biceps and shakes her lightly—"have some fun."

Somehow, he manages to make a compliment condescending. As she storms out of the dining hall, she bumps into Magnus, who looks just as irritated as she is.

"Sorry," she says, looking down.

The Icelandic pilot grunts, then pats her on the back, and she thinks she catches his face twisting into something like a smile.

Everyone gathers in the common room that night and tries to relax and watch a movie. But the internet connection is too slow, and when *Beetlejuice* glitches one too many times, they end up playing Worst-Case Scenario instead.

Genevieve watches from a beanbag in the corner, visibly amused. Eila bows out, saying good night, eager to get back to her father's journal. There's only one entry left. She doesn't know what she'll do when it's over. It feels like another goodbye.

Maybe it's what Genevieve said about bereavement. Maybe it's the weather clearing up or the proximity of returning to her old life, not having to fully adapt at all. The easy way. Whatever the reason, Eila convinces herself that now is as good a time as any to find out what was going through Stefan's mind the last time he wrote. She opens to the last page and, with a deep breath, follows him to the conclusion.

> **Spice Cake**
>
> Sadie brought me a spice cake. Ginger and cloves and extra cardamom because she knows how much I love it. She does this often, but today was different. Today she added extra honey. Because we needed some extra sweetness, she said, to counteract all the mud. She laughed about it. She always hated breakup when spring came, and not just because it had such a harsh and severing name. She was overcome with anxiety when the earth cracked open

and let its gooey insides out. It made her, too, feel exposed somehow.

Just after she left, Vern came by. We ate the cake on the back porch. He said he'd come to give me a pie recipe, which he knew perfectly well I'd never get around to making. I might have tried—why not? But it was a recipe his wife had written out, and as soon as I saw her handwriting on the card, I knew it was something special. He'd found it in a box, he said. It was a peach pie she'd made so many times, the card was stained with water, butter, peach syrup. I told him to keep it, save it for some other occasion. Something vital, because there are times in this world when a good peach pie is vital.

He looked away, pretended he was coughing.

I joked that maybe he could get Sadie to bake the pie for us both, since she seemed to be so good with comfort foods. He laughed, wiping tears from his face. He also looked at me strangely, sort of pained and confused, and I realized that many of the words I'd just said were probably the wrong ones. But I don't have time to go back and revise now. I can only keep going forward.

When Vern first told me what he and Sadie discovered in their greenhouse, I wondered if it was worth it for him, leaving behind his family to come to Alaska. He didn't like to talk about it, but I pieced it together from the bits he was willing to offer. His wife, twice his age, who'd been suffering. His inability to witness it. His denial and recklessness. His daughter, who he never got to know because he was too afraid to be a father.

In the end, he was led to a miracle. He thinks that what they found there, something in the bees' DNA, could put an end to all illness and death.

Does that make it okay? No, I don't think it does. But I do realize now that people do what they're capable of at any given moment, and no one really owes you anything. You have to just take them for what and who they are. And if I don't have time to revise my behavior, why should I bother trying to revise someone else's?

Anyway.

From Vern's accounts, he and Sadie fought endlessly about what to do with the bees. Her goal had always been to somehow re-create the flower she'd found in the ash. She'd called it her purpose. But now I think maybe the journey was her purpose. She needed something to put all her energy into, but she never thought she'd actually find it.

So many things could've happened if they'd shared the discovery, perhaps good, probably bad. Vern was ready to hand it over, right then and there. Duty and responsibility, he called it, as if he knew anything about either. Sadie was sure a discovery like that could actually destroy the planet. Not just disrupt the balance of nature, but devastate it.

Sadie won the argument, and Vern promised to keep it a secret. It's still there, it all exists, but who knows what's become of it. They hadn't spoken of it in years.

Then it all came back up again, stubborn as a rosebush, and Vern couldn't let it go after he heard about my illness. He's begged me so many times these last few months.

But it's not for me.

Do you remember the place, Eila? You were so small then, but you helped me build it. It was where you first used a hammer. Most mornings, we walked down to the river, just you and me. Not another soul in sight. Just the bending trees and the sunlit water.

Vern wants to save me. I get that. And he's so sure that those bees could do it. The thing is, it's a beautiful idea until it isn't. Only until you realize that no matter how long you might live, you'll never get to do everything you wanted. And if you got to live forever, you still wouldn't get a chance to go back and do things over.

When the end of your life is an imminent thing, suddenly all of your flaws are more visible. Your scars, the scars you've given others. And your secrets pound on the inside of your skull. You want to confess everything all at once.

There is a balance in the world shutting down, then waking up again. People are no different. One of us closes our eyes forever so that another can open theirs. The darkness exists so the light can be cherished.

The fires burn so the forest can regrow.

The antlers fall every spring so they can return, new again, each winter.

39

This idea of Vern and Sadie discovering the key to immortality seems so absurd, so far fetched, Eila has to wonder if it's something her father made up. Something, perhaps, to explain the great surrender he was about to undertake.

But there are elements that make Eila think he may actually have been telling the truth. That perhaps it *is* all real, that there is some great discovery that could either save or destroy the world. First, there's his ability to write so lucidly about it, to get things right. Just before he stopped communicating verbally, he had a hard time stringing sentences together and landing on the right words. But here, despite the shaky handwriting, his thoughts are organized, thoroughly documented.

There's also a map. It's not much clearer than his handwriting, but it's obvious enough—the bend in the Yukon River, the proximity to the Dalton and the nearest villages. And though the place itself is at the edge of memory, she knows of its existence and was told stories of being there with him. When Eila closes her eyes, she can picture morning sunlight filtering through spruce trees, reflecting off rushing water.

And then: Eila's dizzy remembering being in the garden with her father. Of course he tried to tell her about this. It makes sense now. His "ramblings" about the lupine, the "ash flower." She thought he'd been mixing up words again when he said she could have fixed Vern and Sadie's "anomaly," their "abomination." She thought it was nonsense.

But he'd been more focused and clear sighted than ever.

Suddenly, Eila's angry. Truly angry. Angry that her father would choose not to take Vern's help when it was offered, that he would so casually mention something as miraculous as this and then so easily let it go. Angry that neither of them had given her the full story, given her a say in what happened. Mad at Sadie, who's always treated her like a grown-up yet also said nothing, even when they stood around that bonfire like awkward teenagers at a school dance, no one wanting to be the next to have to mumble some incoherent, poorly constructed tribute. It's hard to buy into what her father said about people only doing what they're capable of at any given time. There has to be some accountability.

But most of all, she's mad at herself, because her father *had* tried, albeit in a subtle, quiet way, and she made assumptions and chose not to really listen.

All her life, she's held herself to certain standards and played by the rules. But then the world stopped making sense. Trying to take care of the earth's creatures doesn't immunize you from tragedy. This time, things have to be different. She needs a new strategy. She can't stay put any longer when all she really wants to do is run. And run fast, too, like Jackson used to. While she never understood his desire for constant movement, suddenly she feels driven, pushed, *propelled*.

Vern's discovery, however terrible it may seem to some, could cure the lichen of the parasite and, in turn, save the caribou. Maybe it's nothing. Maybe her father did begin dreaming too much in the end. Either way, she needs to see for herself.

Eila passes the common room quietly. She gathers what remains of the lichen samples, then packs her bag and goes in search of the only other person who might understand.

PART 4

40

Lark Audette

One spring, when the birds hatched, two ornithologists captured one from the nest. They took this bird, an alder flycatcher, to another nest—the nest of a captive willow flycatcher they were also studying. There was nothing in appearance to distinguish the two songbirds. The alder flycatcher spent two months learning the call and songs and ways of the willow flycatcher. They became, from the outside, identical.

But the following spring, the alder reverted back to its native call. With colors and markings perfectly alike, the only thing that differentiated the two birds persisted naturally—they couldn't be anything other than what they were.

Lark watches the flycatcher from the long bench of a fallen tree. The sound is like a zipper being pulled back and forth. The pitch goes up quickly, then slides back down. Every few seconds there's a hurried "pip" from the bird's throat. The flycatcher glances around hastily from her loose, messy nest.

An olive-colored back, with three white stripes across her wings that look like military achievement. The bird flies from the nest again, dips urgently through the air, and opens her beak to snap up an insect. Then she circles around and returns to her perch.

She is part of the tyrant flycatcher family, a name that has always seemed unjust. She consumes to survive, like all things do. She is irritable and nervy and critical of birds much larger than herself, like many other creatures. She pushes her way through the world and takes what she needs. This doesn't make her a tyrant, Lark thinks. Only more courageous and respectable than some humans she's met. She writes this in her notebook, alongside a few other notes about boreal songbirds.

She jumps at a sound coming from behind. Footsteps on the trail. It's the woman who works in the visitors' center. She walks the trails by herself every afternoon wearing knee-high rubber boots. Lark knows now that these are called breakup boots, because they were marked as essential on the list of supplies she was given. She understands why, now that she's slogged through the muck.

The woman waves to Lark as she passes, a look of recognition in her eyes. And though it's a kind look, there is also something sorrowful, as if it hurts her somehow. Lark can't imagine what she's done. The woman makes it ten steps past where Lark is sitting before turning around with a sigh.

"I'm Sadie," she says.

"Lark." She stands. The flycatcher takes another swoop through the air, passing between the two women, and then returns to her low nest, a small cup of loosely strung twigs and string.

"Have you caught anything?" Sadie asks.

"I'm just going to check. I think there's a swallow in the net down there. I was waiting for the kids that wanted to watch the banding." She looks at her watch. "But I don't think they're coming."

"I'll come," Sadie says. "Maybe I can lend a hand."

"Sure."

The swallow caught in the mist net looks like it's resting in an invisible hammock. It bobs on the gentle breeze until Lark lifts it out. She tips the bird onto its back, then leans forward and blows a steady stream of air onto its stomach. The light, wispy feathers part to the side, revealing a pink belly. Lark examines the fat stores, then holds the bird out for Sadie, the delicate transfer of life from one pair of hands to another.

The swallow between them, Lark wraps an aluminum band around its leg, then writes the serial number on a log sheet. She glances up to see that Sadie is looking at her, not the bird, and they both smile, though it's hard to say who is more awkward.

"Have you lived in Fairbanks long?" Lark asks.

"All my life," says Sadie. "My great-grandparents were homesteaders. My grandparents moved to Fairbanks later in life. My parents were both born here." She hesitates. "How about you?"

"I'm from the Southwest. New Mexico. Just here for the summer."

"A long way. And your family? They're in New Mexico too?"

"My parents are dead. Well, my mother is dead. I'm not sure about my father. I grew up with my aunt. She's also a birder."

"So you don't know where your father is?"

"Nope." Lark uses a tiny measuring tape to check the wingspan of the sparrow. She tries to be gentle, but her hands are shaking and she doesn't know why.

"Have you ever tried to find him?"

Lark keeps her eyes trained on the bird. The wind ruffles its feathers. "Wouldn't know where to start. Could have asked my aunt, I guess. Maybe I just wasn't ever ready."

"What do you think you'd say if you saw him again?"

Lark's eyes flick up at the forwardness of the question. She has no idea why a woman she's just met cares about her family, her past, but she decides she'll humor her and gives as cryptic an answer as possible for her own amusement. "Do you know the alder flycatcher?" Lark asks. "Have you ever heard their call? It's impossible to break them of it. Their call is always going to be their call. They can never be anything other than who they are. People are like that too. I never understood why people apologize so much for doing the best they can with the tools they have. Does that make any sense?"

"Yeah, but if people do bad things . . . you can't just forget that, can you?"

"I'm just saying." Lark sighs, turns the bird over, and lets it tiptoe to the edge of her palm. It flies into the trees, out of sight so quickly it's a dream it was ever held captive. She wonders briefly if her outlook on the world is a sign that she's well adjusted or simply lazy, but she decides quickly that it doesn't matter. Things are what they are. "I'm just saying that there is room for growth in this world, and people are so busy holding grudges, they don't take the time to consider what someone might have been going through when they did XYZ... Doesn't make it right, but I guess, if I saw my father again, I'd ask him what kind of song he's singing now. Is it the alder or the willow? The one he was born with, or the one he learned later."

Sadie blinks tears from her eyes. "So, how did you end up here?" she asks.

Lark thinks about how she actually got here. The drive up the Alcan, the emptiness of the road. The bag of chips she had to eat when she passed the only food stop for over a hundred miles. The diner that touted the best grilled cheese on the highway, where she watched a mother nursing her baby and briefly missed the mother she never got to know. The convenience store where, between dusty VHS tapes and plastic sunglasses, she found a red-tailed hawk carved out of wood, its wings spread in flight. The family who breezed through that store. The mother and father stretching their arms over their heads while still holding hands. The kids who begged for quarters for the gumball machine that spit rainbow-colored spheres down an elaborate spiraling tube. Lark bought the hawk quickly then and left, stepping outside to find a dog lying on the porch beneath a sign that read NO DOGS ALLOWED.

A place full of contradictions, she thought, bending to pet the dog.

Just like the letter had said.

"They invited me," Lark tells Sadie, waving her hand in the general direction of the buildings. "Someone from here. After college, I never really figured out what I wanted to do with my life, so this seemed like a good plan. I don't know who sent the initial letter, but whoever it was, they were so enamored with this place. I had a hard time getting it out of my head once it was there."

41

Eila Jacobsen

Eila waits for Magnus on the airstrip before anyone else is awake, taking advantage of the fact that they all stayed up too late and will probably sleep in. The one variable Eila isn't sure about is Isaac, who tends to be up at any hour. She stands alone at first, the sky dark behind the mountains' silhouettes, the early-morning breeze sending ripples of dusty snow across the paved strip. A mix of snow and rain splatters on her jacket. Her backpack is on her back, her sleeping bag hugged to her chest. She wonders if this is too much to carry but acknowledges that, while she might prefer to head into the great unknown with very little, it would be stupid, and she isn't stupid.

On her way out of the station, she stopped by the gear room, where she found a tent that hadn't been used in ages and likely wouldn't be missed. She also took some rain covers for her gear and a first aid kit. She signed out, too, but decided against taking a radio. Good to let them know it's intentional, but she doesn't want to be reachable.

For a brief, heart-stopping moment, she wonders if Magnus changed his mind, if he's turned her in and Lucas is going to march out and write her up, tell her she's never coming on a trip like this again. Well, she probably isn't, regardless.

She feels suddenly guilty, realizing that she's pulled Magnus into her delinquency. While she doesn't have a problem dealing with the consequences, she doesn't know what will happen to him, to his pilot's license, once he gets back.

But then she sees Magnus crossing the airstrip, and his usually hunched-over figure is walking tall. He's wearing a bright-yellow vest over a hoodie and a black beanie over his chin-length hair. He's smoking a cigarette and holding a ceramic cup of coffee, and, as he gets close enough, Eila sees that he's smiling.

A sight she's never seen.

"Perfect weather," he says, dipping the half-smoked cigarette into a shallow puddle before stuffing it into his vest pocket. He climbs into the cockpit and nestles the mug between his legs, and Eila lets out her breath, a stream of fog releasing.

Eila pulls her gear into the plane and sits next to him. He hands her a headset and says, "We're going to get reamed for this."

"I can pay you," she says. "I'm sure you'd get a few hundred at least if this was a charter flight."

"Nah. I was waiting for an excuse to get out of there. I could have just left, you know. But they kept saying they needed me. 'Hang on, hang on, don't go yet.'" He huffs at the absurdity.

"Are you sure . . ."

"This is going to be the best day in six months. You know what you're doing, though, right?"

Eila nods.

"What's in Cloud Creek again?"

"A cabin. Really."

He eyes her, like he's still concerned she might walk off into the wilderness alone, without a plan. Which is accurate, kind of. She may not have a plan, but she does have a goal. She knows exactly what needs to be done, even if she isn't sure how to do it yet. "I'm just saying. In case. You sure you want me to leave you there?"

"Yes, I definitely am." She notices a scar at the corner of his mouth. When he smiles, it pulls back into a crescent. "My family has a cabin an hour's walk east. This is literally what I do for my job, don't worry."

"All right then. No more questions. No more worries. Let's rock and roll."

When he starts the plane up, panic runs through Eila. There's no turning back, and she feels urgency, the need to go now. Someone has surely heard the propellers whirring and the engine revving. Her feet press into the floor as if this might lift them into the air. Her hands are sweating.

And then they're up, the plane shaking and vibrating. Rocking and rolling, just as Magnus said. It's a forty-five-minute flight, most of which is too loud for them to talk. The plane hits turbulence so frequently, Eila couldn't speak if she wanted to. She's scared in a way that's shockingly unfamiliar. But Magnus grins through it all, so she plasters her hand to the window and tries to smile too.

The ground below turns to widening valley and mudflats and glassy, serpentine rivers. The land is painted with swells of garnet and gold, with drifts of summer snow clinging to the mountainsides. Her eyes follow the river tributaries, the dots of green shrubs, the sweeping valleys that tilt in dizzying angles.

"All my life," Magnus shouts into the headset, "I've seen this view. My world is this great expanse. I can't stand small spaces. And so many people. It's suffocating."

His energy is so contagious that Eila finds herself getting excited, too, until the weight of what she's doing hits. The reality that they will have to come down, and she will have to keep moving on her own. All she has left are the caribou. But they are slipping away, and saving them is too important to lose sight of the mission.

Across the plain below, an animal is running, and Eila strains to make it out. It's too big to be a mountain goat or wolf or caribou—it has to be a bear—but its coat is so light and it looks as if it's gliding, floating above the earth.

42

Every bump of the landing in Cloud Creek fills Eila with simultaneous fear and relief. The plane rolls to a stop and Magnus says, "Man! I needed that. Thank you." Before Eila can say she hasn't done anything, Magnus's radio comes alive with static and they hear Lucas's voice. Magnus switches it off quickly, shoves the radio into his pocket, and shrugs. He says, "It's easier when you have someone else to blame, you know?"

"I thought you were going to say you never saw me," she teases.

"I need coffee. Don't die, okay?"

As Magnus heads to the café, Eila yells after him, "Hey, thank you! Please tell Lucas I'm totally fine. I know how to take care of myself. But give me a good head start first!"

He holds up two thumbs as he backs toward the café entrance. Then Eila is once again alone with a backpack, a tent, and a sleeping bag. She heads toward the general store for some food, scanning the dirt roads between houses for signs of life. There is no one in sight. The store itself sits like a fat, happy hen on its nest. Settling in for a long sleep.

A dog sniffs around the perimeter of the store's foundation. There's an outhouse behind the building, with a ceramic toilet seat set upon a wood plank and a sign on the door that says **IMAGINE THIS AT 40 BELOW!** The woman working inside the store has a name tag that reads **DOLORES**. Behind a curtain of gray-black hair that falls over her broad shoulders, long gold-and-purple earrings catch the light. Dolores gives her a gentle smile.

Eila waves, then wanders deeper into the store, lingering around dimly lit displays and picking up Arctic-inspired souvenirs: salmon-shaped key chains and snow globes and cartoonish ceramic moose. There are handwoven baskets and baby clothes and patterned blankets draped over railings. Eila stops herself from aimlessly wandering. She is here for specifics—food, something hot to drink, a moment to regroup. She fills a blue-and-yellow ceramic mug with coffee and collects as many canned goods and pastries as she can fit in the crook of her arm.

Dolores, brow furrowed, is looking out the window when Eila approaches the counter. Because she already feels guilty, Eila immediately thinks she must have done something to annoy her. But then she sees through the glass the view of the airstrip, where another small plane is landing, its propellers spinning as it wheels to a stop. The guilt dissipates, and Eila is struck with panic, though she tries to appear calm.

"Thank god the weather cleared up," Dolores says, still staring out the window. "My grandkids have been playing inside for, oh, ages, it seems. Summer didn't used to be like this. So much *weather*."

Eila smiles, even though she's sure it's not the correct response, and drops the armful of baked goods, canned fruit, beef jerky, a bag of ground coffee, and a jug of water onto the counter, and Dolores turns to face her. Eila taps the side of the coffee mug in her hand, a little red stirrer spinning. "This, too, please," she says.

The woman looks Eila up and down with narrowed eyes, making some kind of determination. "Hmm. Yes, you're going to be Bear Child," Dolores says, and Eila can feel her own heart rattling. Her hand shakes as she passes Dolores some folded dollar bills. "I have a nickname for every person who's come into this store, and I remember every single one of them."

"That's impressive," Eila says, sipping the coffee, though it's still too hot.

"Usually, people come through here twice. Once on their way up, and once on their way back. I haven't forgotten a single nickname." She holds her hand up, swearing solemnly. "I think people like that. I also think it makes them want to buy things, if I'm being honest," she says with a wink.

"Well, people will want to buy things anyway. It's kind of what they do. Go to the Arctic, bring back a stuffed moose." Eila pauses, hesitates to ask: "Wait. Why Bear Child?"

Dolores shrugs. She says, "Someone in the diner says there's a white grizzly around. Been spotted a couple of times. And you have that vibe. Love of nature. Free spirit."

"I think I saw that bear," Eila says.

"A ghost bear," Dolores whispers.

"What did you say?"

"Ghost bear," Dolores repeats. "If you follow it, it will take you to this magical place in between here and the spirit world. Where we can talk to the dead again."

"Really?" Eila says.

"Nope! I made that up. It's a good story, though, right? I'm a writer. My imagination is strong. But maybe you should follow that bear anyway, just to see. Where you headed now?"

"Um, east, I think," Eila says. She zips her jacket up to her chin and burrows in, not wanting to give away too much information, despite Dolores's kindness. "At least I think that's where this trip ends."

"You following the caribou?"

"Why, have you seen them?" Eila asks.

"A few passed by." Dolores looks down at her hands. "Not nearly as many as other years."

"Where?" Eila asks. "Which direction?"

"Hmm." Dolores squints out the window and her wavering finger finally halts, pointing due east.

Eila thinks for a moment. What *is* she following? Is it caribou, a bear, a dream of healing the planet, some abandoned cabin she's only seen as a child? An answer? Regardless, the internal drive is the same—so she nods and sips her too-hot coffee again. "Good," she says. "That's where I'm going."

"Well, take this," Dolores says, sliding a jar of fireweed jelly next to the rest of her groceries before slipping a pocket-size notebook with a bear on the cover into the bag. "Write yourself a good story. See you next time, Bear Child."

Eila thanks Dolores and carries the bag of food out to the parking lot. The dog is still there, a black-and-white husky, and it noses its way over to her. He's older, his muzzle graying. As she looks up and down the empty streets, she concludes that fireweed jelly on banana bread for breakfast isn't the worst thing in the world. The land is dry, scrubby plains, speckled with patches of snow, with a few very small, spindly trees dotting the horizon. It seems to stretch on forever, though eventually it will come to an end, as all things do. The sculpted peaks of mountains surround the town, and between them is clouded space, like a fog that one could disappear into and never return.

A portal, maybe, to Dolores's in-between world.

Eila stands at the east edge of town, eating her breakfast quickly. The dog has followed her and is now sitting at her feet, looking around the town just as she is, as if they are a pair that has always been. She tries to shoo him back, but he looks at her as if he doesn't understand. He's not wearing a collar and looks like he could use a few more meals. He walks slightly sideways but seems intent on sticking with her. Eila intentionally drops a piece of jam-slathered banana bread.

The urgency to leave creeps up on her. Every moment she isn't walking is a moment she might be caught. She slings her pack onto her back, pulls on a baseball cap, and begins the trek across the endless snow-swept tundra. The dog remains dutifully trailing behind.

"I suppose I asked for this," she says to him over her shoulder.

Every once in a while they encounter a short, jagged spruce, and the long stretches of tussocks are broken by the smooth dark wells of unnamed lakes. The clouded sky breaks, and a faint orange brushstroke sweeps over the mountains. Eila and the dog follow a stream, a tiny forked tributary of the Yukon River. They continue moving forward, looking for the caribou, looking for the impossible bear, looking for the cabin, the bees, the flowers.

She is certain she'll find all of it, if she keeps going.

43

Vern Graves

When Vern receives the flyer in his mailbox, he almost throws it away. It's one of two items that arrive that day—the other being a utility bill—and he wonders why he put in the effort to walk the quarter mile from his cabin.

The leaves have turned yellow overnight, and he suspects they'll all drop from the trees just as quickly, as is the fall in this part of Alaska. But at least he's out now, while the sun is at its highest, warming his shoulders through his heavy sweater. He opens the door to his cabin and pauses in the Arctic entryway, where he keeps the recycling bin, pocketing the bill. He's about to toss the flyer in the bin, but something about the photo catches his eye. There's a group of teenagers sitting in a field, all with binoculars hanging from their necks and little green badges on their chests. A blond woman stands in the center, her hair tied up in two knotted buns. Her freckled cheeks are red with sunburn, and she has a canvas bag slung over her shoulder. It's the woman from the hardware store. The one he mistook for Lenora.

Vern gasps, then covers his mouth and shakes his head, tricked again. He looks more closely now. She's striking, startling. He's sure there something to her familiarity, but he's afraid to find out the answer.

Her arm is outstretched and a falcon is perched there, dark and sleek, its head turned and its glassy black eye focused on the woman.

Junior Birders Take Flight, the headline says. Beneath the photo, he sees her name—Lark Audette—and he nearly faints. How is it possible that he's run so far, sure he would never hear the name again, only to have her so close, right here in Fairbanks? Well, at least he isn't totally crazy. He was found once, by his sister-in-law, Esther. She promised not to tell anyone where he was, only because she believed it was his prerogative to reach out to his daughter or not. Still, how has he let himself grow so comfortable, so complacent? How has he not seen this coming?

The flyer is advertising a migration event. The sandhill cranes have already begun their journey south, and a group of bird-camp birders will attempt to follow some of them for the day. It's meant to demonstrate the unpredictability the cranes experience during their migration. And it's also in honor of Lark.

Vern doesn't know what to do. His shaking hand, still clutching the flyer, hovers over the recycling bin. He feels frozen, afraid to break free because that would mean making decisions and taking action, however small. Even walking through the second door of the cabin feels like a commitment he's not ready to make.

He looks again at the photo. Lark, smiling and bright. What would seeing him—after all these years—possibly bring to her life? What joy, what resolve, what closure? And even if he was going to see her, introduce himself, explain perhaps why he abandoned her as a baby, he couldn't do it at her birding event.

Vern places the flyer on the windowsill in the Arctic entryway and forces himself back into his cabin before he has a chance to think about doing anything else. Then, he begins doing the only thing he knows how to in these situations.

He grabs a suitcase and starts filling it.

44

He's almost finished packing when Sadie pulls into his driveway. She's bundled in a puffy black jacket and bright multicolored hat and scarf.

She bangs on his door with such force that he's afraid she already knows everything. How? Any number of ways. She's Sadie, for god's sake. Somehow, she always traps him. That day when they left the homestead, he tried to sneak past her with a flower that he'd stolen from the greenhouse—an Arctic poppy that he'd named the lemon butter poppy because its petals formed a pale-yellow cup like a bowl of buttercream icing. Of course she'd been right there watching. He couldn't bear to leave that flower behind, but Sadie caught him hiding it in an empty yogurt cup. "We can't take anything, Vern. You swore."

Vern already has two suitcases by the door. In the rush, he decided to leave behind a lot of his possessions—he was surprised, really, to see how much he'd accumulated over the years. But things like dishes and appliances and knit blankets and all the furniture would have to stay. The hanging plants too. There just isn't time. They'd never survive the drive anyway.

He's attempting to stuff his toothbrush into a toiletry bag that's too small when Sadie bangs on the door again. Then she rings the doorbell. Once, twice, three times.

"All right!" he screams.

He opens the door and Sadie immediately spots the suitcases, then peers behind him to where he's attempting to hide the little zippered bag with the bottom of his toothbrush still poking out.

"What the hell is this, Vern?" Sadie demands.

"What?" he says. "Nothing. I thought I might go on a trip. What's it to you anyway?"

"We've got a problem," she says. Sadie stands in the Arctic entryway, transferring her weight from one foot to the other. Vern glances at the windowsill behind her, where the flyer rests precariously. She must have gotten one too. But would she connect the dots? He's briefly mentioned his daughter a handful of times, but he's positive he's never told Sadie her name. And why would she care? It's his problem.

"It's Eila," Sadie says. "I got a call from the research station up north. Apparently, Eila took off, left her post without telling anyone. She didn't take a radio or anything. But someone in Cloud Creek said she came in on a plane, and then just started walking. The woman at the store in town talked to her, apparently, said she only had a hand-drawn map and was following caribou."

"Caribou?" Vern says.

"Yes, caribou. That's actually the least surprising part of all this."

"What direction?"

"East."

"Oh."

"I'm not sure what to do, Vern. She listed me as a contact, I guess, but how should I know what the hell she's up to?"

Vern looks down. It's all coming at him at once—his daughter, his meddling in Eila's life. "Well, we both know where she's going," he says.

"What?" And then her shoulders slump. "Oh. But why would she . . . how would she . . ."

"I might have told Stefan about the bees. And I might have tried to convince him to use them to save himself. And he might have told Eila."

"You what? Why didn't you tell me?"

"I'm sure that would have gone over well. What does it matter anyway? He refused to talk about it. He agreed with you, you'll be happy to know, despite my best efforts."

"So, Stefan told Eila, and now Eila is going there, to what? To see what could have saved her father's life? She must be furious with us, Vern. Jesus. We have to go up there. She might be angry enough to open the place up. No wait, of course that's what she'll do. She doesn't know what we know."

Vern tosses the little bag of toiletries he's holding across the room, thinking maybe Sadie won't see what it is. But it hits the heater, bouncing back out and falling directly in the center of the room.

"So, what exactly are you running from this time?" Sadie asks, but Vern is already reaching for the flyer. It's going to come out, one way or another. He points to Lark, shrugs, attempts to mumble some sort of explanation.

"I see," Sadie says, although she doesn't seem to understand the gravity of the situation. "Well, you're not running away just yet. We need to get to the greenhouse before Eila does."

"Well, I wouldn't—" Vern begins, but Sadie cuts him off.

"Oh my god, no one cares, *Vern*. Come on. We have to go."

The world is getting more brittle every minute. Vern shivers as he grabs a flannel blanket and some extra layers. He reaches into his car for a hat and gloves, and Sadie is visibly impatient, but he won't compromise on the cold-weather gear. He learned the hard way—a punctured tire in the middle of nowhere at forty below zero—to play it safe, no matter the season. Always keep the hat and gloves in the car.

Toward the edge of town, dead brown grass slopes on either side of the highway. Ahead, dense spruce trees open a path, like an artery leading from the heart of the North to its frozen edges. They turn onto the Steese Highway; the only thing certain is that, if they keep going, they will reach the ends of the earth. A vast ocean of nowhere and nothingness.

A few miles outside Fairbanks, they reach the Fox General Store—a bright-turquoise building. Sadie stops to get gas, and Vern waits in the car while she stands with one hand curled around the pump and the other on her hip. He tries to think of some way to be useful, but her windows are all clean and he can't find a bit of trash anywhere in the vehicle. He runs his fingers beneath his seat, a place he'd be afraid to search in his own car, but there isn't so much as a gum wrapper.

Ravens skip around the parking lot, picking at whatever they can find. Sadie disappears into the store, and Vern wishes he'd thought to go in first and come back with some nice treat. Something to ease into the conversation he needs to have. But what would accomplish this? Chocolate? Sour gummies? Just thinking about this makes his teeth hurt, and how does he not even know what kind of candy she likes at this point?

She returns a few moments later with a gallon of windshield washer fluid, a bottle of water, and a bag of peanuts. As she gets back in the car, Vern says, "Before we go any farther, I need to say something."

"More?" she says, relaxing in her seat and taking a long drink of water. "Let's hear it."

Vern adjusts himself, stretching his legs as much as possible with the little room available. He averts his eyes and fiddles with the door handle.

"Eila getting to the homestead, maybe letting the bees out. It's . . . it's so much worse than that."

He pauses.

"Come on, Vern," Sadie says, slapping the steering wheel. "Out with it."

"Okay. It's just. After we left the greenhouse, you know, a few years ago."

"Five."

"Five years ago, yes. Around that time, you know, that same year, something else happened." Vern wants to vomit. He closes his eyes, gathers every bit of his courage, and blurts it out before he can change his mind: "Jackson's there."

Sadie blinks many times. So many that Vern wonders if she's in shock.

"Wait, what? Jackson's where?" she asks.

"You know, the homestead. Your homestead."

"Jackson," she states flatly.

"Yes."

"Jackson Hyder?"

"Yes."

"What the *fuck*, Vern? You're telling me that Jackson Hyder is alive? Not just alive. Alive and living in *my* cabin? And you *knew*?"

It feels absurd, repeating the one word he's already said too many times, but Vern winces and says it anyway.

"Yes."

45

Sadie drives, eyes narrowed and locked on the road, sighing once in a while in a labored way. Shaking her head. She doesn't speak. It's torturous for Vern, who's never been comfortable with tension, especially when there's no escape.

Eventually, Sadie turns on an audiobook, clearly somewhere in the middle, without any explanation of the story and with clearly no intention of turning it off. Vern tries to follow the plot and gathers that a man is about to commit a murder, but he loses the thread when a bizarre cosmic event enters the narrative. Vern feels reality slipping. Once, he slyly attempts to turn down the volume when Sadie glances in the driver's side mirror. But she only reaches over and turns the sound back up. All his attempts at conversation—especially regarding Jackson Hyder, back from the dead—are met with rolled eyes and breathy harrumphs.

The grumbling and dirty looks continue for over an hour. Then it begins to snow. Violent gusts of wind blow it directly into the windshield, and the wipers do little to help.

Sadie sighs dramatically and says, "Open that glove box, would you?"

Vern does it quickly, a yellowed envelope spilling out into his hands. He stares at it.

"Go ahead, Vern. They're yours anyway."

He slips two fingers into the open side of the envelope and draws out his glasses, lost years ago in Sadie's field, the frames melted, the lenses charred. "I knew they were yours as soon as I saw them. There's a piece of paper in there too. Go ahead and dig that out while you're at it."

"Sadie, I honestly had no intention of . . ."

"I'm sorry I didn't remember you the day you found me at the farmers market," she says, waving off the end of his sentence. "I remembered after that little piece of paper came fluttering down while I was watching the fire burn. And, well, Stefan told me the situation afterward. You know, about you being in the field."

It takes a moment to sink in.

"You knew, all this time?"

She keeps her eyes on the road, her mouth cinched like she's trying to stop herself from saying more.

"But, if I'm responsible," Vern says, his cheeks burning, "then why have you been my friend all this time? Why work with me all those years, side by side like that, after I'd done something so terrible to you?"

"A couple of reasons," Sadie says. "But I'll tell you the one that's most relevant. I wanted to punish you. Not just punish you. Punish you in a way that would be hard for you. With love. And I have done that. Well, Stefan and I have."

He still doesn't understand, but he doesn't know how to ask her to explain. He feels stupid and flustered.

Sadie's eyes flick up to the sky. A group of sandhill cranes is flying through the snow, circling a field by the highway. She swings the wheel and swerves into the parking lot of the Livengood Diner, the last stop for more than a hundred miles.

46

Vern positions the salt and pepper shakers just so, each in its own square on the checkered tablecloth. He also aligns the plastic sugar packet holder within a rectangle of red and white squares, his eyes scanning the room as he waits for Sadie to return from a counter where she's ordering pie. When Sadie asked what kind he wanted, he only waved in the general direction of the counter and said, "Anything. Surprise me. Pie is pie."

She'd disappeared before he finished speaking anyway, and he turned back to the table with heaviness, because pie is not just pie at all. It seems to be taking her an incredible length of time to decide, and Vern isn't sure if he should be glad or anxious that she's stalling. He'd just as soon let Eila get to the cabin and do what he's desired all along. But then, who knows if she's going to get there. And when he imagines her wandering alone across the tundra, he decides the world has already lost enough Jacobsens.

Sadie comes back with three small plates, one hand awkwardly gripping two at once, and sets them on the table, sweeping the salt and pepper shakers up against the window.

"I've got Dutch apple, peach, and some kind of chocolate caramel cream," she said. "I know you claim pie is pie, but that's just not true, so you're welcome to have whichever one you like."

Vern looks at Sadie across the table—her silver hair, the fractured crystal blue in her eyes. He watches her stab at the apple pie with a backward fork and notes that her wrinkled hands don't look old, but worked. They're the hands of someone capable and strong. Of course, strong doesn't mean invincible. Somewhere in those wrinkles are the moments she became a guarded person, less free, and he wishes then that he knew her more deeply. That he hadn't resisted her friendship, that he'd let her in so she would let him in too. Perhaps reveal herself—the real her—rather than remaining at such a distance.

Sadie keeps glancing out the window like she's willing the snow to stop. "We need to get back out there," she says. "I don't like the idea of Eila walking across the tundra like that. If the weather is like this here, I can't imagine what it's like up there. It's got to be treacherous, and she doesn't even know where she's going."

"We'll get there," Vern says. "One way or another. I mean, it's almost a certainty that she'll make it first, but we'll get there eventually."

"You'd like that, wouldn't you? For Eila to just open up the greenhouse and let them all out. You'd get what you wanted, but you wouldn't have to bear the responsibility. Jackson, on the other hand . . ." When she says his name, she flinches, like she's witnessing something painful. She covers her mouth with her hand and looks away. "What were you thinking, Vern? I just don't understand. All the pain she's suffered. And you just let it go on. Kept this whole thing a secret."

"I had good intentions," Vern says, his mouth watering for a bite of the caramel pie but knowing the timing would be truly terrible. "Sadie, I swear that I did."

47

It began in the butterfly house. They were visiting the botanical gardens in Montreal—as a horticulture teacher, he liked to wander through, trying to find some unique species he'd never seen before—and Vern knew his wife was wandering a Japanese garden somewhere, their six-month-old daughter, Lark, in a stroller. The little girl looked out with an enchanted sort of fascination with the flowers and sprawling leaves that surrounded them. It was terrifying. And Vern was so overwhelmed with her innocence that he ducked down a side path, mumbling half an explanation to his wife, promising to find her again in a few minutes. He could hardly breathe.

Even as he walked farther from his wife and daughter, the sound of delighted giggles seemed to magnify, a child in rapture. He stepped quickly through the first door he came to, a glass leading to a glass room, and the sound was replaced by the flapping of thousands of tiny wings.

Light filtered into the room from above, illuminating every leaf and blossom around him. Vern felt something tickle the back of his neck. And while his instincts told him to swat at it, he was glad he didn't when the tickling traveled to his cheek and then to his forehead. The butterfly's wings fluttered with the most delicate lightness against his skin, as if magnetized but also pulled away by some other force of gravity. Then it floated off to a leaf.

On its back, it was mostly black, with pale-yellow dots in a diagonal pattern across its wings. The underside looked almost exactly the same, but in reverse. Vern paged through the book at the center of the garden.

Giant swallowtail.

Not the rarest. Quite common, in fact. And once he knew what to call it, and once he recognized its colors and patterns, he saw them everywhere. They stood out against the vibrant blues and purples and greens. They gathered around puddles, as if collectively swallowing the small bodies of water. Vern began to count them, lost track, and began again. By the time Lenora found him, he was lost in numbers, whispering to himself.

He didn't hear them come in. He didn't notice them standing behind him. He'd picked up the dribbling end of a garden hose and let the slow trickle empty into a depression in the concrete. The swallowtails hovered, and Vern was on his hands and knees in a puddle before he realized Lenora was watching. His daughter smiled wide, looking back and forth from her mother to the butterflies.

For a moment, Vern was full of love and joy and weightlessness. He had Lenora and Lark and they all had the butterflies.

And then everything changed.

"Let's bring them home with us," Lenora said.

"Who?" Vern asked.

"Your new friends. I'm sure all we have to do is ask. Let me go find someone."

Vern stood up and dropped the hose at his feet. His butterflies scattered and Lark stopped smiling, perplexed.

"What are you talking about?" he asked, the magic evaporating with her ridiculous suggestion. "They're just butterflies. They don't belong to us."

"Oh, but they're not *just* butterflies," she said. Her eyes grew vacant in a way Vern had never seen before. "Well, fine then," she said. Then Lenora straightened the straw hat on Lark's head and wheeled the stroller out of the butterfly house.

Vern knew her question should have come across as sweet, and light, and full of Lenora's charm. But somehow, it hadn't. He could tell it was tinged with too much sincerity, too much weight. And like those butterflies gathered on the puddle, something flapped frantically against his heart until it hurt.

48

This is supposed to explain something, but by the time he reaches the end of the story, Vern realizes that Sadie doesn't understand. Nor is she impressed. In fact, he wonders why he decided to start so far back. But it seems important to get all the details right, to explain his wilderness of good intentions, somehow tangled with cowardice.

"I'm not saying I was right," Vern says. "I was obviously wrong. Very, very wrong, and selfish." He pauses for a moment, then adds, "Obviously."

"Yes, I get that," Sadie says. "The selfish part is clear. I just don't see how it's relevant to this moment. We're about to get on the dang Dalton. The weather sucks. Eila might be lost somewhere in the middle of nowhere, and you're rambling about botanical gardens and butterflies. Jackson—who everyone has presumed dead for the last five years—is living some reclusive life in my cabin, and you've known that, all this time. And of all the explanations you could give, I get *butterflies*? Goddamn it, Vern, I wish you'd just order some pie, eat it quickly like a normal human being, and then get to the damn point."

Vern looks out the diner window at the highway, a trail boring a hole directly into a bleak horizon. "Okay," he says.

Sadie sits back and sinks her fork into her second piece of pie, the coveted chocolate caramel.

49

She'd been collecting furniture as long as they'd lived together. Vern couldn't have cared less about the accumulation of "stuff." That their Maine farmhouse was crowded—understatement of the century—was the least of Vern's worries. It made Lenora happy, and to make her happy, he'd have filled all the rooms in the house, floor to ceiling, with anything she asked for. But slowly the household dynamic changed. More and more he stayed downstairs, where there was room to breathe, and Lenora spent many of her daytime hours—nighttime ones too—upstairs, dusting and arranging the pieces she'd found at antique stores or flea markets. A desk went from one room to another, then back again only a few days later. A chair completed the look of one corner, but moments later another chair was absolutely necessary.

Vern repeatedly asked if she wanted something moved, yet inevitably he heard the scraping of wooden legs on the upstairs floor as he sat down to read the paper and drink his morning coffee. She dragged the furniture around all morning, all afternoon. He had to take her by the hand and lead her downstairs for lunch or she wouldn't eat at all.

Once, she had been a master with fried chicken and she was proud of it. Her peach pie—well, most of the time he couldn't even think about it without tearing up. At one time, she'd been a magnificent dancer; she'd spun circles around him at the VFW on Friday nights. And my god, could she sing.

But after a while, she seemed to remember nothing of those times. Vern thought that she'd gone crazy up there, moving furniture from one place to another and then back again. It wasn't until he'd had enough and gone upstairs to tell her so that he realized the problem was bigger than he'd imagined.

"Listen," he said, clutching the rolled up newspaper in his hand. "What's wrong with the chair over by that desk, where you had it before? It looked just fine there. No one is coming to see all of this stuff anyway."

Lenora looked confused.

"Why not just pick somewhere and stick with it?" Vern asked.

"I don't know what you're talking about," Lenora said. "I'm having company, and this is just where I think it should go. And this piece is new. It's the first time I've placed it anywhere, so what do you mean *just pick somewhere*? If you're mad at me for spending the money, it's going to be worth a lot more someday and . . ." She paused for a moment, thinking, then said, "Lark will probably benefit from it one day, and if it's the noise, then just go put in some earplugs and let me do my thing in peace. Or go for a walk!"

"What?" Vern said. "What in the hell are *you* talking about? You've just gone back and forth with this chair about ten times in the last . . ."

Lenora looked at him blankly, then crossed the room and gripped the back of the chair with both hands. She bent and began to push. The newspaper fell from Vern's hand to the floor, worn with scratches, and unfurled.

In the next few months, Lenora underwent a number of medical tests that all revealed the same thing: early-onset dementia. She was forty-six. She'd just had a child. It seemed impossible, a mistake, too cruel to comprehend. Vern felt too young and unequipped to handle this.

He couldn't accept it and spent many nights in the front porch rocking chair with a bottle of bourbon. He'd ask Lenora to join him, realizing that she'd forgotten the night they'd met and shared the Salty

Darling. She always declined anyway and retreated to the second floor, her space, and Vern rocked and drank and listened to the sounds of desk feet scraping the hardwood. Rectangles of light lit the grass in front of him, and every so often he saw Lenora's shadow pass over as she drifted from room to room. Lenora was becoming a ghost—a ghost who switched around the furniture, leaving him disoriented in the morning. Except she was just as disoriented as he was.

It was Lenora's sister, Esther Audette, who suggested the nature walk to clear his head. It was about all the plants in the area, but the walk leader had a specific love for the pollinator-friendly varieties. The group passed through creeks and marshes and climbed hills to get a better view. They saw marsh marigolds and jack-in-the-pulpit and trout lilies. There were plants that Vern didn't even know the names of, right there in his town—like the *Aureolaria pedicularia*, the fern-leaved false foxglove, a parasite, he learned. They even saw a field of fireweed, which sent the walk leader into an unexpected tizzy.

When the hike was over, Vern hung back. He wanted to know how the woman had started leading these walks. He'd taken a sabbatical from teaching and thought he could see himself doing something like this too. The woman told Vern about where she'd grown up in Alaska, where she'd fallen in love with flowers. Their resilience was so admirable. Their ability to adapt and survive so inspiring. Like the fireweed, which grows in places of literal destruction. When she saw fireweed anywhere, she couldn't contain her joy.

For that one afternoon, Vern felt let loose from the terrifying responsibility of caring for someone he loved deeply and ultimately could not protect. Two somebodies really.

The woman wrote her name—*Sadie*—on a ripped piece of paper, in case he ever found himself in Fairbanks, Alaska. She could usually be found, she noted, at the farmers market in summer.

A few months later, Vern walked in on Lenora in the basement, packing up a box of antique champagne glasses to send to her mother—who had died many years before—and the doctors suggested Lenora move to a facility where she could get better care. One of the hardest things Vern ever had to do was tell Lenora they were going to lunch with her mother in order to—being honest—trick her into going to the facility. It killed him that when they arrived and checked into her room, she didn't even ask about the lunch plans.

Vern sat next to her bed, holding her hand, his insides dissolving, his skin prickling with a cold sweat. He couldn't swallow. When Esther peeked into the room holding Lark, Vern almost passed out. He could no longer separate his various sensations, the somersaulting emotions.

Was he losing Lenora, or had he already lost her?

Since the night she'd baked him that peach pie, he'd grown to rely on her to lift him up. She was both parachute and safety net. Now, he was falling, terribly fast, and she was neither of these things. In fact, she was falling, too, even faster than he was, and he had absolutely no idea how to be savior to them both.

He couldn't explain why, but this made him irrationally angry with her.

He had become a single parent, and he had no clue what this role looked like. Esther said, "It looks like whatever you want it to look like," with a matter-of-factness that made Vern feel like a child. "Plenty of people in this world are faced with difficult situations like this, and they are far less equipped to handle them. You just do it."

Lark was sitting in her stroller, crying, and Vern couldn't, for the life of him, figure out why. Lark was only just learning to put sounds together. How could she possibly understand what was going on? Vern threw up his hands. Esther knelt on the concrete in front of Lark and held out both fists. When Lark tapped the correct one, her aunt uncurled her fingers to reveal a miniature bird figurine.

He could have thought of that, couldn't he? A way to distract and delight his daughter. There he was, a helpless twentysomething. And there was Esther, who claimed she could teach Lark the mechanics of flight. This was the rest of his life. Constant questioning, endless doubt. Relentless inadequacy. Inevitable failure.

The morning after leaving Lenora at the care facility, Vern woke up and was shocked to see himself in the bathroom mirror. His hair had gone almost completely white overnight, and wrinkles tugged the corners of his eyes, as if he'd aged a decade in the span of a few hours. His eyesight—perfect just yesterday—was suddenly too blurry to read the wall clock.

It was impossible. He panicked.

It wasn't a perfect science, and to this day, Vern still can't rationalize what he did. Sometimes he tells himself he was young, and young people make stupid mistakes, and they can be forgiven because of their stupid youngness. But even this, he knows, is no excuse for placing all his hope and loyalty into one scribbled note from a woman he'd met once.

He labeled his trip *professional development*—he had to see the fireweed in Alaska and further clear his head—and drove away on a long, zigzagging route to avoid facing the truth of what he was doing. He told himself he was not running away. It was simply one stretch of a migration—one that he would soon complete in the reverse when he returned. He chose Alaska because it felt like it belonged to him somehow. And it was far and remote, a place to think long and hard about his resilience.

Vern went in search of fireweed, of beauty, of transformation.

50

Sadie scrapes the plate with the side of her fork, gathering the crumbs and leftover pie filling into a mound in the center. Vern leans back in his chair, hands in his sweater pockets, fingers fiddling with a folded piece of paper. It's the smooth-as-silk card on which Lenora wrote her peach pie recipe. The one he tried to give to Stefan. The one Stefan gave back to him, told him to hang on to for some other, more important person. It seems strangely cruel that he should be sitting here, staring at pie like this. Like some force of the universe has brought him straight to it.

Vern imagines what Sadie is thinking: *How could you do something like that? How could anyone do something like that?*

"So, that's why I didn't recognize you when you got here," she says. "You looked different when we met."

"It was terrifying," Vern says. He wants to tell her she saved him, which is how it felt at the time. But the story has changed. "You inspired me."

Sadie scowls. "I don't think that's how inspiration is supposed to work."

"It was a monstrous thing, what I did," Vern says.

"You can say that again."

"But then I met Stefan. And Eila. I'm not incompetent—I saw what I missed. They had it all. The lightness I was striving for but somehow couldn't accomplish."

"Your past is your past. It's not that I don't care about your old life, and what has become of your wife, and where your daughter is. We're going to get to that."

"But . . ."

"But, first things first. What I still don't get, Vern, is how it came to be that—"

"Okay, okay. Jackson Hyder. Got it."

Vern's mind drifts to five years ago—to that first time he and Jackson spoke about love and loss and the terrible weight of living. He remembers Jackson's attempts at getting him to exercise, to feel more "in his body." That was before it all became too much—even for Jackson.

51

Vern and Sadie had only recently left the homestead behind, but Vern didn't give up. He was studying the genetics of both bees and flowers in his little cabin, trying to determine if there was a solution to what they'd found—a way to use it for good, some happy medium—or if they'd truly created a Godzilla of a species that would destroy everything once unleashed. He'd hardly left the house in the weeks since they'd returned to Fairbanks, only stepping outside his small, square cabin to use the outhouse and empty the slop bucket.

But that day, something inspired him to be closer to nature again. He held a seed between his thumb and forefinger and thrust it up to the light, astonished by what he saw—or, more precisely, what he *remembered* seeing so long ago, when horticulture was new to him. He'd always understood the science of it—in the most simplistic sense, sunlight and warmth and water would make this seed burst and sprout once planted in the ground. But knowing something and really feeling it are different, and the feeling is what came back to Vern then. It shouldn't have seemed so mysterious, but it occurred to him that this thing he and Sadie had been doing every day—growing strong, resilient flowers—was happening naturally all around him, all the time. It was, quite simply, *nature*.

That in itself was no grand epiphany. But after weeks of torturing himself, trying to find a loophole in Sadie's argument, he realized she might be right. He had accepted her terms of absolute secrecy before they were even barreling down the Dalton back to Fairbanks. But until now, he'd never found any reason in those terms.

Nature would survive, he realized, with or without him. Humans might not. There's no telling the future of a species hell bent on destroying itself. But nature would endure.

Realizing the futility of what he was doing, Vern broke out of his weeks-long daze and went for a walk. Fireweed blazed purple along the edge of the road. Yellow butterflies congregated around drying mud puddles. He was still wearing his slippers, and the dry, gravelly dirt caused Vern's awkward, shuffling feet to slip. He felt like he'd been gazing into a cup of tea for far too long and was now finally swallowing and feeling its warmth slide down his throat.

In the distance, the figure was recognizable only as just that—a figure, nothing more. Man, woman, kangaroo, he couldn't tell the difference. Vern's eyes distinguished very little at a distance, even with his glasses. As he got closer, Vern saw it was Jackson, turned to face the woods, hands pressed against a tree, his head down and his shoulders shaking. The way he likes to remember it, Vern began running toward Jackson, but of course, he's kidding himself. Vern was never a runner. He wasn't even a fast walker, especially not in those slippers. Still, the urgency was there.

"What happened?" Vern sputtered.

"Oh shit," Jackson choked, his muscular shoulders looking slack and shapeless. "Nothing, nothing."

Vern gave him a stern look. "Tell me."

Jackson used both palms to wipe away tears and muttered just two words: "Eila. Dead."

Vern's heart did a thousand leaps, from adult Eila to Eila as a child to what was surely a devastated Stefan. As Jackson stepped back, Vern noticed the tree was not one, but two trees twisting around one another. But then everything was spinning, and he couldn't trust himself.

"I keep seeing it, Vern. Every night that I close my eyes. And every morning I try to run it off, but it just comes back. I can't stop seeing it. She's going to die, Vern."

Vern let out the breath he'd been holding and nearly passed out. He looked down and saw that his shirt had a spreading inkblot of sweat around the collar. He stumbled to respond. "Wait, so Eila's not actually dead? Right?"

Jackson's sweatshirt was soaked through. He used his sleeve to wipe his glistening forehead. "No," he said. "Not yet anyway. But in my vision, she dies, on her research trip. She's in the river, and the caribou trample her, and she's just gone."

"Oh," Vern said. "But that's just a dream."

"It's not a dream," Jackson said. "It's a *premonition*. This has happened before. I've had visions like this, and they've come true. I saw that dead loon, too, before it actually happened. I saw myself running into the university room, harassing that poor woman."

"I see."

"The thing is, Vern, I don't know what I'm supposed to do. Last winter, it became perfectly clear that Eila was part of me. Not like when people say 'my better half' or 'you complete me.' Nothing cheesy like that. I mean this literally. I think if something happened to her, I might actually die myself. I've grown incredibly knowledgeable about my body and how it works. I could point to the place where she resides within it."

"This is why you're running?"

"It worked last time." Jackson shrugged. "At first."

"But the vision still came true eventually."

"Yep. You can only run for so long, it seems."

Vern felt something flip over in his stomach. "Well, maybe this time it won't happen," he stuttered. "Maybe this time will be different."

Jackson shook his head. "No, I know for sure. Because the first time, with the loon, there was a preceding event. My shoelace came untied—which never happens because I double-knot them—and when I knelt down to tie it, a fox ran across the road in front of me. I kept behind it and it led me to the pond. Anyway, all of that happened in the vision, right before I found the loon. It's the same now. Something's going to happen first, and the devastating part will follow. I'm running because it tires me out, but also if I keep moving, she can't grab me by the hands and tell me that she's invincible because of me. Because of *us*."

Vern's eyes began to tear up then, as he thought of Lenora and the severing he'd felt when they'd discovered her illness. He didn't intend to cause more despair, truly, but what Vern said next felt very true at the time. Words he could not take back. Promises that, in the years to come, he would not allow himself to break.

"The only way that I know," Vern said, "to avoid that kind of heartbreak, is to look away. Turn your back on it and go. Leave it all behind for good."

"You're saying I should leave?"

"I'm just saying, if you're so sure about the vision, and if you're trying to avoid her pinning you down and confronting you about your love—we're talking about love, I assume—then maybe if you go somewhere she really can't find you . . ."

Jackson considered. He started to speak many times but stopped himself. Then he said, "But she wouldn't know. It sounds selfish."

"It is," Vern admitted. "All I know is that if you look away from the darkness, your eyes will find the light."

"How do I just leave? Where would I go?"

Whatever it was that had rolled over in Vern's stomach did so again as he saw the solution to two problems at once.

"I think I have a place."

52

"I promised I wouldn't contact him, no matter what," Vern says, as if this makes it okay. The promises he *has* kept. He almost repeats Sadie's words back to her—you know what *no matter what* means, right?

"What about saying 'Hey, Jackson, by the way, Eila *didn't* die'?"

"I thought about it. But every year, Eila went back up to the North Slope, and so how was I to know if his vision just hadn't come true *yet*? It wasn't my place."

"But it was your place to give him horrible advice? The man was distraught. You could have said something nicer, more optimistic."

"But it wouldn't have been true. At least not at the time."

Only sticky crumbs remain of the pie. Sadie presses her fingers into them, licks them clean.

"Well, we've got Jackson out of the way," Sadie says. Her eyes narrow. "Now do you want to tell me about the other thing?" She doesn't wait for an answer, only reaches into her jacket pocket, pulling out a shiny piece of paper. Vern recognizes it before she finishes unfolding it—it's her copy of the flyer. "You can't run away this time, Vern. Because your songbird is here. So, what now?"

Vern studies the patchwork of photographs on the flyer, the logo that looks like handwriting. Suddenly, he makes the connection. Sadie working at Creamer's Field, and Lark spending the summer there too. "Wait," he says. "You've known, haven't you? That's why you wanted to get me to the refuge for a walk."

"It was Stefan's idea," Sadie says. "He tracked her down and wrote to her. I just made the arrangements."

"You've wasted your time. It's not that I can't handle it, although for the record, consider your punishment a success. I feel thoroughly loved, while at the same time extremely uncomfortable. I just don't think she's going to want to see me."

"I'm not sure you're the authority on what she wants. Or what anyone wants."

"Look, Sadie, when I was at your house those nights—"

"It's fine, Vern."

"I should have walked away to begin with."

"Well, we shouldn't have kept it from you. That's not what friends do." Sadie sighs. "It was just such a brief thing, and it was complicated. Stefan and I, that spring . . . At that shindig, I hadn't told him yet about the baby because I was terrified. I didn't get another chance to tell him until the night that we lost her, which is probably what you saw."

The baby. Vern feels a new wave of disgust. He knew the moment he'd witnessed was private, but he didn't understand the gravity at the time. He tries to remain steady and focused now as Sadie continues.

"You remember that summer, when we rebuilt the cabin and set up the greenhouse? All those nights we spent sitting in the living room, you reading something, Eila using kindling like building blocks, Stefan drawing. I think I was knitting then, or some other stupid thing to keep myself busy. Stefan made some ink drawings, one of Eila and one of our little would-have-been child. He couldn't imagine what she would have looked like, so he drew her as a caribou."

"I remember those," Vern says. "I didn't think anything of them at the time, though, other than that they were quite nice. And also, that he had so much more talent than me."

Sadie looks at the ceiling, as if debating whether or not she wants to continue. She takes a deep breath before going on, like she's giving in to something.

"We said we were going to write little notes to ourselves and stick them in the frames behind the drawings, like time capsules we could look back on one day. Like this fun surprise for our older selves. I don't know what he wrote, but I could see it was a good page long."

"And yours?" Vern asks. He expects her to reveal some big secret.

Instead, she says, "I couldn't think of anything to do the situation justice. So, I just wrote the name I was going to give her. Hannah. After my great-grandma."

Words rise into Vern's mouth, and he realizes he hasn't said them in many, many years. He says them for Sadie and Stefan, for Lenora and Lark, for his secrets and misguided promises: "I'm sorry. I'm so, so sorry."

"Do you know the alder flycatcher?" Sadie asks. "It's a bird."

Vern shrugs, shakes his head, wondering what this has to do with his apology.

"There's this other kind of flycatcher, the willow flycatcher. Both these birds have distinct songs. You can let an alder flycatcher hatch in a willow flycatcher's nest, let it grow up with a family of them. But that alder is still an alder, and it will always be its true self. It can't be anything else. You're not a bad person, Vern. You were kind and honest once—I've seen it. That part of you is under there somewhere. You've just been trying to be something you're not for so long. The world's a dark place. It's ugly a lot of the time and it hurts. But even when it hurts, you have to take it and then let go and get on with living."

Vern thinks of Esther outside the care facility. *You just do it.* The cold creeps into his bones. He sees Eila, running farther into the wild. He sees Jackson, doing whatever it is he does up there. He sees his daughter, following the cranes. He imagines Stefan, all those years ago, bent over a moose skeleton in the middle of a mountain trail. The things they'd talked about, while they were both so young and directionless, seem to have come around full circle.

Adaptability, resilience, the act of searching.

"Nobody really knows how to do it, do they? Being a parent. But how would I even begin a conversation with Lark at this point? Why would she even want to talk to me?"

"It's your story to tell, Vern. It's your song. The question is, Which song are you singing now? The one you've been singing the last twenty-plus years, or your true one? The original."

They both turn to the window, where the sun has broken through the veil of gray clouds. He considers this—what his story is, how to balance all the elements. What does he have to offer? Vern puts his hands in his pockets and feels for the recipe card, his thumb running over crusts of flour and butter. The card Stefan had handed back to him, told him to save for a more meaningful occasion, one he was sure would come.

"Listen," Sadie says. "We have to make sure Eila keeps the bees a secret. And we have to make sure she's okay. And I think it goes without saying that she needs to know about Jackson. But first, let's go across the street and see those cranes."

Vern nods. "Why don't you start the car, and I'll meet you out there."

"Just be quick," she says.

The bells on the door clang when she leaves. Vern walks past the spinning case of pies, buys a pack of gum, some peanuts, and a bright-purple scarf that says *LOVE* in big letters, the *O* replaced by an image of the state of Alaska. He goes outside to find Sadie standing in the parking lot, the pavement wet, snowflakes falling on her shoulders. Behind her, the sun is setting, the sky melting into ripples of blue and orange.

As he wraps the scarf around Sadie's shoulders, he says, "My daughter, by the way, is not named for the bird. That's one thing no one else knows. She's Larkspur, really. Named for the flower."

53

Lark Audette

The board is filled with projects—paper cutout birds and handwritten paragraphs—created by the third graders in Lark's summer class. Lark is proud of every nuthatch and red-winged blackbird and boreal chickadee. Every carefully penciled letter describing the birds, their diets, their habitats. Not all the students in her summer camp started out as bird lovers. A lot of them weren't even nature lovers. But the kids grew so much during their two months together that they don't feel like students anymore. They feel like family.

She knows this is the nature of summer camp. It gathers kids who might not normally become friends. It allows freedom to explore. And the aspect of play, the idea that they are there to have fun and not to be graded, makes it inherently easier to elicit their participation. It feels a little like cheating. In fact, some nights she's gone home with voices in her head, nagging that she's an imposter. Not a *real* teacher. Not a *real* classroom. But it is real learning. Every morning, she walked to work reminding herself that what she does matters a lot to these kids. Who cares how it was designed? Who cares that they aren't graded?

The bird camp ended a month ago, but she has stayed at Creamer's Field as a volunteer, though she hasn't quite figured out why. She is unexpectedly sad to be leaving soon and has considered staying in

Fairbanks many times. She's heard the other camp instructors talk about winter—how they prepare their cars and their minds. How they settle in or try to keep moving. How the darkness is like a blanket that becomes more and more comfortable over the long months, hard to crawl back out of come spring. She wants to be a part of it. She could become a teacher—the next steps of her education and career are wide open at the moment.

Lark sits on one of the classroom tables, wondering at how much she's become like her family. Her aunt, the birder. Her father, apparently a horticulture teacher. And here she is, loving the birds, loving teaching. She can't help but wonder if she'd have found this path without their histories. Is it all her own?

Imposter syndrome creeps back in.

The cranes have been starting to leave, migrating along varying routes. One of the high school students suggested aligning Lark's going-away party with it.

"We'll send you off with the birds," the students said.

Lark couldn't argue, especially when their reasoning was twofold. A goodbye to her was also a way to honor the birds' unpredictable migratory behavior, especially the previous few years. It would be next to impossible to stick with them. You never knew when they would take flight, and you never knew which direction they would go. She imagines her own flight back to New Mexico, following the cranes. Not an actual flight—she'll still be driving. But her migration will take her back to old patterns, the same set of possibilities.

A group of older campers presented her with the flyer during one of their last camp days, just before school began again. The dates had yet to be filled in. When the sandhill cranes started to migrate in groups, they would pick a day and follow them. Today is that day, and Lark isn't sure yet if she'll actually continue with them, or if her migration will take its own form and direction. She will have to wait and see.

For the hundredth time, she studies the letter that invited her here. The handwriting is shaky, a little falling off the lines. Initially, it made her question the validity of the invitation, but that doubt was overshadowed by the message.

Everyone enters Alaska the same way—with no idea how it's going to change you. It's different from other places, maybe because of the space, the expansive emptiness just waiting to be filled. You can fill it with your desires, or expel what you no longer want, but it will never be full. It is big enough to hold all of you.

Everything your heart no longer needs.

You'll find something here that you can't find anywhere else. It's a place of wild contradictions. That's the gift that this land gives you.

54

She has no memory of her parents. She was so small when her aunt took her in and set her on the path of the birds. Her earliest memories come in disconnected fragments—butterflies, flowers, and pie.

Why, when she closes her eyes, does she see thousands of yellow swallowtails? Why, when she opens them, does her vision flicker with pink rose petals? Maybe these things could be explained, if she had the guts to ask. Maybe they are embedded in her psyche, or one night as a child she had a particularly vivid dream.

Except for the pie. Her aunt explained the pie without any prompting, recounting for Lark all the times that her sister had made peach pie. Any occasion, any excuse, and there was peach pie.

"Funerals, weddings, summer barbecues, baby showers, Fridays," she said, the corners of her eyes creasing in bittersweet smiles. "If you had a bad day, or a particularly good one."

When they went anywhere, they had to try the pie. Peach, if possible, but it really didn't matter what kind. When they were in Pennsylvania, they tried the pie. In Nebraska, they tried it. In Australia, they tried it. None of it ever came close, in her aunt's opinion, but Lark had no frame of reference. She hadn't even turned one when her mother was taken to the dementia-care facility, where she died just a few short years later from pneumonia. That was also when her father left without saying goodbye—so she was told—for some great unknown.

Lark's childhood was punctuated by pies. They were not intended as a substitute for memories, but that's what they became, a vicarious childhood lived through over two decades of peach pie filling and sweet, flaky crust.

Pie became a source of comfort for Lark, a reminder of her mother, even though she'd never actually tasted her mother's pie. Her aunt once told her that she'd pay a million dollars for a copy of her sister's peach pie recipe. Her aunt did not have a million dollars, but that didn't matter. Just down the street from Bosque del Apache, back in New Mexico, a café has begun making peach pie at her aunt's request. The owners have taken humbly and generously to all her aunt's recipe tweaks and suggestions.

Despite her desire to travel and find herself, Lark is momentarily homesick. She parts the blinds in the classroom and peeks outside at the group gathering. Homesickness is replaced by panic. When the birds are gone and winter does come, then what?

The cranes that are left have gathered in the field. Some have already begun to leave, but there are still many to follow. The junior bird watchers club—all twelve of them—stand by the fence, holding mugs of hot drinks, waiting for the birds to take flight.

It was a little silly, Lark realizes, to assume that any group of birds would take off on any particular day, but she couldn't let go of her feeling about it. Something in the air, in the way the birds were calling out to one another. She felt the urge to be daring—to predict what the wild might do.

A few of these cranes have been fitted with ankle bracelets for tracking. Lark opens an app that allows her to see a map and the yellow dots that represent the birds.

They wait.

Finally, after the campers and a few other Creamer's Field staff return with lunch from their local Thai restaurant, the cranes take flight. Sixteen of them lift off and circle overhead before flying—as Lark worried they might—north.

Lark gets into her car, wondering what she was thinking having this event. Even with the tracking devices, how on earth is she going to follow the birds if they set course over undrivable terrain? How are all these people going to follow her? She drives down College Road, then up on the Steese Highway, leaning forward over the wheel and peering through the windshield to see the arcing shapes above.

They keep flying, up through Fox and, miraculously, along the Elliott Highway. Lark wonders when they'll decide to change direction, when they'll head south, because south is where they're supposed to go, and it's where she's supposed to go too.

She picks up the radio and asks the rest of the group if they're still with her—their car has fallen behind—and they say, "Yes, but what the hell? Where are we going?" Lark doesn't know the answer. Where is she going? Doubt sneaks in again. Perhaps the birds took a wrong turn and have led her astray. Their compass is broken. Her compass is broken.

They drive for more than an hour, and as they near the turnoff for the Dalton, the road turns to dirt and early snow begins to swirl around the car. Lark checks the rearview mirror to see the line of cars behind her. The walkie breaks through with static, and one of the students comes on, saying they should probably stop at the diner in Livengood. It's the only place to stop for an unnervingly long time. Lark agrees. She decides that, wherever this café is, she'll declare it the end of their journey. They've followed the cranes far enough. They can say their goodbyes and move on to whatever the next season brings them.

One of the wipers sticks to the windshield. She rolls the window down and reaches out to free it. The cold air stings her eyes and nostrils but wakes her up, so she leaves it open. When she reaches for the glove compartment to find her winter hat, the book Jude gave her falls to the floor. She's read it three times in the last few months. And yet, they haven't spoken all summer. It occurs to her that she never even tried the number he'd given her, and a line comes to her from the book, one that has been circling her mind ever since she arrived in Fairbanks.

In the North, there are no edges, no boundaries. Direction is meaningless. Trust it, though. One way or another, you will get where you need to go.

Mounted to the dash, Lark's phone blinks as the cranes' dots change position. Through the open car window, she can hear them trumpeting as they circle and careen down to land in a field. She passes the illuminated sign for a café ahead. Beneath it is a second sign. She finds herself caught between overwhelming relief and startled wonder. Encircled by an arrow made of blinking red lights, the three cursive letters of the sign read: **PIE**.

She pulls into the café parking lot. When the rest of the group arrives, she tells them she's going to have a look at the cranes, but they're welcome to go inside where it's warm. They've been staring at cranes all summer, after all. She'll be quick. Lark hops the guardrail and walks off the shoulder to a clearing where the cranes have gathered. She raises her binoculars, watches them prance in the snow and call out to one another.

When she turns back to the café, two figures are walking toward her. She recognizes one of them. Sadie, from Creamer's Field, throws her legs over the guardrail, then turns back to help the man. They hook elbows with one another in a way that even someone who's basically a stranger can tell is awkward yet extremely familiar.

Sadie raises her hand when she sees Lark, and Lark lifts her hand in a half wave but is quickly distracted by the man. She has no memories of what he looks like, but somehow, she just knows who he must be. The fact that Sadie is there confirms it, and everything begins to make sense: the afternoon they banded the bird together, the questions about her father and how she ended up here. She suspects now that Sadie had at least some hand in that.

A gust of wind passes between them, shaking the alders and taking with it a good number of fluttering leaves. "There goes autumn," her father says.

"I was just heading in there for some pie," Lark says, because she doesn't know what else to say, and it's the truth. Her throat feels like it's closing. A storm of emotions travels through her at once—anger, frustration, hurt, regret. The missed opportunity of growing up with a father. She should kick snow at him. She should shout at him to leave; these are *her* cranes.

But if she's being honest, she doesn't want to do any of these things. She loved her childhood, and she loves her life. There's something to be said for embracing your path, however it was set forth, and the circumstances that brought you here. Lark doesn't know if she's always felt this way, or if it's something she's absorbed recently, perhaps from Jude's book. Either way, she makes a mental note to call and thank him, then focuses again on the flustered man before her.

"I'm . . . I'm . . . ," he stutters.

Sadie buries her chin in her scarf and closes her eyes like she's praying he'll pull it together. He's such a bumbling mess that Lark feels sorry for him.

"I know who you are," Lark says quietly. The cranes behind her make high-pitched creaking calls. They tiptoe closer, dance away. Her father pats himself down like he's forgotten which pocket he left his glasses in. Eventually, he pulls out a folded note card and offers it with a shaking hand. "Here, here," he whispers. "Don't even bother with that pie in there. That pie is nothing compared to this. This is the cure for everything."

Lark takes the recipe, blinks at the looping letters. She knows they were written by her mother. "I'm not much of a baker," Lark says.

"Me either," her father says.

"Well." Lark glances at the back of her hand. Jude's words are no longer there, but she remembers them very clearly. *Perhaps the future.* "We'll probably screw it up, but we might as well give it a try," she says, tucking the recipe card in her jacket pocket.

55

Jackson Hyder

Jackson had watched Eila skiing across the lake. First, she was behind him, so he had to turn to keep her blurry shape in his periphery. They shushed along in canvas Carhartt pants, hoods cinched tightly around their faces. The world glistened silver. Something caught Eila's eye, and she veered off toward the ice-tipped black spruce. Jackson had to stop completely so as not to lose sight of her.

This was Eila. If something interested her, she followed, especially if that something was an animal. He tried to guess what it was—marten, fox, hare. She glided over the lake surface, the idea of friction simply nonexistent. There was no separation between her legs, the skis, and the ice beneath her. *Effortless* was the word that came to mind.

Jackson instinctively noted the muscle groups and rhythm involved in her movement. He began calculating her stride frequency and length, then estimating velocity and how long it would take for her to reach the tree line. His feet started moving involuntarily, and before he'd had a chance to think about his own stride—length or frequency—he was behind her. They stood a few feet apart, large, rounded lynx tracks stretching across the snow between them.

A million thoughts began running through his head, but they all disappeared when her lips touched his. This was Eila, too—seemingly impulsive, but not really. There was an underlying thoughtfulness to everything she did. Their lips pressed together. Then they were lying in the snow. The cold never bothered her, but still his impulse was to take off his coat and lay it beneath her. The steam from their combined breath rose between them. He placed one hand on either side of her face, not so much holding it as framing it.

Terms like *anaerobic threshold* and *movement economy* seemed idiotic just now. The body's oxygen consumption has to do with the heart. Its limitations are the heart's limitations. As his body moved over Eila's, Jackson felt like it was bursting full of air.

He found the freckle on her abdomen, the one he'd seen so many times when they'd shed their clothes to swim in the pond behind his cabin. He'd long ago named this particular freckle the *north star*. Her back arched beneath him, against the packed snow. When he pulled his nose away from the hot, damp hollow of her neck, he found her black hair fanned out, ice clinging to the strands. She reached up and framed his face as well.

Afterward, he leaned against a tree, and she leaned against him. She told him about the trip she would take in the spring, less than two months away. How the world always broke free of this winter encapsulation with such speed, he still couldn't quite fathom. Suddenly, everything he thought he knew so precisely seemed to lack foundation. He was caught between wanting this new thing to last forever and wanting to return to the steady, predictable life he was used to, where all things were part of a list, everything calculated. This—whatever it might be or become—didn't have a term in an anatomy book or a diagram. That this made more sense than any anatomy book or diagram was what troubled him most.

A panic began to rise in his throat, and his heart considered closing. But he wouldn't allow it, not with Eila. And so, he leaned back farther, pulled her closer. He closed his eyes and tried to breathe the imploding feeling away.

It would pass, like all things. This change in rhythm and pattern, it would all resolve, return to normal, as soon as they stood up, brushed the snow from their pants, strapped their skis back on, and shush-shushed off toward home.

56

It's taken five years, but Jackson's lungs have learned a new rhythm. His heart has too. Since that day on the bridge—his last day in Fairbanks—he hasn't run a single mile. He recognizes the running now for what it was: a simple distraction. It did nothing to resolve the vision of the loon. In fact, once he thought about it, it had actually led him right to it.

He tests his body in different ways. Carpentry, yoga, climbing, swimming. He's just finished swimming across the river and back, a thing he will do until the surface freezes over. It's getting close. Ever since he and Eila were kids, he practiced pretending that he wasn't cold, trying to keep up with her. Eventually, he built up a tolerance to it. But it's harder now, each year that he's away from her.

Jackson stands on the gravel shore, icy water trickling from his long hair down his forehead. He closes his eyes and focuses on the beating in his chest. Where he used to obsess over the quick hammering of his heart, the force that came from constant movement, it is now equally fascinating to see how slow the beating can become. How still he can be, while waiting.

The caribou have yet to come. It's later than usual for their migration to pass through. He knows this because he waits for them each fall, and their arrival is always tinged with both joy and heartache. They bring Eila with them—her memory, her face, her scent, her visions.

He's waiting for them, but what arrives instead is a woman.

Jackson breathes deeply, taking in the smell of drying leaves and the smoke curling from the cabin chimney. When he opens his eyes, there's a white-haired woman in front of him, wearing a heavy wool cloak. For a moment, he thinks she might be a spirit, but then he sees the shotgun hanging by her side and his four dogs bound down the hill, circling her. Silently, and without taking his eyes from her, Jackson picks up his T-shirt and shorts from the rock where he left them and pulls them over his wet skin.

"You just swam across the river," the woman says. It's a simple statement that might have come from anywhere—a voice in Jackson's head or the wind. But it comes from this woman, her pants muddy and her hair like a spiderweb caught in the breeze. She points to the slick current behind him, as if in a trance.

"I did," Jackson says. "Where did you come from?"

"I'm from the village," she says, straightening and shaking herself back into the present. She rests her hand on one of the dogs. "Norma Wolfe. They say they haven't seen you there in a while, so you wouldn't remember me. I only came last summer."

"And?"

"And, what?"

Jackson pauses, water dripping from his beard, soaking through the collar of his T-shirt. "Never mind. Let's go inside, Norma Wolfe. Are you hungry?"

"Not really," she says. "What's that sound?" She glances around.

Jackson nods toward the greenhouse. "Comes from in there. Bees, I think." The buzzing in the greenhouse has become the background music to Jackson's life, alive as a beating heart. Though it was unnerving when he first arrived, he barely notices the sound now. When Norma turns to look, Jackson sees the stitched outline of a wolf on the back of her cloak.

Inside, she gets comfortable right away, as if she's in her own home, organizing wooden spoons and spatulas on the kitchen counter, wiping crumbs from the kitchen table. She pauses, tracing her fingers over the stars engraved in the wood surface.

Jackson makes a plate of smoked salmon and crackers. He pauses with the plate above the table, all four dogs congregating by his feet, noses in the air.

"Grab the door?" he asks. "They're better behaved outside."

They sit on the deck facing the river. Jackson positions salmon on a cracker and holds it in his palm, then passes the plate to Norma. Because small talk is difficult, especially when he has company so infrequently, he almost asks how she ended up in the village. But most people aren't like him, and he gets the sense that there's something emotional driving her—as there was for him. He'd have hated if anyone in the village had asked that question when he'd trekked through himself.

He almost asks why she's here too. Instead, he says, "I expected the caribou to come through by now. But I haven't seen a single one." The words feel like too much—mentioning the caribou out loud is somehow like telling this strange woman about Eila—but it's all he's been thinking about. Eila and the caribou are one and the same in his mind, which is how he knows they are late. He watched them cross the river last year, farther upstream, where the water breaks apart and gets shallower. He was overcome with the image of Eila on the opposite bank, calling them toward her. Leading them on.

"I watched them last year," Norma says, as if reading his mind, "from the back porch of my cabin. It was the first time I'd seen so many since I was a kid. I was afraid they were all gone."

"So many of them are gone," Jackson says. "But there are still enough to—" A raven swoops into a tree above them, followed by three smaller birds, loud hecklers. Jackson uses the distraction to change the subject. "Did you walk all the way here?"

He realizes then that, whether she walked or not, she's going to have to spend the night. The sun is already dipping low.

"Canoed mostly," Norma says. She takes a long breath, like she's preparing to submerge herself, then sighs. "But now the canoe is busted—hit some sharp rock about a mile back. I shouldn't have just left it there."

"Why did you?"

Norma reaches for some salmon, slipping it to the dog by her feet, then readjusts the shawl around her shoulders as she sits back. She shrugs. "I guess I felt like a walk."

"Where were you headed?" Jackson asks.

Norma squints at him, calculating something. "Here," she says, like that should have been obvious. "I was on my way here. What's going on, by the way, in that greenhouse?"

"I don't know," Jackson says.

"You haven't checked? I thought you'd been here for years."

"I have. It's just part of the agreement. I don't open it. Don't ask questions."

Norma scoffs. "Sure," she mutters, rolling her eyes. *"Don't ask questions."*

There is a bed in the back room, which Jackson offers to her. Norma insists that even though she's in her seventies, she doesn't need a "fancy-ass bed." Jackson explains that he's never slept in that fancy-ass bed because he prefers to sleep in the loft, where he can see the river and climb out the window to the kitchen roof.

That night, the howling of wolves rises from the hills across the river.

57

He had the first vision when he was sixteen, just after his mother drove her packed Subaru down to the Lower 48. She left him alone in the two-room cabin, and he lay in bed at night, staring at the whiskey-colored ceiling beams. There he would see the bird. Twisted in wire, bleeding, gasping for air. He took it as some kind of symbol, perhaps of himself being left to take care of himself, or perhaps of his mother and whatever she had been dealing with that drove her away. Regardless, someone was trapped.

Jackson tried to shed the vision, but it wouldn't leave him. So *he* tried to leave *it*.

The night he began running, he was at a bonfire, ten drunk men and women he hardly knew huddled in a circle. It had warmed to ten beautiful degrees but they were standing shoulder to shoulder, as if remembering colder times. Swathed in wool, yet tossing logs into the pit with glove-free hands.

Someone said something about the winter nights seeming so endless. But how, eventually, you crawl into them like a den, and suddenly it's like warmth and light aren't welcome anymore. When they return, they just leave you nervous; you're forced to emerge from your comfortable, frozen world. The brightness is too revealing. Every action foreign, every movement awkward.

Perhaps it was simple disagreement with the opposition to movement. Perhaps it was claustrophobia. Jackson's chest thumped and argued: *flight is necessary.* Well, it was worth a try. He moved his toes inside his boots, tapped his heels on the ground. No one noticed when he backed away from the circle and disappeared into the host's cabin. He'd come in XTRATUFs because it was spring and mud was unavoidable, so he groped around in the dark, trying on one pair of sneakers and then another, until he found some that fit well enough. He didn't know who they belonged to.

Jackson laced the shoes up blindly and stepped out the front door. He took off into the night. He'd never run more than a mile in his life, only when it was required in middle school. It felt as if he were shedding a past existence, creating a new one. He was free now, independent. He looked forward, and the stagnant life around him fell away like chiseled-off stone, leaving behind something new. Happily, he found that the nights after he ran, he was not awakened by the image of a dying bird. That's how he started jogging across town day after day after day.

For a short time every morning, Jackson was still lonely and angry—a lonely anger that collided and tangled with his desire to be free. Breathing momentarily became short and slightly painful. His knees ached with tightness from the day before, despite his methodical stretching. Briefly, the earth below became his enemy, then transformed into his partner for the next few hours. He felt his lungs expand. His breathing finally eased and leveled. His body began to catch a rhythm. He was aware of everything moving through him—blood, air, water. A power radiating from his core, propelling his body forward.

Jackson's vision narrowed. There were, suddenly, no spruce lining the edge of the road. No clouds in the sky. No birds in either trees or sky. All distractions disappeared. Instead, he just saw a tiny pinpoint on the horizon ahead.

A target.

Something rose to the surface. A rhythm of aloneness that was not lonely at all. It was not filled with terror or painful images. In fact, it was a happy kind of solitude.

But running was not the same as outrunning.

It was mid-June. Jackson rounded a bend on Ballaine Road and stopped by the lake. He unzipped the nylon pouch he kept strapped to his upper arm and pulled out his cell phone. The number for the pizzeria was on speed dial. He waited for it to ring once, twice, and then a woman answered in a rushed voice.

"Large pizza, please," he said between long breaths. "Pepperoni and sausage."

"That all?" the woman said.

"And bacon. Thanks. I'll be there in twelve and a half minutes."

"Twelve and a half exact—oh, sorry. I didn't recognize your—it'll be ready."

"See you in twelve," Jackson said. He hung up and continued jogging.

In the pizza shop, the woman behind the counter asked, "How long you going today?" Jackson shrugged, accepted his pizza, nodded his thank-you, and found a table outside. As long as it takes, he thought.

A number of advertisements were taped to the shop window. A cello concert. A group of D&D players looking for new members. A book reading at the gallery. A talk about birds—the migrating sandhill cranes. Eila and Stefan were sitting on the patio, absorbed in conversation. And for a moment, he missed his mother and her homemade pizzas shaped like Salvador Dalí's clock, which only made him antsy to move again.

Jackson crushed the cardboard box as best he could and shoved it into the trash bin. He paused to give Eila a sweaty, one-armed hug as he passed—jogged away in silence. He crossed the train tracks and cut straight through the center of campus. Then he plunged down the hill to Farmer's Loop and felt the gravity and silence of his cabin pulling at him.

A few miles later, just before he reached home, it happened. His shoelace untied, the fox, the path by the pond. Then a horrible, resolved feeling came crashing down as he heard the faint wailing. He stopped, parting the low bushes. The loon's neck was twisted, wings bloody. The barbed wire encircled its body. When Jackson approached, it began to flail but gave up when it became more entrapped. It breathed heavily, its red eye narrowed and focused directly on Jackson's calculating brow.

Sweat trickled into Jackson's eyes as he leaned over to remove the wire, tearing the skin of his fingers in the process. The bird didn't struggle. Its wings were punctured multiple times and there were crisscrossing gashes on its chest. Downy feathers scattered across the ground.

Jackson didn't know how it happened. He couldn't tell who was to blame. He carefully lifted the soft gray bird from the tangles of wire. A tiny call, almost a growl, escaped from its rust-colored throat.

He remembered seeing the poster for the bird talk at the university. It was a long way, especially considering he'd run twenty-four miles already, but he knew that the bird wouldn't survive if he didn't do something. Jackson took off his shirt and wrapped the bird in it, then started running with the loon under his arm like a football.

When he reached the science building at the university, Jackson shoved the door open and scanned the bulletin boards for the flyer advertising the woman's presentation. Esther Audette. She was an ornithologist from New Mexico. That information seemed unnecessary at the moment. He just needed a room number.

The lights were off, and an empty nest was projected onto a screen. Jackson flipped on the lights, and Esther stopped in the middle of a sentence. Every head turned, but Jackson ignored their surprised faces and walked directly to the podium. He unwrapped the bloody T-shirt and took the loon in his hands.

The woman shot a panicked look around the room. "What the hell are you doing?" she whispered, covering the microphone.

He held the loon out to her like an offering, its neck limp. "I need you to fix this," he said, pushing it toward her. "Please."

"I'm just giving a . . . I'm not a . . . That's not what I do." Esther stumbled for words, but she took the loon and lifted it gently.

"Just fix the bird, Esther. Please, just fucking do something."

He could tell this made her angry—the use of her name and the expletive and the suggestion that she wasn't trying—but he was angry too. At what, he didn't know. The universe, perhaps. Esther laid the bird on the table and bent over it, its gray feathers sticky and matted. She put her hand on its chest, as if listening through her fingers. Its eyes were closed, but Jackson remembered the way the loon had locked on him pleadingly and followed his movements. He wanted to tell Esther—tell everyone how much it had needed him. He wanted Eila to know this too. He'd noticed Eila and Stefan in the back right away, and wished he could run over there now, to hide behind them both, to let Eila take over this whole situation in which he had no idea what he was doing.

Esther bit her lip and looked as if she might cry. "It's dead already," she said, shaking her head. "I'm sorry. I can't . . . there's nothing to be done."

Jackson leaned against the wall and wiped his bleeding hands on his shorts, noting how peaceful the loon looked. Jackson's calf muscles twitched. His chest burned. He knew, then, what it felt like to go too far. To push too much. To fight a battle that he was never going to win.

"It was worth trying," Esther said.

Jackson wanted to take the loon back, to wind the T-shirt around its body again and hold it close. Maybe run out of the room. "I'm sorry," he said.

Esther hovered over it like it was hers now. She said, "It's a red-throated loon. They're different from other loons. They can take flight from anywhere, land or water, without space for a running start. That way they have options. That way, they're never stuck in one place."

58

The loon vision was powerful—it had shaken him. But it was also dispassionate in some ways; he hadn't known the bird. Following the day on the lake, his vision of Eila was too much.

In early March, it was still cold enough that the glass of water he left on the porch turned to ice within minutes. After seeing Eila's death again, he stepped outside and the northern lights were out. Out of instinct, he turned to run back inside and call her, let her phone ring once, like he used to—their signal to go outside and look up. But he couldn't bring himself to do it. Instead, he poured whiskey into a ceramic mug, went out to the road, and began walking, his head tipped back to the green waves above.

It was silent except for the remaining snow—a high-pitched creak-crunching beneath his boots. Gnarly black spruce waved on either side of the road.

The stars blinked at him, delicate snowflakes falling onto his forehead.

His breath rose into the sky, disappearing into the cold, dark night.

The whiskey burned as it slid down his throat and made all his limbs tingle, slowly numbing his terrifying thoughts. He walked faster, the moon brightening the stretch of dirt road to an opulent, shining path. But that led to more darkness, where he wanted to send this new vision to rest.

Jackson felt dizzy and lifted the mug to his lips again. He heard the howling of sled dogs through the trees, and their frantic heartbeats mingled with his own.

In the end, the alcohol only made it worse. He collapsed into bed, sure that he'd exorcised the vision, but only woke again in the early hours sweating, the dream still hanging in the air like specks of dust caught in the rays of moonlight. He kept seeing Eila's body, broken by the creatures she loved most, the river's slick current dragging her away. Trying to erase her.

In the morning, hungover and feeling only half-alive, Jackson wandered out and saw a dog running away with something from his shed. His head pounded, mind on a loop of too many memories. Eila in bed with pneumonia, him sneaking to the woods to complete her research project. Eila gliding across a frozen lake. Eila's warm body beneath his.

His mind jumped from envisioning her beautifully alive to the certainty that she was going to die. And then his feet began moving, and suddenly he was barefoot and hurtling down the snow-packed road. His head cleared and he remembered trying to outrun his vision of the dead loon.

If he could stop her from holding his hands and saying those words—that as long as they were together, they were invincible—perhaps he could stop the whole thing. If he just kept moving. The cold air caved his chest but he couldn't stop, tears streaming and freezing on his cheeks. He begged this to be the answer. Either way, running seemed like a better answer than whiskey.

For the next few months, he tied his laces in the morning and didn't stop running until evening. Didn't stop when his knees burned or when Sadie left him doughnuts at the end of her driveway, or when—gods forgive him—Eila tracked him down. He didn't stop until the day he ran into Vern. Vern, who always seemed to have an excuse not to exercise, was walking the road that afternoon, like he'd only just discovered that nature was beautiful.

Jackson stopped—*momentarily*, he told himself—to tell Vern that seeing him out there moving made him proud. He didn't have time to think about how patronizing he sounded. As soon as his feet stopped moving, he glanced to the edge of the road and there they were: the two birch trees, intertwined in perpetual embrace. Jackson nearly collapsed. He might have, but his feet felt cemented to the road. He couldn't stop the violent, furious sobs from coming.

This is the state he was in when Vern approached.

Jackson felt like he should say something, but it would all sound so insane—the visions and the running, despite knowing it wouldn't really solve anything. He wished he could start the scene over again, go back and hold it together, just pat Vern on the back and congratulate him for moving his body.

But there he was. There was no pretending Vern hadn't stumbled upon him at his most vulnerable. So, rather than make something up, he simply told the truth, though it came tumbling out in disjointed fragments. Simply, "Eila." Very simply, "Dead."

Standing in his slippers in the middle of the road, Vern looked as if he might fall over. His hands came to rest on his thighs and he bent forward, sucking in air in great gulps.

"What happened?" he panted. *"Tell me."*

"No, no," Jackson said. "I mean, she's not dead . . . yet. It's the vision. I see it all the time."

"So," Vern tried to reassure him, "nothing has actually happened. You're simply having a dream."

"Not exactly," Jackson said. "It's not a dream. It's more like . . . a prophecy. Oh god, that sounds stupid. It's happened before. I swear, I'm not crazy."

Jackson attempted to explain the loon incident, and the feeling of dread before he'd found it tangled in the long grass. Vern's head tilted slightly when Jackson mentioned the bird talk at the university and the poor woman he'd harassed.

"Well, if you're so sure," Vern said, "then you'll never outrun it. Not while you're here, and she's here too. It will just follow you around, endlessly."

"Only until it happens," Jackson said. "But if—when—it happens, it will kill me. Well, it won't actually kill me. That I could deal with. It'll just leave me here, alone and lost and . . . well, fucking shredded, Vern. But yeah, technically, then the vision will go away."

Jackson expected Vern to say something encouraging, hopeful, sappy. Instead, Vern—who was now upright and arching his back, wincing in some kind of aged pain—stared wide eyed at a puddle in the dirt road. A congregation of yellow swallowtails had gathered. They flapped against the surface of the water, agitated and graceful at the same time. In slow motion, Vern pointed at them, his mouth open, but no words came out. Goose bumps rose visibly on Vern's arms and he began crying as well. The two of them stood there, sobbing, holding one another's shoulders.

Finally, Vern said, "Oh, dear god, help me." Jackson thought he might be having a heart attack, but Vern pulled it together long enough to tell him that the only way he knew to avoid the horror was to run away from it.

There was only one thing Jackson had to do in return for the cabin and promise of silence. He had to make sure the greenhouse stayed securely closed. What was inside must never see the light of day, at all costs. And no questions. Jackson didn't have the wherewithal to think of questions at the time anyway. He clasped his hands behind his sweaty neck and looked at the sky. It was a way out.

"Sure. Okay. That's fine."

It wasn't until he'd made it there, hundreds of miles north in the remote Arctic nothingness, that he realized he actually did have some questions. There was an enormous buzz emanating from the greenhouse, and when he pressed his face against the overlapping layers of plastic, he thought he could make out a faded kaleidoscope of color. Of course he wanted to know. But it was too late. He'd promised not to ask. And it was a small price for the peace he'd secured in that distant, wild, unknown place.

59

Departures had never been simple. But once he began moving in a direction, he usually didn't have any trouble continuing. Until this time. Jackson had built a shield around himself. But as his boots—crunching through hard-packed snow—took him north, that shield fractured, revealing all the soft, unrecognizable pieces beneath.

All Vern had given him were some handwritten directions, a map, and coordinates. There were no photos, so he just assumed he'd recognize it when he saw the mysterious greenhouse. He'd hitchhiked up the Elliott and Dalton Highways, choosing not to pass through Coldfoot. Instead, he turned northeast and hiked through white boreal forest and across the frozen wetlands, carrying only a backpack and his drive to reach a piece of land he wasn't allowed to ask questions about.

When he arrived in Cloud Creek village, population thirty-five, Jackson stood for a long time at the edge of the river, looking back at where he'd come from. It was not something he was fond of—looking back—but for the first time in his life, he was having trouble deciding if going forward or back was the right decision.

Cloud Creek seemed like a good resting place, after which he would again take off toward the unnamed tributary. But Jackson found himself standing with his backpack at his feet, his right foot pointing slightly ahead and his left slightly back, as if each had a different idea about the next step. Should he just turn around and retrace his path? Go back to his cabin with its empty bird feeders and garden beds?

This, it occurred to him, is what a person *should* feel. Trepidation. Hesitance of the unknown. But this is exactly what he'd been chasing his whole life, exploration of his body's physical and mental limitations. This, he realized, could be the last of the unknowns.

He pointed his toes upstream and stepped like the humbled stranger he was toward the tiny village. Houses were dispersed along a single main road, stocky log structures adorned with moose antlers, lanterns, snowshoes, and a variety of rusting metal tools he'd never seen before. Jackson passed a post office and what he guessed was the school. A few narrow trails led to a few spread-out cabins. A young girl, a teenager, bundled in a parka and wool hat, was sitting backward on a plastic tricycle, watching a younger girl dig in the snow. A man exited the post office carrying a stack of boxes he could barely see over. Dogs ran back and forth inside fenced kennels, some resting on snow-covered porches. Otherwise, Jackson saw no one.

After walking this far, he wasn't sure when to stop, or what—man, beast, deathly quiet building—he should stop for. So he kept going, very quickly finding himself on the opposite side of the village.

The boarded-up feel of the village betrayed its inner generosity. It didn't take much longer for a man to come bursting through one of the cabin doors, skis strapped to his back, the small herd of dogs behind him scrambling over one another to get to the front of the pack. The man's pace slowed as he tucked his chin and cupped his hands to light a cigarette, the dogs running ahead.

He squinted through the gray snow-light at Jackson and said, "I'm not going to ask where you've come from, because if you're wandering into Cloud in the middle of September with nothing but a backpack, I'm guessing you'd rather not say."

Jackson opened his mouth but nothing came out. He hadn't heard his own voice in days. Before he could try again, the man said, "And I'm not going to ask where you're going, either, because if you're wandering into Cloud in the middle of September with nothing but a backpack, I'm guessing you don't have a clue."

The man pulled the earflaps down on his fur-lined hat and blew a visible mix of warm breath and cigarette smoke into the icy air. He nodded and said, "I'll see you around." Jackson watched the man trudge along after his dogs, the packed snow groaning beneath his boots.

When Jackson had left Fairbanks, he had no idea how long it would take to get where he was going or where he might stay along the way. One night on the Elliott he'd slept in the bed of a truck that belonged to a man who'd given him a ride, while the man slept in the front seat. Otherwise, he'd pitched his tent under snow-laden spruce branches. And the night before he found the village, Jackson slept at the edge of a tiny lake, though he didn't really sleep, thinking he could feel the permafrost shifting beneath his cold and tired body. *Something hibernating deep in the earth is rolling over in its sleep.* He cinched his sleeping bag tighter around his face. When he woke, he watched a bull moose through the mesh door of his tent. The moose grunted and nibbled on saplings, his thick neck stretching to reach the highest branches.

After the skier's greeting in the village, Jackson felt the unusual inclination to stay close to the man's cabin. Though it was possible, even likely, that the man would have offered him a couch to sleep on, instead he spent the cold night camping in the cemetery between the town and the river, his tent wedged between rectangular swatches of fenced-in land with wooden crosses protruding at odd angles. This time, Jackson was lulled to sleep by the water gurgling beneath the ice.

In the morning, shadows moved outside his tent. He heard whispers and the scraping of a shovel against snow. When he emerged, he was dizzied by the sun's glare bouncing off the white earth in all directions. The river ice gleamed, nearly blinding him. As his eyes adjusted, he saw a small girl behind his tent, bent over something and giggling. A black-and-brown husky ran circles around her. Smoke rose from the ground.

As she backed away, Jackson saw that she'd cleared the snow and built a fire. She faced away from him, and for a brief moment, Jackson forgot everything. He lost all sense of time and physical space. It could have been years in the past. It could have been some possible future that had yet to take place. The girl's black hair was braided, trailing from beneath a thick wool hat. Jackson studied her innocent way of standing, her weight on one side, the other boot tip grazing the snow. She was almost floating. Jackson blinked away the image—Eila as a child—the awkward, quiet girl she was when they'd met.

"Little fire starter," someone said. Jackson turned to find the skier walking toward him. "That one's mine. You wouldn't think it, though, would you?"

"I don't know," Jackson said. "I don't see why not."

"That's Angela—she was born here. Her mother grew up in this village. Angie doesn't speak much, out loud anyway. I'm Clark."

"What about you?" Jackson asked. "Have you lived here all your life?"

"Oh, no," Clark said. "I'm from all over. I never quite knew where I wanted to be until I got here. Then something in me just said, 'Hey, it's time to stop moving.' So, I stayed. She's building that fire for you, by the way. She wanted to make you coffee."

Jackson watched as the distance between the little girl and the image of the woman he loved grew wider and wider. Angela nestled the cup into some snow, then used two gloved hands to lift the saucepan from the fire and carefully pour the dark coffee. When she turned and presented her brew, he saw a girl he'd never met, smiling and proud and blissfully new to the world.

60

Jackson had spied on Stefan Jacobsen hundreds of times as a child, seen enough to know his work wasn't as simple as it looked. After school, Jackson often followed the bear of a man down various paths to the future site of someone's home, watched him lift timber and stone that weighed more than any man should be capable of lifting. Jackson kept a close eye on the structure of Stefan's body as much as the architecture of his cabins, the places where it tensed as he engaged certain muscles. The strength of his legs, the flexibility in his back. His form.

The man was superhuman in so many ways.

Stefan would climb support beams, gripping them like a gymnast, swinging his legs over and pulling himself up. He sometimes hung upside down, his knees hooked over a beam, banging in nails from this position. Once, while he was walking across the main support like a tightrope walker, Jackson saw him drop the hammer he was carrying. His arms went straight out to his sides, and one foot shot out. He then caught the hammer with the top of that foot in a precarious one-legged balancing act. You wouldn't know he was so agile—given his size—unless you watched him like Jackson did.

Not too long after the hammer, Jackson and Eila sat on the living room floor, waiting for Stefan to finish making his signature "carpenter's pancakes"—*a little sawdust is good for the heart,* he'd say. As he stirred in some wheat germ, he repeated the miraculous move. In the middle of flipping a pancake, Stefan jolted his leg upward, his slipper flying into the air and completing one full rotation before he caught it on the tip of his foot. So, it hadn't been a miracle after all.

He intentionally wove lightness into his life.

Jackson took notes and made sketches, all while hidden among the trees. Sometimes Eila came with him, though if she did, she was usually engaged in something like following small-mammal tracks. And as he watched, Jackson realized that each time Stefan built a new cabin or outhouse or backyard shed, he developed some new style, a new detail, to make his work a bit more beautiful. He carved stars and moons into front doors. He built a loft railing to look like a setting sun—a half circle of rays radiating upward. He hauled a tree from Two Rivers once, finished it, and fixed it in the center of a cabin so that the kitchen island was built into the trunk. The rest of the tree extended up through the loft floor, and the top nearly pierced the peak of the ceiling.

It wasn't always aesthetics. Each new project he took on revealed greater function—drawers built into the space beneath a bed, rows of open shelving built over the kitchen counters, hooks for hanging pots and pans driven into the ceiling beams. Jackson witnessed what he believed was a kind of magic, the way Stefan was always making life a little more artistic, but also a little more purposeful.

When Jackson arrived at Sadie's homestead, it was this sense of lightness and artful living that he found himself pondering. The cabin needed some work, mainly because critters had burrowed into the insulation, but also because, at some point in the few months between when Vern and Sadie had left the place and when Jackson arrived, someone had ripped the front door off. Jackson assumed it had been a bear when he found claw marks next to holes in the walls and tufts of fur caught in the broken windows. The place was mostly empty, so all that the bear would have found were some paper, old clay pots, and framed drawings hung over the fireplace. The paper had been shredded, and the pots were broken and strewn across the floor. Trails of soil left the place looking like someone had tramped through in muddy boots, dragging their feet intentionally through a patch of damp carpet at the center.

When Jackson looked up, he saw the loft railing had been broken as well. And then he tipped his head back, noticing the leak in the roof. A drop of cold water fell and landed directly on his forehead. He wiped it away with his jacket sleeve and went to check on the rest of the property.

Outside, where the greenhouse had been boarded up, Jackson found claw marks in the many layers of plastic, and cracked boards, as if the bear had been curious but then got bored. Somehow, it was still tightly closed. When he pressed his hand against the plastic, he felt the whole place vibrating, an agitated sort of energy coming from within. He couldn't see much, but, squishing his nose to the plastic, he saw hints of colors inside, all blurred together.

He reminded himself of his job—not to ask any questions, and to make sure that, above all else, he kept the greenhouse secure. All Vern had told him was that whatever was inside had no business out in the world. Vern had given him these instructions in a halfhearted way, and Jackson wondered if he was perhaps hoping for failure. But *failure* was not a word that Jackson took lightly, or easily.

He retaped the plastic in every single place the bear had scratched it, and he reinforced the boards that held the plastic in place. He cleaned the floors inside the cabin and rehung the door. He patched holes in the walls with mosaics of plaster and broken pottery shards. He fixed the loft railing, too, adding a flourish of diagonal boards that fanned upward, a nod to Stefan's sunset design. He stapled layers of plastic over the broken windows, but when he finally got back to the village for new glass, all he could find were scrap pieces in various colors. So he made a pattern across the many small windows—pale red, green, light blue. Repeat. Over each of the windows he hung shutters hinged to open in different directions so the light could enter at any time of day, in any season.

The last thing he did was build a round kitchen table with salvaged wood he'd also hauled back from Cloud Creek. He sanded the rough surface, but when the notches and ruts couldn't be fully smoothed, he spent days carving a multitude of tiny stars.

61

When a new vision appeared last winter, Jackson was sure he was crazy. This one—the bear—seemed to replace the one of Eila's death, which only increased his anxiety. He wondered if he had changed the outcome of the Eila vision, and that was what had brought on the new one, or if it was all just superstition and coincidence to begin with. What had he done? Perhaps by leaving, he had saved Eila after all, or perhaps it had never been necessary—a stupid, irreversible mistake. But if that was true, how could he ever go back and confess what he'd done to her?

Norma stays for six days without the slightest mention of leaving, and Jackson is surprised to find he's okay with this. She hasn't asked him any questions about his past or his future. Each of those six mornings, Jackson has climbed out the loft window onto the roof, where he sits and sips his coffee and watches the ice beginning to stretch across the river. The sunrise flickers across the glassy surface. He watches Norma sneak off on those mornings as well, down the path toward her stranded canoe. She disappears into the spruce and is gone for hours. When she returns, she brings nothing back with her.

When Jackson offered to help haul the canoe closer to the cabin, she refused. She maintains a certain guardedness. On multiple occasions, he's stopped himself from asking what her original plan had been paddling here—how she'd expected to get back without a strenuous paddle upstream that even he wouldn't undertake. He suspects she is somewhat like him and likes to feel her own strength when possible.

She keeps her shotgun underneath the bed while she sleeps.

The river is freezing more and more each day, and if Norma waits much longer, the two of them will end up spending the winter together in a cabin built for one. One night, while they're sitting on the deck eating a whitefish stew that she made, she says, "I have a husband named Mitch who I walked out on a year ago. It's why I left Whitehorse and came to the village. I told him straight up I was leaving. I even stupidly told him where I was going, although he probably could have figured it out—my son Clark lives in Cloud Creek. My granddaughter too. They're the ones who told me about you. The mystery man at the old homestead."

Jackson can't help thinking that if anyone else had called him "mystery man," he would have been terribly annoyed. But something about this woman's independence, and her disregard for his opinion, delights him. It also makes him wonder about his own grandmother. Since he's never met any of his grandparents, he decides to silently assign Norma this title. His very own shotgun-toting grandmother.

"I'm not all that mysterious."

"Well, I've been here six days and I still don't know what you're doing here or why those buzzing bees are locked in there. I can usually pick up on things, form some kind of story. But not with you."

"Well, you've been here for six days, and I didn't know about Mitch or why you left him for Cloud Creek. What made you decide to start somewhere new?"

"I'm still not convinced that I didn't destroy something good in the process of restarting. Who knows? But I just got sick of the constant assumption that I wasn't capable, even though I literally did everything. Sometimes it was worse than that. The names and such. Things not worth repeating."

"I've destroyed good things for less," Jackson says. "Houses. Birds. Perfect relationships."

"It's just that, I heard someone say on the radio one morning, 'The grass is greener where you water it.' And at the time, I was scrubbing at that dark ring that forms on the bottom of the coffeepot and just never seems to go away, no matter how much elbow grease you put in. And I thought, 'Who the hell would want to water *this* life?' So, I bought a canoe, learned how to use a shotgun, packed, and took off down the Yukon, almost died a few times—bears and rapids—and eventually landed in Cloud."

"How long were you married?"

"Forty-seven years."

"Jeez."

"I loved him once," she says. "I remember the first time I saw him, yellow-and-black-plaid shirt, playing bass in a local band. The Tumbleweeds. Honky-tonk western swing. That's what they played." Norma laughs, pretending to play the air guitar. "I danced. So stupid."

Not having any idea what Mitch looks like, Jackson inevitably pictures Stefan in a flannel shirt, sitting in the corner of the bar with his guitar. Then he sees himself grabbing Eila's hand that one time when they were twelve or so, and spinning her around. He shifts back to Norma, pushes a little further. "I've had loads of love in my life, and I've managed to wreck every bit of it."

"You've got the dogs," Norma says. "You found them somehow. There's got to be some love left, no?"

"The dogs found me," Jackson says. "When I hike out to a village, there's always some stray that a musher couldn't use any longer and left behind. And somehow, that dog always knows that I'm the one to follow home. I've gone back to Cloud Creek four times since I moved into this cabin. I have four dogs."

"Anyone who thinks affection has a limit never had a dog," Norma says. "What are their names?"

"They don't have names."

"No, no, of course. Because grief is limitless, too, and the quickest way to that is giving something a name. Better to keep your distance, don't let yourself get too attached." She stares flatly at the dark water lined by thin black tree silhouettes, the lantern on the tree-stump table between them flickering. "My mother used to take my sisters and me on fishing trips in Nunavut. We'd tie our tent down to beach rocks and build fires to cook Arctic char. Those beaches, the smooth rocks worn down by the hooves of thousands and thousands of caribou, always traveling from one destination to another for centuries—it was reflecting on those trips that made me realize I could do it on my own. Do you think you can grieve a part of yourself that's lost?"

"Yes," Jackson says. A cold wind rushes through the birches. The thin bite of cold in the air fills him with longing for winters in Fairbanks. He pushes his hair behind his ears and pulls the hood of his sweatshirt over his head. "But I think you can always find it and bring it back to life again."

62

Norma gets up earlier than usual the next morning, but Jackson is already sitting on the roof. He woke before the sun rose, the cold slipping through the loft window, the sound of ice creaking and groaning at the edge of the river. He saw it again last night. The vision in which Stefan Jacobsen is on his hands and knees looking for something in the grass. Stefan begins to laugh, Jackson blinks, and then Stefan is gone—replaced by a roaring white grizzly.

He watches as Norma descends the cabin steps, assuming she's going out to her canoe again, but instead she turns and heads directly for the greenhouse. She cups her hands around her eyes and tries to peer in through the plastic. She stands back, surveying the whole dilapidated structure. When she grips the wood plank securing the door and pries, Jackson has no choice but to yell "Don't!"

Norma looks around, trying to assess where the voice is coming from.

"You can't open that," Jackson yells.

"Why not? I'm not afraid of bees." Norma has one hand on her hip and another shielding her eyes, and she squints into the sun with a bit more drama than is probably necessary. "I'm not afraid of any—"

"Just don't," Jackson interrupts. "It's boarded up for a reason."

"Which is . . ."

A long pause. "I don't actually know. But I know that it's meant to stay shut at all times."

"I need some wire. Stainless steel. For fixing the canoe. I thought maybe there was something in there I could use."

"There isn't."

"Well, how do you know, if you don't even *know* what's in there?"

"It's toxic." He's pretty sure that is a gross exaggeration of what Vern actually said, but he needs to sound convincing.

"Do you know that for sure? Or is that just what you were *told*?"

Jackson sighs. He's tired, maybe because of the bear vision, maybe because of the rapid onset of cold weather and the promise of snow. His body always tries to slow down before he's ready to give in to it, even though it's the right thing to do. He takes a long sip of hot black coffee, the steam rising, obscuring Norma's figure in its cloud. "It was implied. All I know is that my job is to keep it closed, and to not ask questions."

"God, I'm sick of *not* asking questions. All that *Play nice*, and *Don't rock the boat* shit. You know, my favorite is *That's just how it is*. If I were you, I'd at least try to figure out what's in there. How do you know you're not harboring something illegal? Aren't you even curious?"

The thought has occurred to Jackson. Of course he's curious. The fact that Vern was involved at all makes him suspicious, but the fact that Sadie also had a part means it's definitely not illegal.

"It's not," he says simply. "And you're not."

"I'm not what?"

"Me. You don't know anything about me, or why I'm here, or what this place is."

Norma rushes to get out the words "Well-it-sounds-like-you-don't-either" before holding her hands up in surrender. The wind picks up, whipping her white hair into her eyes. She peels it away and says, "I'm going to go check on my things. See if I can do without the wire. I really should be getting out of here."

"You're not planning on paddling upstream, are you? You won't make it, especially now with freeze-up."

"Of course not," she says. "I'm going to hike back, but you don't just abandon a busted canoe. That just makes it someone else's problem. I believe in responsibility."

Jackson watches her pull the heavy cloak tighter around her shoulders, and the image of the wolf disappears into the birches.

That night, when they're eating on the porch, it's almost too cold, but neither of them seems willing to say so. They dip homemade bread into mugs of hot broth and sit silently until the moon flickers in stark white ripples over the river. There is a constant buzzing coming from the dark greenhouse—a low hum, like a soundtrack for the night.

Jackson looks at Norma and wonders what she's waiting for. He can't think of what he could possibly have to offer her. A place to stay, some food. But he still hasn't given her anything of himself. Anything true. He decides to test the waters. "Have you ever been so scared of something all you can bring yourself to do is turn and run like crazy?"

"Like they do in horror movies?"

"No. Not like in horror movies."

"You mean like I did? Scared of a life with a man who used me for verbal target practice?"

Jackson hasn't thought of it that way—that Norma ran because she was scared. Of course, bravery is most itself when wielded against fear. But what he did, that was something else entirely. It was a dark void, buried beneath his ribs, a hole that still doesn't have a name. He suspects it's something like cowardice but doesn't want to admit that. How would he explain running from something good? "No," he says. "Not like that either."

Norma doesn't ask for more. Perhaps she's thinking about her own messy journey, just as Jackson did when he stood at the edge of Cloud Creek. He slides a notebook out from under his chair and opens it in his lap. He scans the columns, the dates, and all the data he's tracked.

"The caribou should have come through." He thumbs through the notebook's pages, then stops at his most recent entry. Dates of first arrivals, dates of final departures. "In fact, every year, for the past five years, they've been long past this place by now. Getting to their wintering grounds. But I haven't seen even one. I did see cranes the other day."

"All the way up here at this time?" Norma asks. "They're too beautiful for this world, in my opinion."

"They should be going south about now."

Norma's white hair drapes around her shoulders. She wiggles her hands free of her shawl and presses them together. She turns to him, her eyes brimming with a kind of sorrowful joy. "The cranes—it's like they *actually* become one with their lovers. They move together, call out together. When they mate, they create their own language. That's what I wanted."

Jackson clears his throat. "Yeah. That's what we had." He still can't bring himself to say her name out loud.

Norma's eyes spark in the moonlight. She looks like she might ask *Who's "we"?* But of course, there's no need. She gives him a nod that means *finally* and says, "Ah, I see. So, what happened to her?"

Something invisible and accusatory wraps its fingers around Jackson's throat. He swallows hard and admits, "I don't know."

"You say that a lot. Which is strange, because you strike me as the kind of person who knows a lot of things."

And then, before he knows it, he's rambling—about the visions and his certainty that his best friend and love of his life was going to die. About how leaving was supposed to stop the cycle. When he finishes, Norma is staring at him, the river reflected in her eyes, her mouth open.

"You just *left*? Like ran away and let her assume that you'd *died*?"

Jackson shrugs. It's an inadequate gesture for the embarrassment and guilt he feels. He says, "Basically, yes. But only to keep *her* from dying."

"Or," Norma says, leaning forward in her chair, "to keep yourself from having to deal with her dying. Because you don't know if you've helped or hurt the situation, do you? All you've done is force her to deal with the exact thing you were too scared to confront in the first place. Alone."

He's never thought of it in these terms. The reverse. Jackson feels weak and broken down suddenly, and he tries to gather some semblance of courage again.

"The visions are real," he says. "They've come true before."

Norma spends a long time shaking her head and making incredulous hand gestures. She starts many sentences before finally saying "This is the most ridiculous thing I've ever heard. I'm sorry, but it is. Not the vision part, because I believe in visions and dreams and spirits. But leaving like that? That's . . . I don't even know what to call it."

Jackson has no response, but he knows exactly what to call it—cowardly. That certainty has slowly crept up on him. He thinks of Vern, telling him it was the only way. That he had to put distance between himself and the horror. And he felt whittled down enough at the time to accept that.

But there's something that's been nagging at him, something that tells him Eila hasn't died; he'd have felt some sort of severing in his body if it had happened. He would know it in fiber and bone. And he doesn't, hasn't felt anything of the sort.

He says, simply, "I didn't know what else to do."

"Well, it's not for me to say what you should have done instead," Norma says, "but I do know fear is the goddamn worst reason to do anything. Especially when it comes to love. Yeah, it's scary, but it's the only thing that's going to save you."

Jackson's head hurts, and he's so tired. When the warmth of the sun left, it took all his energy with it. "The worst part is," he says, "if she's still out there, I think maybe she's gone through something terrible, and I wasn't there for it. I've been having a different dream now." He pauses, then adds, "It's about a white bear that used to be a man."

Norma flinches, her eyes wide and her brow furrowed. She puts a cold hand on Jackson's arm and nods her head. "I knew it," she says. "I knew you were the one I needed to see. We're going to have to go back for the canoe. I brought something for you."

In the morning, they walk up the river. Norma rummages through a dry bag in the boat, letting out a shriek when she finds a heavy black radio. She turns and hurls it unceremoniously into the river. In the abyss of moving water, it makes an unsatisfying splash, floats for a moment, then disappears.

"Useless," she mutters. A few curses follow, her eyes fixed on the spot where the radio sank moments ago. No trace of ripples. "I've been carrying that thing around for the last year," she says. "I thought I might want to call Mitch, you know? Just a week ago, I was having serious thoughts about going home. But I heard the wolves the last few nights, and I know I can't do it."

Jackson wrestles with something inside. He's not sure what he's doing here anymore—if he's meant to help this woman make a decision, or if she's meant to help him. She shakes her arms like she's shedding an old skin and says, "Okay." Then she's digging into the canoe again and unstrapping a pair of wooden skis from her pile of gear. She holds one in each hand. "Here. These are for you."

Jackson takes one, doesn't need to examine it for long before recognizing the woodwork. "Stefan," he says, goose bumps traveling his limbs.

"You knew him, didn't you?" she asks.

He runs his finger along the edge of the ski to where the wood curves into a wide, rounded tip. He's seen Stefan make skis before, splitting the trunk of a birch with a wedge and a maul, soaking the wood for days to make it flexible enough to bend into shape. *Patience. That's the most important thing in this task . . . and in life.* That was Stefan's mantra.

"These were hanging over my fireplace when I moved into my cabin in Cloud Creek," Norma says. "They told me they were made by a man who'd restored this homestead years ago."

"Oh, he's not here anymore. He's back in Fairbanks."

"Yeah, they told me that too. Said he left a long time ago, and that only some young hermit lives here now. Thing is, lately I've been having dreams, and not exactly nice ones."

"What kind of dreams?" Jackson asks. He is now sure that Stefan is gone.

"Usually it's a bear," Norma says, "banging down my cabin door. Looking for something that isn't food or the usual kind of thing a bear would want. At first, I thought it was Mitch, or some symbol of him anyway, coming to find me and drag me home. Those anxiety dreams. I always wake up terrified. But last time, it told me its name. It's a giant white grizzly bear named Stefan Jacobsen. I thought maybe I should bring these back. They don't belong in my cabin. I think they need to be here, to restore some kind of balance."

PART 5

63

The Braided River

In the month between skiing on the frozen lake and Eila's first research trip in the Brooks Range, Jackson began running. In that time, Eila was only able to catch sight of him when he was on the road. He ran most of the day, every day, needing to move all the time. And he refused to talk to anyone when he was doing so, even her. At first, she was happy he was treating everyone else the same way he was treating her. Then she realized that he was treating her just like everyone else. It happened so suddenly, Eila could only assume it had something to do with the day at the lake, the day everything happened.

She tried to bump into him when he wasn't running, but it proved impossible. All she needed was an answer. Not why he was running so much. Not why he was avoiding her. Just why he was running and avoiding her *now*, why he was hiding *now*, after they'd finally been together, in what she knew was the kind of harmony only nature could contrive. Perfect symbiosis.

Since she couldn't pin him down, she found herself furious when she saw him on the road, so she began avoiding *him*. Somehow, that proved just as difficult. Inevitably, she would be driving to the research station and there he'd be, his muscular legs springing him forward, sweat glistening on his neck. As much as she tried not to turn her head as she passed, she inevitably did.

She wanted to understand his motive, but he wouldn't give her the opportunity to ask. The next-best solution was to find the answer herself. Research is what she did for a living, after all. She got into her truck one day and drove north, where no one—especially Jackson—would see her.

She stood in front of the sign at the Dalton Highway. The gateway to the Arctic. The dusty road before her carved through short trees, climbing and then dropping over the hill and out of sight. One hand gripped the wooden signpost, the other clasped her ankle to stretch her quadriceps, and she knew that one way or another, this was going to bring her a sense of resolve.

What she didn't know was how much it was going to hurt.

As a child, she'd run through woods, marshes, fields. But back then, she wasn't thinking about the running. She was thinking about something ahead of her, even as it moved farther and farther away. A butterfly. A fox. A floating dandelion seedpod. The running she hardly felt, simply an act her body was engaged in to achieve some other goal. There had been lightness in it, and joy. This is what Eila imagined she would feel again, and what she imagined Jackson felt every day that he took off from his front porch.

Why else would he do it? Because after years of searching for new experiences, he'd finally found one he loved more than her?

She focused closely on the rhythm of her breathing, the forward angle of her torso, the length of her stride—but the variables didn't seem to work together, not a smooth machine like Jackson. Her heart didn't feel lifted, only tighter and heavier. She was painfully aware of her body. The dirt road stretched on endlessly, and even though she struggled to breathe at times and her legs ached, she persisted. At some point, it would all have to make sense. That was the thought that was getting her through, at least.

A tour bus passed on its way to Deadhorse, pumping charcoal gray exhaust into the air around her. People turned and gawked out the back window, some giving her a thumbs-up or a slight wave. She'd expected to be embarrassed—as if they'd know why she was running, see the torment and heartbreak in her stride—but she wasn't.

The bus grew smaller as it crested a hill, and Eila turned around and began to run back. When she reached her truck, it had been one hour and forty-five minutes, and she hadn't felt a single thing aside from pain. And no gain.

The following day, when she passed Jackson, she had to squeeze the steering wheel firmly to keep from pulling over, jumping out, and demanding of him to answer: *What could possibly make more sense than us?*

64

Eila doesn't know how far she's come. Though she's tried to continue moving east, following the river, there are so many bends and forks that she's lost track. It makes estimating the actual miles she's traveled nearly impossible. She has the GPS, displaying the tangle of squiggling lines that has been her path, a compass she took from the TFS station, and her father's hand-drawn map, but they're not as much help as she'd hoped in the open tundra.

Yesterday, when she left Cloud Creek, she and the dog walked for six hours before the sun set, and she was forced to pitch the tent in the dark. She lay in her sleeping bag, the hilly earth beneath her. And though she didn't need the dog's heat for warmth, she didn't move when he pressed himself into her side. They got up and started walking again before the sun rose. Eila skipped breakfast, but she offered pieces of a croissant to the dog as they trudged over the soggy hills and tussock-laden fields.

Somehow the mountains they are heading toward never get any closer. As the sun rises over those purple snow-streaked peaks, Eila glances over her shoulder and smiles at the dog's crooked run. *Coulda-been-a-sled-dog-but* . . . She can't afford to slow her pace, but she also doesn't want to let him fall behind, so she stops and waits, reaching down to scratch under his graying chin. When she searches into her pack for a can of sausages and her hand brings up the half-finished jar of fireweed jelly first, the dog begins jumping over and over, his front paws off the ground. She puts some of the jelly on the sausages and lets him eat the whole can, wincing at her poor judgment. He's got to eat something, she thinks.

For the next hour, Eila and the dog follow a patchy trail of infected lichen, gathering more samples. There are now multiple bags inside her pack. The lichen feels like the lightest thing in the world—and also the heaviest. She expected to see at least some caribou, too, but since the plane, there have been none. The landscape, in fact, has seemed starkly free of wildlife.

Of course, that should change. Once she finds the cabin, the greenhouse, the bees.

The homestead should be here, somewhere, but Eila is so tired she begins to wonder if she's seen particular trees before. And when it starts to snow, her eyes can no longer tell the difference between mountain and sky. Her legs shake in a way they never have before, and her back burns with the weight of her pack. Eila sits on the cold earth, trying to summon any kind of strength, and the dog seems grateful for the pause too.

Strength like when she was learning to drive and she buried the front third of the car in a snowbank. Her father lunged in waist deep and began digging with his bare hands. When he pressed his weight against the front bumper, his eyes were bright and determined, but it was the bulk of his shoulders, the arcing of his back, that made Eila so certain he would succeed. With what seemed like superhuman force, he pushed the car out of the snow and onto the road.

Strength like that.

And strength like he had near the end, when all his words eluded him and he wasn't able to turn over in bed. When Eila turned him on his side to change the bedsheets, he'd hide any signs of shame. Instead, he told her stories of the Lower 48 and the other places he'd lived before moving to Alaska with her. All those stories came spilling out, but try as he might, he couldn't remember the word *vacuum*. And yet he laughed—that roaring, selfless laugh.

Strength like Stefan Jacobsen, conjuring a smile, even as his cheeks puffed and he lost his hair and he grew heavier than ever from the medications.

Strength like that too.

In pictures when he was younger, before Alaska, his size was always the most surprising thing. He was so small, skinny even. The young man in the photos would have had a hard time lifting five gallons of water. But she only ever knew the giant Stefan—sturdy and gentle.

He'd come to the North as one person and transformed into another.

As she conjures all this strength and resilience and lightheartedness, she notices movement on the other side of the river. A flash of white that disappears as quickly as it appeared. She pulls out her binoculars, catching the shape of a white grizzly barreling down the bank. It isn't impossible. The bear splashes through the shallows and turns back to her once—a prompting pause. She needs no convincing—unafraid, she's already running, zigzagging through the low shrubs and the birch saplings along the river. She keeps sight of the bear on the other side, its pale shape weaving between trees—disappearing behind hummocks and then reemerging.

Her breath rises ahead of her as she runs, as the bear lumbers farther away. Her stride lengthens. She feels an urgency to catch it, to look in its eyes, but the distance between them continues to grow. Eila lifts her chest higher, her lungs still quite accustomed to the piercing cold. They fill with air, but it isn't painful. It feels like life itself, its purest form, entering her body. This is what it is to be alive. Muscles she never knew existed stretch and wake. Muscles in her legs, her back, her shoulders. Even her heart expands. Her feet are lighter and she hardly notices them touching the ground, as if they are floating just above it—the earth rising to meet her.

She hardly notices, too, when she breaks through a thin sheet of ice in a shallow section of the river, closing in on the bear's diminishing shape. And then, in the flurrying snow, with the river gripping her ankles, the bear slips into the trees and out of view for good.

Eila's veins feel hot and flood with adrenaline. But as it wears off, she remembers the dog, and her eyes search the landscape. "Shit," she whispers, feeling guilty for allowing him to follow her, only to leave him behind out in the open. She whistles as best she can with dry, cracking lips and yells, "Hey, Dog!" For a moment, she wishes she'd given him a name, but it's not like he could have learned one so quickly anyway.

Her mind scrambles for a moniker, and just as she's about to yell "Fireweed!" she sees him lilting over a hill toward her. It's a relief not to have to give him a name just yet. When he's close, Eila crouches to pet him, but he's running so fast he slams into her and knocks her over, his wet nose in her neck. "Okay, okay," she says. She laughs, stands up, and brushes wet brown grass and mud from her pants. "Sorry. I won't do that again. I promise. We're partners now."

Then Eila sees the ground around them—the ground she was lying on—and finds it is covered with the infected lichen. Black-speckled lichen extends in all directions. Opening her hands, she finds her palms are stained black as well. "All right," she says, "it truly couldn't get worse than this. Now we just need to find that greenhouse. Come on, Dog."

When Eila reaches the next bend in the river, she realizes just how turned around she is and finds herself walking downstream on yet another unnamed fork. The snow around her eddies, and her vision becomes tunnellike. She puts one foot in front of the other. Unable to trust the river or the mountains or the ground beneath her, she relies on her instincts instead. She trudges onward, her feet sinking into ground that looks deceptively dry. The infected lichen is still thick.

She imagines Jackson walking beside her, tries to conjure him in the spiraling snowflakes. She remembers that night in the tree house, when they shared their first beer and he showed her the maps of Whittier, so certain his mother was going to take him on that trip. But it was Stefan and Eila who took him to kayak Blackstone Bay.

They'd driven ten hours south of Fairbanks to the Anton Anderson Memorial Tunnel, a one-way, two-and-a-half-mile tunnel through a mountain. It was the only way into and out of Whittier. Once on the other side of the mountain, they rented two kayaks and pushed them into the slate gray water of the bay, then paddled into the fog—Stefan in one boat, and Eila and Jackson in the other.

They spent three days paddling, camping on marshy islands, spotting eagles with their binoculars, reaching out to let their fingers graze crystal-blue icebergs. The farther they got from the mainland, the more silver-pink jellyfish they saw swimming alongside their boats. At night, all three of them squeezed into one tent, listening to the low sounds of humpbacks singing.

One day, Eila and Jackson walked together along the smooth, slippery rocks toward the looming glacier. They'd brought sketchbooks and made a game of seeing who could draw the fastest. They drew mussels and driftwood. They drew the tiny, translucent mushrooms that curled up like fragile little chimneys from tree bark. Jackson's drawings were better than hers, and he drew them faster too. She was self-conscious and hesitant.

They closed their sketchbooks and Jackson said, "Your dad. He's a really good one. You're lucky."

Eila twisted her braided pigtails, her hair frizzy from the humidity. "I think your mom did want to take you on this trip" was all she could think to say.

Jackson shrugged, picked up a slick black stone, pulled his arm back, and sent the rock skimming over the water's surface. "Maybe," he said. "I'm just saying. Sometimes I wish he was my dad. I don't even know my dad. I barely know my mom. Stefan's just so big, so strong. I'm going to be that strong one day."

Just then, Stefan bellowed from back at the campsite, "Eats are up!" And they scrambled back over the rocks to find a campfire, sharpened sticks, and hot dogs waiting. "Do you hear that?" Stefan asked as they ate and dusk approached, the mountains around them more intimidating in the darkness. The sound of thunder boomed across the bay, the glaciers calving. As they fell asleep, every half hour there was another crash, more ice breaking and dropping into the bay. Eila and Jackson both jumped at the sound.

"Nothing," Stefan whispered into the dark, "can make you feel quite so small and insignificant as standing in front of a glacier. And that's the best feeling in the world." Jackson was on his back, hands clasped over his chest. He smiled in the moonlight.

Eila tried to catch Jackson's eye then. She dreamed that night about the two of them hiking across a glacier, their bodies tiny specks crossing an immense frozen landscape. They got smaller and smaller as they walked, until eventually they disappeared into the blue ice. But somehow the smaller they became, the happier they were, and they felt incredibly calm as they drifted into nothingness.

Eila shakes herself awake and blinks against the hypnotizing snow and lull of memory. There's something on the edge of the river, and she strains to make it out. It's a canoe, with all the gear piled next to it on the bank. After scanning the area and seeing no one, Eila drops her backpack and sits on one of the wicker seats. She has the urge to crawl into the hull and fall asleep there. The snow dampens all sound around her—she closes her eyes and the world is silent.

But then the dog barks and there's the cracking of branches and a cream-colored shape bursting through the aspens. It's the color of the bear, and Eila's heart is far too expectant—and then disappointed—when she instead sees a white-haired woman in a woven cloak tramping through the trees. The woman stops abruptly, swearing at top volume, pressing her shaking fingers to her chest.

"You scared the shit out of me," the woman says.

Eila tries to speak, but her voice doesn't seem to be working. What comes out is the scratching of a record needle, rough and restless. "You're not . . . ," Eila says, trailing off.

"I'm not who?"

"I'm sorry," Eila says, unzipping her pack and retrieving the crumpled paper on which her father drew the map. She heaves the pack over her shoulder again, holding out the piece of paper. The woman takes it, hesitant but curious, inspecting the hand-drawn map with narrowed eyes. She shrugs.

"Let me take you back to the cabin where I'm staying," the woman says. "We can figure it out there. There's water and food and a fire. The guy who lives there might know where you're trying to go. Can you help me carry this canoe? It's not far."

They each take one end of the canoe and lift, the woman in front and Eila in back. The dog weaves through the trees, seeming to know where they're headed. His upright tail, all wispy black fur, waves back and forth. The woman straightens her back and steadies herself, and they trudge upstream along the gravel beach with the canoe rocking between them. After a while, the woman shouts over her shoulder, "I'm Norma."

"Eila."

"And him?" Norma asks, nodding ahead to the dog.

"Doesn't have a name."

"Seems to know the way."

Norma has to drop the canoe and rest after a while. Her forearms are burning, she says, her wrists aching. She's breathless. "Sorry," she says.

"It's fine," Eila says. "At this point, what's a little more time?" She rubs her knee where the canoe has been banging with each step.

They're surrounded by fluttering yellow aspens, the leaves dropping in great numbers with each strong breeze. "You're just walking out here?" Norma asks. "How long have you been lost?"

Eila shuffles through the moments that could answer this question. The Tumi Field Station, the spring when her father died, the winter when they learned of his illness. Five years ago, when Jackson disappeared.

She's about to put together some kind of answer when a vibration like thunder shakes the earth beneath them. Ravens fly overhead and the air around them grows still, the way it does before a storm.

"I saw the map. But what is it you're looking for?"

"There's a greenhouse," Eila says, "where some friends used to do research. Experiments."

Norma lifts her eyebrows. "What kind of experiments?"

"All kinds. Botanical, specifically. I'm just hoping that whatever it is, it will do some good. Maybe a lot of good."

"Huh," Norma says. "Okay." She bends her knees to lift her end of the canoe again, and Eila catches her eye before doing the same. She senses a trace of resistance, like Norma is protecting something.

This woman wasn't part of the plan. But she's here now, and it's going to come out eventually. A few more steps and Eila says, casually, as if addressing the trees, "As far as I know, what these friends found was some kind of mutation in their bees. The bees became indestructible. Immortal, *apparently*. They observed them for years in their greenhouse."

"Like actually immortal? Like the 'living forever' kind of immortal?"

"Yep," Eila says.

Norma blurts out, "I think where we're going now is where you're trying to go. I mean, I'm staying in that cabin."

"What?" Eila says. "Really? It's supposed to be close. But I assumed I'd gotten too far off track. How far is it?"

"It's just up there." Norma gestures with her nose. "Past that stand of trees."

Eila almost drops the canoe and runs. But she maintains her composure and doesn't abandon Norma, breathing deeply as she hoists the canoe higher and adds determination to her pace. She says, "I'm going to use it. You should know that. I'm going into that greenhouse and taking what's there and I'm going to use it to help the caribou."

"What's wrong with the caribou?" Norma asks. "I mean, besides the obvious—fewer of them all around, climate change, and infrastructure and everything."

"The last few years the population decline has been enormous. They're literally dropping off the map by the second. All of that lichen in my pack is infected with some kind of parasite, and I'm positive it's killing the caribou. So, I'm going to figure out how to use what's in that greenhouse to fix this lichen, and then hopefully the caribou as well. Bees, flowers, whatever it is. I'm a biologist—I can figure this out."

"The person who lives here . . . I don't think he's going to be keen on you opening up the greenhouse. Just saying. You're going to have a hard time convincing him. He bit my head off for trying, and he claims there's something toxic inside. Course, he doesn't know anything. He's just telling me what he was told."

"Told by who?"

The homestead comes into view and Eila forgets the question, feels herself shaking. She thinks she might fall to the ground with exhaustion, but instead she begins running, Norma shouting after her to make herself at home and maybe put a log on the fire.

65

The wind picks up crisp, yellow birch leaves and blows them around the yard. Meandering flakes of snow drift down. The caribou should be passing through, like stocky, snorting ghosts, but they are not. They have always crossed the river just before it freezes over, driven toward a place where they are held by winter. It is also the time of year when Jackson sees Eila everywhere. Although his visions of her don't plague him as they once did, this is just when the dull ache of missing her is the hardest. With the fall migration. When his body hasn't moved enough.

He feels a presence coming, even if he hasn't seen the caribou yet. And lately, he hasn't moved nearly enough. If he could swim, he would. But the river is icing over, and he is acutely aware of how his body feels the cold these days. It's not like how it used to be. Not like when he was younger, observant and eager to experience the intensity of everything, good and bad.

Jackson shoves off in his kayak and skims across the river, to where the water pools in the shallows of a gravelly beach. He uses the paddle to break a hole through the thin layer of ice and stands with the water gurgling around his knees. A moment later, he can't feel the lower half of his legs. This is what he can manage. A brief ice bath to shake loose the trickling regrets, the clinging doubts.

He takes long, slow breaths—three of them—and just before he plunges beneath the surface, he sees something running along the riverbank, darting between trees. A bear—*the* bear. Massive, white, like some kind of Arctic spirit. Jackson sinks under, the water taking him in.

66

Eila's shoulders feel numb; her fingers tingle. She pushes her sleeves up to her elbows, wipes sweat from her forehead. The greenhouse is boarded up but buzzing with a fury. She has a flash of hesitation. Eila is reminded that her father chose not to do exactly what she is about to, to use this—science, phenomenon, whatever *this* is—to save himself. She only ever trusted him, and she knows his reasons were probably wise. But she can't lose the caribou, too, so she finds her hands pulling the boards from the door. When the boards and nails refuse to budge, she dislodges an axe driven into a stump by the woodpile and uses that to pry them off. The first one snaps, then the second, until there is just a thick plastic sheet separating her from the inside of the greenhouse.

Eila pauses again, realizing the chaotic scene that would unfold if she simply flung the door open and let the bees burst out. Instead, she uses a pocketknife to slice through the plastic, making a large enough opening that she can slip her hand in and unlatch the door, then slide her body through the gap. Inside, the bees are a thick, raging cloud. They fly in all directions, an unpredictable swarm, and it's terrifying. Eila crouches and covers her head with her backpack, goose bumps prickling her skin. Having been comfortable around animals—even including most insects—all her life, the world is suddenly disorienting. The sound comes in waves, a deafening roar that rises and falls as the bees cyclone around her and crowd toward the edges of the greenhouse.

When she's able to breathe steadily again, she stands up and takes in the greenhouse. The garden beds are bursting with red, orange, and purple—nasturtiums and alpine daises and Arctic lupines. There's a workbench with pots and soil and gardening tools. Eila finds a notebook wedged between two stacks of clay pots. She flips through it, scanning for some indication of what Vern and Sadie were up to. There are notes about every flower they apparently tried to crossbreed, with the characteristics they were aiming to combine—all Arctic adaptations for resilience. It looks like they were attempting to create a flower that could survive anything, which is, in a way, exactly what they did. So why did they leave it all behind?

Then she finds the page with the notes on lichens. From what she can tell, they tried to use cells from the lichens' fungi to create a regenerative compound in their lupines. In careful handwriting, the notes describe what happened when they attempted to pollinate the lupines artificially, and why they used the live bees instead. The compound they created worked magic for the flower but passed something back to the lichen that killed it. Seeing it as yet another failure, they must have disposed of the lichen outside, not realizing it would spread and infect the reindeer lichen across the tundra.

What Sadie and Vern did doesn't seem intentional. Perhaps they'd missed it, this simple alteration of the compound. They clearly left in a hurry, too quickly to witness the extent of the damage. Then she notices the empty columns they created for listing anomalies. There's only one entry: *a great abundance of calcium.* The very thing missing from the dying lichen.

Eila sets her pack down and reaches inside for a bag of the lichen samples. She spreads the black-fringed leaves on the ground. Hundreds of bees instantly move toward it, a whole group shifting and twisting and landing to cover it. They seem hungry, drawn to it for some reason, though, in theory, they shouldn't need anything to survive. Still, they are older than bees should be and have gone without for so long. They crawl over the lichen like desperate creatures.

Please work, Eila pleads silently, even though she has no idea what "working" would look like. She doesn't know what she's waiting for, or what she hopes will happen, if it will be instantaneous, or if it will take time, but she crouches, trying to catch a glimpse of whatever is happening beneath the bees. If it works, she feels certain that, despite any notions of right or wrong, she will let the bees out. It can't be wrong to cure the infected lichen that's devastating the caribou all over the tundra.

She knows that—though her father had good, noble reasons for refusing to be saved, and Sadie had good, moral reasons for wanting to keep this a secret—she can't bear the thought of the caribou dying when she could have done something to save them.

It's the only way.

When the first group of bees lifts off the ground, they hover, as if confused about where they should go next. She inches close to one as it hangs in the air, and then, all at once, its wings shrivel and curl in on themselves. Then, almost in unison, all the bees that swarmed the lichen cease buzzing and fall to the ground, silent. Their tiny bodies lie dead in the garden beds. Yet, the lichen is a luminous green.

Eila lays out another piece of lichen and watches the whole scene unfold a second time, the bees amassing over the leaves like ravenous creatures, bringing life back to the lichen and then dying almost immediately after. It's not what she expected, but of course, this is balance. This is nature working itself out—the bees undergoing the natural process of death, and the lichen returning to life. Without even trying, they've cured each other.

Eila takes a deep breath, the smell of wet earth and fertilizer filling her nose. She lets out a laugh and then finds herself crying, although she isn't sure if it's with relief or joy or sadness anymore.

Flinging the greenhouse door wide open, Eila watches the thousands of bees spill out. The air is thin and wet with snow. The dog is sitting outside the greenhouse, nose sniffing the air as the bees pass. Most of the bees fly west toward the trail of black lichen, like they know exactly where they're going, as if they've been waiting ages to be released for this very purpose. Some of them land on the lichen around the cabin, and others hover, as if confused about where to go. Eila catches sight of Norma by the river and wants to tell her what she's just witnessed, but the cabin is between them, and she notices a pair of wooden skis propped against it.

There are four old huskies sleeping on the cabin porch, and they all lift their heads when she and the dog walk past. She's tempted, briefly, to see if they know how to sit, shake, roll over. But she just rubs each one behind the ear before opening the door.

Eila has only flashes of memory of her summer here, when her father renovated the cabin, but when she steps inside, she sees traces of him everywhere. In the functional elements, the many shelves and hooks—all ways of saving precious space. And in the aesthetics—the exposed, rustic ceiling beams and the sun radiating from the loft above. In the clay mosaic patches in the walls, the way the windows open in multiple directions, depending on where the sun is—the colored glass that lets in a rainbow of light. The kitchen table, adorned with carvings of tiny moons and stars. All these details take her back to her father's sense of beauty and lightness and joy—something he managed to hold on to even at the very end.

The fire has almost died out in the living room. As Eila crouches to add a log, she notices two ink drawings over the fireplace. One is of a small girl with a long braid, running behind a fox. The drawing is rough yet elegant, composed of simple lines—the only part that's fully colored in black ink is her hair. The other drawing is of a caribou calf, curled up on the ground beneath a tree, flecks of snow drifting around it. Eila takes both drawings from the wall and lays them flat on the kitchen table. In the bottom-right corner of each, her father's initials are brushed in thick black curves.

The first drawing is obviously of her. But the caribou seems like some cosmic coincidence, as if her father had seen the future and known that she would love them, that they would be her friends, that their souls would be tied to her soul. With her thumb, she lifts the metal tabs on the back of the frame and slips the drawings from between glass and cardboard. There is a folded piece of lined paper behind the drawing of her, with her father's handwriting—much steadier and tidier than in his journal, but clearly his. The top of the page reads "The Sunlit River" in the same neat print he used to pen the lyrics to the song, and she can't help thinking of his musings about wild minds and wandering. Two things that seem to have brought her here, in this moment.

Eila isn't sure if she wants to devour this new page immediately, save it for later, or never read it at all. She folds the page and zips it into the front pocket of her backpack, then checks just to be sure and finds another slip of paper behind the caribou calf drawing. But this one simply says "Hannah" in a lilting cursive that is decidedly not Stefan's. Eila slides the drawings back into the frames and replaces the cardboard. She presses her thumb down on each metal tab, hangs the drawings back over the fireplace, and scans the cabin one more time before leaving for the river. To tell Norma that she was right, that even after everything she herself—and Vern—had been ready to do, after everything her father—and Sadie—had not been willing to do, none of that really mattered. It wasn't up to any of them to begin with. Nature didn't need them deliberating and making decisions.

Nature was prepared to take care of itself.

67

Instead of the water freezing his doubts away and allowing him to feel as if he's inside his body again, it grips and shakes him. An involuntary thing. Jackson remembers going to the middle of the lake with a fishing pole and a power drill when he was ten. The ice cracked and he fell into the breath-sucking water, and a moment of excitement was replaced instantly by panic. Suddenly, his body would not listen to his brain. None of his limbs were behaving properly, and he'd never been quite so scared.

And when the hand reached in and pulled him out, in his delirium he thought it was some mythical beast, with paws large enough to haul his body from the water with the ease of someone pulling a carrot from the garden bed. But, of course, it was Stefan Jacobsen, in a fur-lined parka, his cheeks red and his thick beard frosted with ice crystals. In his memory, Stefan let out a fierce growl as he heaved Jackson's convulsing body onto his back and carried him to the truck. Jackson remembers the heavy parka being wrapped around him and the heat pulsing from the dash.

Stefan had been driving to unlock a tenant's door, he explained. But how he'd seen Jackson in the lake and reached him so quickly was a mystery. He talked some more, his voice gruff and muffled—all Jackson could hear was the sound of the blood pounding through his head. Riding in the truck, swathed in Stefan's giant winter coat, Jackson spread his pale fingers in front of him and wondered if he could ever be that strong. He expected Stefan to yell at him, to demand to know what he was doing out there. Demand to know why he was such a stupid, careless kid. But he didn't do any of those things. It was only afterward that Stefan's words echoed in Jackson's head, like a dream he wasn't sure he'd really had.

"The cold is merciless," Stefan had said. "The dark can be hard, but there's always the promise of light returning. The cold doesn't make such promises. The cold is hard, too, and it's relentless, and it'll kill you, and it won't think twice. That doesn't mean you need to be afraid of it. You just need to make sure you're the one in control. Right here." Stefan's hand left the steering wheel to pat Jackson's chest through the coat. "And here," he said, resting a hand on the top of his thawing hair.

Jackson feels the blood rushing in his ears again now. His control is slipping away, his body surrendering. His life has been a series of tests—one attempt at mastery after another—leading him here, where he knows absolutely nothing. And it's here, immersed underwater and seized by the cold, that he realizes she gave it a name for him. Norma Wolfe—who washed up on the riverbank with her white hair and ice-blue eyes and all the fight in the world if you tried to tell her what to do—has named the gaping hole in his chest. The thing that's missing, leaving only an empty shell that consumes not just things, but everything.

The thing that he's lost, the thing that would save him, plain and simple and terribly complicated.

Love.

He makes a decision then.

Now, it's the only thing that makes any sense. He has to go back. He has to see her and he has to take responsibility. If Eila's gone, then she's gone, and he'll have to face that horror. If she's still there, he'll have to face what he's done to her, too, which is a different kind of terrifying. The kind that involves walking up to her cabin and knocking on the door and waiting for as long as it takes. It involves bringing her the porcupine quills he found by the river and the notebook where he's been taking careful notes every day for five years—cataloging the timing and numbers of the caribou as they migrate through. Their colors, their scents, the sounds they make. The secret names he's given them.

He owes her so much more, but at least, even if she's gone, he owes her that.

68

Eila finds Norma sitting in the canoe, attempting to patch the hole in the hull with waterproof tape. The lichen is clenched in Eila's fist, its pale-green foliage now vibrant and glowing with life. When she reaches the water's edge, Eila thrusts the lichen out in her open palm.

Norma looks down at it, then up at Eila, smiling.

"I was going to do it," Eila says, "and maybe it was wrong. But I didn't have to do anything at all. They balanced each other."

Norma takes the lichen, bees circling, their shapes morphing against the darkening blue of the sky.

"My father restored this cabin when I was a kid," Eila says. "He used to say that being lost is the great gift of Alaska. He thought it was a magic place, an endless emptiness waiting to be filled. But no matter what you pour into it—joy, sorrow, feeling adrift and helpless—it never fills up. It's vast enough to hold you, to hold all of its creatures, and it will never change. You, on the other hand, will transform. It will hand you back someone you recognize again."

Eila stares to where the sun, on its downward course toward the horizon, is fracturing the clouds with pointed rays. There's a rumbling from behind, and when Eila turns, caribou surround them, materializing like ghosts from behind a veil of eddying snow. Their knees bend and clack and their heads dip low to the ground, nudging forward in unison like a slow wave.

The pure joy that rises into Eila's body buzzes like the bees that fled the greenhouse. She gasps, holds her breath, afraid this is a dream. She almost faints as they pass so close she could reach out and place her shaking hands on their backs. They weave around her and Norma, crashing chest-high into the water and forging their way across.

One of the caribou stops, looks directly at Eila with her black, glassy eyes. She is familiar in a different way. As if this caribou's spirit belonged to someone Eila knew long ago, or almost knew. A sister that Eila loved or might have loved in an alternate time and place. Eila reaches out, places her palm on the caribou's forehead—against the brown bow of a crescent moon—and time stops.

All the caribou feel like magic, their presence both ancient and yet shining new. Their history is something they know without language. It's in the movement of their hooves, the thickness of their coats, the growing and shedding of antlers. It's in their sense of direction and in the magnetism that pulls them forward. It's in the ground they walk upon, centuries of caribou bones trapped in the permafrost beneath.

Eila has chased that sacred piece of information, the answer to why and how these creatures know where to go and when. How they pass down ancestral knowledge that isn't knowledge at all—simply a form of spirit that they whisper in one another's ears. This caribou whispers to her now, without words, the way Eila and Jackson used to speak.

You just know.

The caribou backs away, and time moves again. Eila's eyes track this sister-caribou and the rest of them, beyond the river to the other bank, where someone has just stepped from the water and is pulling on clothes in the gray snow-mist.

When she sees him—different now with his long hair and beard, his broader chest—her feet begin following the caribou out of instinct. The grip of the river surprises her. Her body finally feels the penetrating cold. It's shocking and thrilling—so very alive.

69

When Jackson rises from the water, he sees them on the other side—Norma, and the crystal clear image of Eila next to her. It doesn't matter that the snow has painted the world an opaque gray. He's imagined this scene enough to recognize the contours and colors on any type of day. He tries to blink it away, but when he shakes his head and rubs his eyes with his palms, the ghost of Eila is blurry but remains. His body tenses with the cold; goose bumps tighten his skin. Perhaps he can no longer take this. Perhaps he stayed in the water too long, and he's delirious.

Jackson wades to the beach for his clothes. He pulls on shorts and a hoodie, then turns again. Not only does the image of Eila remain, but she is now surrounded by caribou. Their otherworldly shapes have materialized, as if from the fog itself.

The sound of them multiplies. Gets closer and louder. The earth pulsates with their steady movement, and then they part around Eila and Norma, all blood and bone and muscle. They break into the water and swim—even the little ones—paddling with their wide hooves, steam rising from their nostrils. Their effort is tangible.

Jackson sits on the beach, hugging his knees. Eila is so constant, so persistently real and alive, that he has no choice but to turn his gaze upstream. He doesn't want to see it, but when he looks, there it is—the wolf, stalking and closing in on the caribou that it will inevitably take down.

He hasn't had this vision in some time, and he wonders again if he's lost his mind. But something is different. This time, Eila is not simply standing there, silent and unaware. This time, she is moving fast toward him, crashing into the shallows alongside the caribou.

And he's moving, too, swimming harder than he ever has, his body propelled by a mythic strength and magnetic force. Part of it comes from somewhere inside him, but more of it—the wilder and fiercer part—comes from somewhere inside her.

They meet at a shallow section of river, the space between them full of everything that could be said but doesn't need to be. Everything that makes sense and everything that does not.

"I'm probably going to be mad at you later. But it's just . . . I'm so cold," Eila says. Her eyes look scared, but her smile is so big it contains his entire world, like the river just before dusk contains all the sun.

Too many questions flood him at once. "I don't know what chapter this is," he says.

"Chapter one," Eila answers. "In which I succeed once again at tracking the creatures I love." She's still wearing her pack, her black hair wild from the wind. The caribou push past on either side, the earth vibrating. Bees fly between them—tiny, determined, impossible creatures.

"Oh no," he says, realizing what she's done.

"It's okay," Eila says, grasping his elbows. "I opened it—I let them all go. And everything's going to be okay." She adds, "I followed a bear."

"It was real, wasn't it?" Jackson asks. His throat is tight and he almost can't say the rest of what he's thinking. "So, then he's gone?" He searches her face and finds a tangle of grief and joy.

Jackson's limbs are numb. But she's still holding on to him, bracing him. The pieces of sky and earth fall to where they belong again, settling into place. "I could feel that the world was broken," he says.

"It was. It is. No one's invincible, Jackson. But we have a few invincible moments, if we're lucky, and I think this is one of ours."

He believes this. If he's ever believed anything in his life, he believes this. Even as he feels that exchange of raw, tender sadness course through his body from hers, and he understands what she's lost.

They're suspended there—the river still trying to drag them down, their bodies shaking and their hair freezing into icicles—and then their hands link together. They wade to the bank and run—fearlessly, the way they did when they were ten years old, sprinting down a birch-lined trail—back toward the cabin, where there is so much to show her. So much to tell her.

How he's been tracking too. How terrifying it is to name everything and how neither of them needs saving. How small he's felt himself become, and how strong in all the ways that matter. How much he still has to learn.

EPILOGUE

The Sunlit River

Centuries ago, when scholars didn't know what was in the far north, they could have left that part of the maps empty. Instead, they imagined what might be possible up there. In the Middle Ages, they drew a line at the top of their maps, and above it, what would later become the Arctic was simply labeled "Inhabitabilis." It was a place of fairy tales and myths. Drawings of monstrous creatures and fictional land formations intermingled with actual places.

What really existed above the Arctic Circle wasn't just mysterious to these cartographers; it was entirely unknowable. Mercator's 1500s map showed the North Pole made up of four clustered islands separated by four symmetrical rivers. Each river flowed north into the center, the top of the world, where they converged and emptied into a central whirlpool. Supposedly, the water fell into the belly of the earth. On this map, the Septentrionalium Terrarum, in the middle of the whirlpool is a magnetic rock cliff, which clearly (clearly!) explains why our compass arrows always point north.

The landscapes on these maps came from tales told by voyagers who claimed to have experienced such wild things. Unbelievable as they may be now, the stories were taken very seriously, even though it would be another few hundred years before any of these explorers actually set foot in the Arctic.

Even though, of course, plenty of people already called the Arctic home, some emerging from a peapod created by the raven, some sharing hearts with the caribou, some learning from the ptarmigan how to travel across the snow.

Perhaps all stories really are true. Anything is possible.

Imagination is powerful.

There is much order in nature. But there is also a lot of magic. I happen to think that the existence of order is the most magical thing about nature. There are so many patterns, and it seems far too miraculous that they are organic. Symmetry in flowers, spirals in the nautilus shell and our very DNA. Waves, arrays, branches. How does the tessellation of honeycomb occur? How can it be real?

The scientific definition of chaos is a type of order that is unpredictable, simple patterns that rise from random circumstances. Irregular heartbeats and weather changes.

A meander: the twisting channels of rivers are meanders, the curves and loops a current makes as it carves through the land. The force of one bend creates the next, causes the river to shift and swing side to side over time. Life is a kind of meander. There is design in the winding paths, a sense of circuitry. It's impossible to know for sure where it's all going as the pieces of your life add up and gather force, but you trust the magic. What's around the next bend might just kill you. It really might.

If I could imagine a perfect life, in a specific place, with certain people in it; if I could map it out, include all the adventures I wanted to have and the monsters I'd encounter along the way; if I could outline the highs and lows, the rising and falling, the moments of happiness and heartache, I think that life would look a lot like this life here. I think it would look a lot like it does when I step outside in the morning with her, and she runs with so much joy toward the river, and the sun splinters into rays, and the coffee is hot but the air is so cold I can barely hang on to the hammer.

I think it would look like that.

ACKNOWLEDGMENTS

Many, many thanks to my incredible agent, James McGowan; to my editors, Alicia Clancy, Laura Chasen, and Laura van der Veer; and to Carissa Bluestone and the fantastic team of editors, designers, and author support at Lake Union. Thank you to my early readers of both long and short bits of this novel: Beth Combs, Will Frey, David Nikki Crouse, and Christopher Myott. Thank you to Katie Orndahl for being such a generous and knowledgeable resource for all things caribou, tundra, and researcher life. Thank you to Derick Burleson, the late poet and mentor who enthusiastically exchanged flower inspiration once upon a time in Fairbanks. Thank you to *Embark* literary journal for publishing an excerpt from this book before it was written.

I'm so grateful to the loves of my life: Jamison, because together we learned it is possible for two people to kick down the locked door of a cabin in Alaska; Elke, because thanks to you, I've had a daily muse for a character so in tune with the natural world; and River, because your jump-scares at six a.m. every morning while I'm writing make sure I never get too comfortable. Thank you also to my family: Donna Bryant, Josh Bryant, and Melissa Colorado, Bethany and Matt Adelman, David Winston, and all the Klagmanns. The creation of this book owes a lot to my departed dog companions: Hazel, who was there for the walks in Alaska that became the seed of this novel, and Ronja, who was there for the trail runs in New Mexico that either cleared my mind or filled it up. And finally, this book is for my father, whose spirit is surely, at this moment, wandering the edge of some wild river.

ABOUT THE AUTHOR

Photo © 2023 Josh Bryant

Jessica Bryant Klagmann grew up climbing mountains, paddling rivers, and scampering through the woods of New Hampshire. She studied writing there and in Fairbanks, Alaska, before falling in love with northern New Mexico. She is the author of the novel *This Impossible Brightness*, and when she isn't writing, she can be found illustrating, trail running, or teaching her two kids the fine art of scampering.